a crumpled ballerina and other stories

A Crumpled Ballerina
and
Other Stories

Neela K. Sukhatme-Sheth

Dedicated to my parents,
Pandurang and Indumati Sukhatme
(I'm the happy recipient of their DNA)

Thanks to my husband, Kumudchandra
for his patient encouragement

Thanks to my gurus, Ellen Hunnicutt, who started
me off in fiction, and Mariann Ritzer, whose
helpful critique encouraged me to keep writing

The morning wind spreads its fresh smell
We must get up and take that in,
that wind that lets us live.
Breathe before it's gone.

Dance, when you're broken open,
Dance, if you've torn the bandage off.
Dance in the middle of the fighting.
Dance in your blood.
Dance, when you're perfectly free.

Jalalu'ddin Rumi
13th century mystic poet

Acclaim for the book

Neela K. Sukhatme-Sheth displays remarkable insight and sensitivity writing about the various cultures upon which her fascinating short stories are based. Her narrative flows with ease, and through her characters, she captures the essence of human strengths, weaknesses and their interactions. Once finished reading this captivating collection, you will feel compelled to start over.

Prem Sharma
Author of novels,
*Mandalay's Child, Karma's Embrace
and Escape from Burma*

Several of the stories have been published elsewhere, some in a somewhat different form and title. These include the non-fiction version of Gio and I (*Milwaukee Journal-Sentinel Wordsmith contest 1990*), A Distorted Web (*In Posse, Internet 2001*), Namaste (*BBC contest 2000, WRWA (Wisconsin Regional Writer's Assoc.) contest 2005*, "Doodh, doodh," (*Byline 2006*), My first Day at Work (*Free Verse Poetry magazine 2006*), A Snake on an Icy Patch of Green (*Common Journeys 1994*), Leather Soles (*India Currents 2003*).

About the Author

Neela K. Sukhatme-Sheth is a retired pathologist who grew up in India and has lived in England, Canada, and the United States for over forty-five years. She has published several essays and short stories, and received awards in various contests, such as the B.B.C Short story contest, Wisconsin Regional Writer's Jade Ring contest, and Milwaukee Journal's Wordsmith contest, wherein James Mitchener, the judge, called her story, "Deceptively simple, sure in the hands of its teller."

Neela blends her East-West experiences with fluidity, and having worked at a Veteran's Administration Hospital, writes about human fraility, the cruelty of war, and human resilience. Neela and her husband travel extensively, enjoy watercolor painting, and spend their time between Florida and Wisconsin. This is her first short story collection.

Music in My Ears

Notes floating out of my beautiful instrument
Bubbling out, painting a picture
Down, down, down they go into the listener's ear.

What am I playing?
I'm in band. I'm playing the flute.
Other flutists join in. The oboe begins.
Then I hear the sound of saxophones and trumpets,
Making our sound fuller and more alive.

Finally, the beat of the percussion.
It all starts with the flute.

by

Kaveri Sheth, my granddaughter, age 11

Contents

Contents (continued)

Prologue: We Four

A cafeteria at 9:30 am on the ground floor of a large Veteran's Administration Hospital. The walls are grey and without contrast. A smell of fried eggs and coffee, and perhaps burnt toast, pervades the air. N, holding a food tray, dodges a fast-moving wheelchair by pressing against the wall, and almost collides with a fellow physician, H, who is entering. Two others will join them eventually. This is a hospital cafeteria; patients must have priority, meaning in this context, the right of way. N's coffee spills in the tray, and she sees it run under the saucer and soak into the paper napkins. Her fried eggs are safe. She signals to H to come over to the Yellow Room, where she has checked that a booth is available. She takes solace in that she will not to have to eat coffee-flavored eggs.

This coffee-cum-breakfast interlude is their daily ritual...has been for the last fifteen years. Four of them, all born in countries far away, all of them now American citizens, take this interlude to discuss old times, families, and the culture they left behind. War invariably comes up, because the patients are veterans.

The sight of old war injuries enters the subconscious of most employees. N hears a familiar "*namaste*" mumbled to her when she walks past. A veteran tells her he was stationed in India for a few months, fifty some years ago. Then a patient with a metal voice walks in and haltingly talks to U, telling him that he was stationed in the Philippines. He sits at the next table drinking his coffee. A man with no legs wheels his motorized wheelchair down another aisle. He waits for a young woman, perhaps his daughter, to bring him his breakfast. R, born in the Ukraine, the senior-most of them, is late coming down; happens sometimes.

This morning they chance upon another new topic, these two men from Korea and the Philippines and the two women from Ukraine and India. What an odd gathering of characters, but also an unusual collection of memories and experiences, some of which are fictionalized in this book. All stories herein are fiction, and any resemblance to real people is purely coincidental.

U has a story about his Filipino father, connected with his own birth, and of course, war...the fight against the Japanese, Pearl Harbor, 7th December, 1941.

N talks of World War II and the war against Germany and Japan from the point of view of an Indian growing up in British-India. Her innocent ballerina image dissolved to dust like the children of Hiroshima.

The stories are varied. H, a Korean, tells us how he believed Korea was a part of Japan, and tells of how the school children followed orders to please the Japanese rulers.

E lost her father when the Russians invaded Ukraine...they said he walked out in the Siberian snow.

We dance to the tune of our births and our aging lives and everything in-between, until we've exhausted the memories; and then, around a small nidus of life's experiences, imagination weaves into a story. We visualize the truth and make it our own; mold it to a character that becomes the basis of a story.

There is comfort in reading fiction from different lands; different people, diverse cultures, and varied problems, with a common theme...we hate war, we suffer in a war, we struggle to be free. There is Grace in human resilience which sustains us. When the world gets too serious, we resort to flippancy and playfulness and music to soothe the pain.

Gio and I

In the barracks in Vietnam, I knew Gio as one of those everyday guys who liked to argue sports, sitting in his armchair. Too lazy to move, but with a strong opinion about everything and everybody around him. I envisioned him at his local bar in some small farming town in Kentucky, discussing his favorite horse, the one he thought he'd make big bucks on, but which always came in second. Gio was the kind to sleep till noon, and then forget to call his boss. He would never be able to say why he'd not shown up for work. His choice would be to fish, or maybe go deer hunting with his buddies in the northern woods. He was not one to venture far from home.

This was the image I carried of Gio in my head for twenty-five years, and then one day through mere coincidence, we bumped into each other, and his first comment to me, in the middle of a noisy bar in Florence, Italy, was "Doctor Mark, make it right for me. I want my arm back."

His tone was sardonic. He staggered sideways in an attempt to salute and I got a chance to take a closer look at him; this man I'd known many years ago, and had not liked even then. What a strange, spontaneous request he had made of someone he had not seen in a long time. There was alcohol on his breath as he stood close to me and grinned.

War had ended long ago and our lives had taken different paths.

Back then, seated on a wooden bench in the big tent, drinking a cup of coffee, our eyes were bloodshot, our brains cloudy, and sleep dripped off our eyelids. He told me how he'd landed himself in 'Nam after he'd had a big fight with his old man. They fought about everything, and in a fit of anger, totally frustrated by his father, who accused him of stealing and playing hooky, which he did, and taking an occasional snort, which he said he enjoyed, Gio enlisted in the Army. He said he wanted to get away from the farm he grew up on, and even further away from the father he hated. At nineteen years of age, Gio was deployed with one of the army's mobile surgical units. With no special skills to boast off, he was given no choice and assigned to work in the triage area as an orderly.

I was already a triage nurse, aspiring to go to medical school someday. I hoped to settle down eventually when memories of battles and guns faded, if they were not erased, from my routine. That's when I planned to marry my childhood sweetheart, Nicole. With a college degree and having been at the war front six months before Gio arrived, I was more experienced and his senior.

For several months that Gio and I worked together, we remained indifferent. Gio washed out grimy sand and scraped grit off bloody elbows and broken legs. He helped carry soldiers on stretchers from helicopter pads and ran them to the triage tents. He felt for bumps over their heads and looked into their bloodshot eyes for signs of a flicker. I heard him brag to his buddies that he'd gotten used to most of the gore. Once, I saw him with his jaws tighten and his knees stiff as he observed a certain terror in a soldier's eyes. Gio explained to me this meant certain death. I nodded. Another time, he was about to throw up when his fingers touched the cracked edges of a broken skull. He said it felt strange to think the soft mush inside the skull was blood and brain tissue.

One morning, I found Gio cowering in a corner of the trauma unit. Slumped back, Gio looked like he was just waking up from a blackout spell. His face was ashen gray and his lips quivered. I had no time for such nonsense because there was work to be done. A man on a stretcher with a bloody shirt and a charred bullet hole above his left nipple needed my urgent attention. The man's breath was rapid and he required surgery right away.

"Move this slob out," I yelled to Gio. "Straight to OR."

Gio would not move. After telling him twice, I moved on to the next patient, seething with anger at Gio's disobedience. I'd seen him put up resistance on other matters, mostly from laziness, I surmised. With all the casualties around us and with new arrivals needing urgent triage, all I could see was pain, turmoil, and death.

"You're drunk," I yelled to Gio again, as I examined the next patient. "Skip this nonsense and move. Get help, quick, you fucking idiot!"

"I'm afraid of blood, sir," Gio retorted in a low-pitched voice I could barely hear. He did not budge his big frame.

It was a hot, humid day and the stench in the tent was suffocating. I gave Gio a long, penetrating gaze. I'll show him, I thought. I'll strip him of his flesh and glory. I turned around and summoned another orderly. He, in turn, called for help and the two of them moved the man with the chest injury to the operating room. When I finished examining the next case, I got to the washbasin to clean my bloody hands. Soon enough, I thought, I'll get Gio's blood instead.

Then my thoughts wandered. Here he was, hardly a man, a boy really! He looked young enough to be dating my teenage sister. There was no sense in his even being here in the middle of a war. I detested him for his stubbornness in defying my order, but I hated myself even more at that moment. I was helpless about the circumstances of war that had brought us together. My bare hands were enough to destroy this emotional weakling. Then again, his youth and big build strangled my feelings of vengeance. I decided to ignore him.

In the canteen that evening, Gio asked permission to eat at my table. We sat opposite one another. This would be my chance to look him straight in the eye and give him my sermon. War was dirty business, just one big mess where there were losers, no matter whom. I'd have to talk to him about doing one's duty to one's country. I would discuss pride and humiliation, ambitions and goals. Obedience and duty would be the long and short of it.

Instead, Gio started to talk with his head down. He said, "I no longer dream of my home town. I have forgotten my anger against my father, but strange vibrations pass through my brain and I can't control them."

He wept softly and I wanted to stop him. He continued in a low, flat voice and said he felt paralyzed by the smell of Vietnamese earth mixed with blood and manure. It followed him around and he despised it. Many things had been said to him and sometimes by him, but he couldn't always remember the details of who spoke to him. No matter how hard he tried, his mind spun with sounds and voices like that of his father; and then, looking up at me, he added," Sometimes like yours, sir. A voice is always telling me what to do." He heard the sound of hooves, and of helicopter engines in the background; the noise was there all the time. He spoke and I listened, waiting for my chance to guide him along the right path.

The chance escaped me because, in the middle of supper, Mac's booming voice came over the intercom calling for our team. Gio took another long sip of ice-cold water before he stood up and walked away.

"Damn it," I mumbled, and followed Gio out.

Gio and I avoided any major confrontations for the next six months that we worked together. I caught him observing me sometimes with almost a jealous look, I thought. It seemed he hated everything around him, like the demons in him consumed him. At times I sensed he wanted to be where I was; to stand in my shoes, wanting to put his heart and his mind to the work I did because he thought it is important. Perhaps he was just a lazy bum, a coward at that; not willing to take any responsibility. The point was he was simply in a war he did not care for. There must be many such people.

Everything changed when I got sent home with cramping abdominal pain. They decided I had a case of severe colitis, an infection of sorts needing long-term treatment. Gio might have liked to be sent home, even without an excuse, I said to a fellow nurse, but such are the breaks in war times.

Twenty-five years later seated at an open-air pub by the waterfront on River Arno, taking in the warm breezy air of Florence, my wife Marcy and I had just finished another good fight of sarcastic rhetoric and she continued to sulk. We were in our second phase of war; the phase of silence for the evening. After a while I suggested we walk down to Ponte Vecchio and see the full moon rising over the city.

"Too many people," she said.

So I started out alone. She said she'd wait for me in the hotel lobby after she'd had another martini.

"Your fourth one," I pointed out to her. My saying so didn't help our cause. Without looking at her, I pushed my way through the crowded bar to exit through the front door.

A heavyset man staggering in through the front entrance bumped into me just as I was leaving. Annoyed, I continued to walk away, but swung around instantly as something in the man's look triggered my thinking.

"Gio! Giovanni Lucca?" I asked hesitatingly of the man.

"Yes, Sir Mark." He recognized me that very instant after I said his name. He attempted a left-handed salute, still staring at me. He clicked his heels to attention.

I held out my right hand. These were peace times after all. He extended his, only it was a large metal hook attached to his wooden arm, which was anchored somewhere underneath a long shirtsleeve. He grinned as he saw the shock on my face. Then he grabbed my right hand with his left hand, which made for an awkward handshake.

That was when he said, "Doctor Mark, make it right for me. I want my arm back." His penetrating eyes stared at me.

I didn't quite get what he meant, but I sensed aggression. A little unsettled, I simply asked, "How have you been, Gio? Looks like we both made it home for the rest of our lives!"

"I want my arm back, sir. You are a big doc now, you can do it." He extended his metal hook out, so it almost touched my face.

Seeing him alone, I said, "Come and join us for a drink. Coffee perhaps?" This way I would get to know him a little, I thought. We could start on a new footing.

He followed me to our table. I introduced him to Marcy, who seemed suddenly happy to be with someone other than me. We talked. He drank three cups of coffee before we ordered a round of Peroni.

"Sir, Doc, we both came home, right," he said eventually, "but my arm got left behind. The rest of me is here."

Gio looked older. He had a few gray hairs around his temple and a receding hairline. His growing up must have started in the triage tent in Vietnam years ago. It was not a happy sight to see this once young man with no hope. I had tried to offer him my friendship, but he wanted more. He was sure I'd fulfilled my dreams and become the doctor I once planned to be. Marcy was laughing at me; there was a smirk on her face. The 'sir doc' title with which he addressed me must have seemed absurd to her. War makes enemies of people and keeps them apart for life. Sometimes even the best of friends, and that Gio and I never were.

Late into the night, Marcy finished her fifth or sixth martini. Then she stood up to go. She gave me a mocking salute as she slid out of her chair and said, "Good night, sir, doc, sir." Then she wove her way out of the crowded bar. We ordered more drinks and talked about whatever we remembered from twenty-five plus years ago. Neither Gio nor I were able to count our drinks, nor did we really care how much we drank. There were tears and laughter; nothing made much sense. Then suddenly, a serious thought must have crossed his mind, because he said,

"Damn you, sir, it's fine and dandy for you, but I need my arm back, the one I left behind in 'Nam."

He repeated his request. He was insistent. How could I tell him about my failures? He just went on saying, "Make it right for me, Doc, I need my arm back, sir."

I wanted to tell him that I, too, carried the aftermath of war on my shoulders all these years. That war blessed me with a wasted life. I detested the sight of blood. I had bad dreams in which strange things happened. Ghastly nightmares which made me drop out of medical school and I never became the doc I aspired to be. Nicole, my childhood sweetheart finally left me. Much, much later I married Marcy and although I loved her, we fought constantly. War had left me empty of bondage and lasting relationships. I had no physical handicap to show for the war, and unlike Gio, I did come back with two arms.

There was no sense in my saying anything so late at night. I had no brilliant thoughts left inside me. The trauma tent loomed large again. I felt sorry for myself and for Gio. Then Marcy came into my thoughts. Her mocking look as she left that evening haunted me. I couldn't change how war had eclipsed my life, just as Gio couldn't change his hook hand. At the very least, I still had Marcy. I could try to salvage what Marcy and I had left in our marriage.

Seated in the bar on the banks of the River Arno in Florence, under the moonlit sky, I told Gio that Marcy was the only good thing remaining in my life. Before it became too late, I needed to go to her. He nodded as if he understood. Perhaps he thought I was a coward, not able to look him in the eye. I hid my souvenir of war well inside me.

The bar noises were dying down. I left him slumped in his chair, looking out onto the peaceful moonlit river. I left him putting away his own thoughts, or so I imagined.

A Worker at a V.A. Medical Center

The edifice stands high
Housing veterans of battle
Sans limbs, eyes, sans spirit
Gear they left behind.

You listen, medicate
Counsel, fill forms
Unable to erase their hurt
A generation crippled by war
.
A seemingly invincible student nurse
Winks at you on the elevator
You smile, adjust your files
And enter Room 2010.

The reality of war at a V. A.

Sukhatme-Sheth 12

A Crumpled Ballerina

In New Delhi, India, a hot day in August, the year 1945. A little girl named Ambika smiled as she thought of her birthday to come in two days. She would be eight years old. Her mother, Aayi, as the children called her, stood before the mirror and vigorously brushed Ambika's dark, straight hair back. Aayi's heavy hand dug the comb's sharp teeth into Ambika's scalp and she winced, stiffening her neck and shoulders. Aayi parted the hair and plaited it into two thick braids with red ribbons at the ends. Once done, Ambika stood still, pleased with herself, and happy about her big day. She glanced up and sideways to check herself. Then, just for fun, she made a clownish face in the mirror, the kind that made her younger brother Rahul roar with laughter.

A few weeks earlier, Ambika had started to make plans for her birthday. Now only two days to go for August 6. Should she invite all seven of her friends for her party at their flat in McCarthy Place, and play hide and seek? No, she thought, the girls may get too rowdy and Mrs. Sinclair, the Anglo-Indian lady from upstairs, would surely complain like she always did. Ambika knew that the Anglo-Indians were a small part of the Indian population, with some British blood; so they considered themselves more privileged than the rest of the Hindus. Mrs. Sinclair's loud groans amused Ambika and Rahul, but they had to be polite. Every few days like clockwork, Mrs. Sinclair would stand in the balcony with her hand on her forehead and call out to Aayi.

"Mrs. S..." she'd say. "Make sure the children keep their voices down today. The planes overhead are noisy enough." Then she'd look at Ambika and Rahul and, wagging her finger at them, say, "I can feel another headache coming on. Don't be noisy today, you understand."

When this happened, Aayi immediately made a serious face and ordered her children to calm down. "Go play a board game. Maybe "Snakes and Ladders." It'll be fun."

The children were obedient and listened. The planes overhead did make scary noises.

Nani, Ambika's grandmother, made a favorite dessert for each of the children on their birthdays. This year, too, Nani had assured her, "I'll make you some juicy *chumchums* for next week."

Ambika had imagined the homemade, syrupy doughnut in her mouth. Then she remembered the round, coconut *laddoos* Nani had made for Rahul's birthday when he had turned seven in June. She tried to push her luck.

"Nani, I want *laddoos* also," Ambika said. "Same as Rahul."

Nani was silent for a while. It would be difficult for their servant, Laxman, to go across town to the market for a scarcity item such as a coconut. Her son-in-law, Ambika's father, did not want them to buy a coconut at the nearby black market, when food items were in short supply. He said it gave people on the street information about who had money and those were the houses that got vandalized. Besides, it was against government policy and Papa would never let them do anything illegal.

That afternoon, Nani simply said, "We'll see. We'll decide about the treats when the time comes."

Ambika felt let down because that was Nani's favorite expression when she didn't want to say no to them.

Ambika and Rahul talked about war all the time. They had heard words like Pearl Harbor, and they did not like Hitler from Germany. Their papa explained, "The Japanese don't like us in India because we support the British."

For the last few years, there had been so many times when the children mistook the noise of military aircraft for thunder when they heard the rumble in the sky. They would hide under their Nani's bed or behind the sofa and pretend there were gunshots outside their windows. Pretend games were fun, but after a few rounds, Ambika worried that the ugly war would really come to their city. Their papa's talk and explanations were too much information for their little minds. Yet, the children knew that America and Britain were on the same side, fighting against Germany and Japan. This bothered Ambika, more so because their elementary school teacher was a German woman.

That whole week, Ambika had been in a pleasant mood because birthday plans were uppermost on her mind. After much discussion, she and her mother finally came up with an idea. She was to invite five of her best friends over for an afternoon birthday party.

Aayi reminded Ambika, "The girls will have to go home before dark."

Another inconvenience. She'd heard these kinds of comments several times before. Aloud she said, mimicking her mother, "In war times, little girls have to be home before dark."

Then back to more planning. Ambika said, "We'll play board games, but first we have to play dress-up. It's so much fun."

Dress up consisted of wearing colorful *saris* of their own choice from the many Aayi would allow them to unfold that day. Then the girls would rummage through Aayi's heeled *chappals* and sandals and find ones matching their clumsily wrapped-around, six yards of sari material. They smeared their faces with powder and lipstick and pretended to visit each other for a tea party. They'd pour pretend tea into little china teacups as they snuggled their dolls, their babies, in their laps. When they tired of this game, they'd discard the clothes and become little girls again. Then they could play, "Pin the tail on the donkey." Ambika said she'd make a big paper donkey and Rahul would cut out a long tail for when they played this game.

After school that evening, Ambika changed into a flowery, yellow cotton dress and accompanied her mother to the bakery. In the small, elite bakery with dim lighting, for that was the norm in those days, Ambika pointed to the colorful pictures of cakes. Mrs. Wendy said, "Chocolate cake or a butter cream frosting on a white cake? Round or square? I can make a swan or a teddy bear shape too. Those are the only two choices, nothing else, sorry. I can't get enough milk to make you an ice cream cake these days. War has made everything so hard."

No matter, these were important decisions for an almost eight-year-old. She continued looking around and took her own time. She spotted a dainty plastic ballerina amongst the decorations Mrs. Wendy brought forward. Quickly, she made her choice of a round cake with a dancing ballerina on the butter cream frosting.

Mrs. Wendy was from England and now lived in India like many other British. She gave Ambika a biscuit while she looked around for colorful candles, but the little girl kept holding the biscuit in her hand, because in their house, the rule was not to eat in a public place. Then Mrs. Wendy wrote up the order and offered her another one to take home to her brother. Ambika whispered to her mother, "Aayi, can I have pink flowers around the ballerina?"

Her mother looked at Mrs. Wendy who simply nodded. "I'll do my best. It'll be a gorgeous cake." Mrs. Wendy, with a friendly smile, wrote down a few more details and then told Ambika to come back on her birthday in two days to pick up this special cake with her name and the dancing ballerina on it. In Ambika's mind, the highlight of her party was the ballerina cake from Mrs. Wendy's.

Over supper, Ambika announced, "I'll tell Mrs. Hilda about my ballerina cake at school tomorrow." She was rather pleased with her outing. Her papa took no interest in her words and continued eating. Then he looked around the table and said, "Eat, Rahul, you can talk later."

"Blackouts can start anytime. Let's get done with dinner." Aayi said.

Papa and Aayi didn't always know if electricity failed or was purposely cut off in the capital city of New Delhi. Laxman, their servant, kept kerosene lamps lighted at such times, and often the family moved around the house carrying little oil divas or lamps. Ambika and Rahul were not allowed to read at night for months because the entire city used low voltage bulbs.

Nani said they would go blind if they read in poor lighting. For years, the windows facing the streets were either painted black or draped with black curtains.

Ambika hated this shut-in feeling, more so at night when she was about to fall asleep and she told Rahul she hated war.

He said, "I do too, it is like being in a dungeon."

Ambika remembered something else she had wanted to ask her papa for a long time. Something Mrs. Hilda had said to them in class.

"Mrs. Hilda is German, Papa. She said the Germans and British don't like each other in this war. Can the enemy hurt Mrs. Hilda because she is German?"

"Well, she's right. Germany and Britain are at war, and America is on the side of the British. Not to worry. She's married to an Indian and she lives in India. Nothing will happen to her here," Papa answered with a smile and a wink.

Ambika idolized her teacher. "Mrs. Hilda says her parents may be put in jail if Germany loses the war. So I want Germany to win, but Rahul says he wants the British to win. India is on the side of the British."

Papa explained to them that India was a part of the British Empire and even the Indian Gurkhas and Sikhs, who were brave soldiers, fought in the British army. The radio from the flats above and in the shops on the streets talked of war all the time, but children like Ambika had school and her birthday to think about this week.

The next day in school, Ambika was particularly pleased with the blue ribbons Aayi had tied at the end of her braids. She kept feeling her braids with her fingers. Then unexpectedly, after lunch, when they were in the middle of finishing some math problems, Laxman stood in the doorway and handed Mrs. Hilda a note from Ambika's father. Through the corner of her eye, she saw Rahul standing outside her classroom, ready to go home. She stared at Mrs. Hilda.

"Your father has some urgent work and wants you home, Ambika," Mrs. Hilda said as she finished reading the note. "Run along. I'll see you tomorrow."

"Yes, Mrs. Hilda," Ambika smiled, kind of excited. "It's my birthday tomorrow. I'll bring sweets for the class."

With her satchel in hand, she walked out, proud and happy, into the afternoon sun. Nearer home, they quickened their pace. Rahul ran up the dimly lit stairs to the flat with Ambika in close pursuit. It was so unlike Papa to send for them.

Ambika saw her parents and Nani talking. There was some secrecy to their talk. Seeing the children, Aayi stopped mid-sentence. She said, "Come children, we're going to Bombay this evening. By train. Nani and Papa will stay here and Laxman will manage the house while I'm gone."

Ambika was shocked. She pursed her lips. "I'm not going," she announced as she made tight fists and held her arms knotted across her chest in defiance. "It's not fair. You promised I could have a birthday party."

Tears ran down her cheeks as she pleaded with her parents to wait till after her birthday; but her father walked away before she could even finish her sentence. He came back into the room with yet another suitcase.

"Nothing's fair," her father said in a matter-of-fact voice. "I want both you children and your mother to go to your aunt's house in Bombay right away. Your aunt has had a heart attack, she needs your mother's help. No arguing, Ambika. Nani should go too, but it will be a long, tiresome journey, so she can stay with me. Laxman will take care of us. You three come back in about a month when we know she's well rested and the war news is good. We'll celebrate your birthday then."

Rahul asked, "By train, Papa, really?" He jumped up and down with joy when his papa nodded to him. He loved to look out of trains and eat along the way. The suddenness of this plan added to his delight. He began to collect his clothes and toys and books right away. Ambika threw her clothes on the floor when Aayi asked her to start packing.

The train stopped for only three minutes at New Delhi station. Papa had to shove them forward through the crowd, staying right behind them; and using the momentum of moving feet, he helped them climb into a train compartment. Ambika and Rahul sat cramped next to each other and Aayi found a place on the seat opposite them. Sadly, they waved goodbye to their papa across layers of people.

A large metal trunk belonging to another passenger was placed on the floor between them, so there was no place for their legs. The trunk obstructed the passage and people had to jump over the luggage to get to the window or to the door. In addition, hand luggage and bundles of clothes tied in jute cloth were placed on the trunk and under the seats, all belonging to people who had managed to get in with them. Within minutes of the train leaving the station, the woman sitting next to Ambika offered to exchange seats with Aayi. Then Ambika and Rahul sat on either side of her, and from time to time, Aayi hugged each of them. She stroked Rahul's hair and asked him to rest his head on her shoulder and close his eyes.

Rahul said no right away because he wanted to see everything.

There was still some sunshine left on this August evening, which made for longer hours of daylight. The train window's dark shutters were pulled halfway down. The adults could see nothing of the surroundings, but Ambika and Rahul saw, at their eye level, the outside sky and long stretches of brown and green whisk past as the train rolled on. They saw an occasional distant plane in the sky. Soon they were bored and fidgety.

Ambika clutched the doll she had carried with her, and her brother, the toy airplane he had managed to bring. It was his fighter plane, he had told her, "For when the Germans come to our town."

"Why did we have to go today?" Ambika moaned, leaning across Aayi's front, to Rahul on her other side. "Just when it's my birthday tomorrow."

"I don't know," her brother whispered back. "Ask Aayi."

The compartment was warm and humid and the smell of sweat soaked the musty air. The constant motion and rhythmic jolting of the train made Ambika doze off periodically. Through sleepy eyes, she saw a man and his wife open up a metal tiffin of food. They broke pieces of *chapati*, the unleavened flat bread, with both hands and scooped up potato and peas *bhaji* into it. The sight of food and the spicy aroma made Ambika hungry and she asked her brother if he wanted to eat. He said later and closed his eyes.

Ambika tried to ignore the noise around her. She took out a folded piece of paper and a pencil from the little cloth bag she carried as her purse and began to draw. She remembered her cake, the one she was to get the next day, and she drew a ballerina with her pointy legs that was to decorate her cake. She talked to her doll, telling her that tomorrow was her birthday and when they got to Bombay, Papa told her they could have ice cream. She hoped her mother would surprise her, and that there might be a party on the train. Maybe a present? Perhaps a twirling ballerina! Wouldn't her brother be taken aback when the strangers in the train compartment sang happy birthday to her! With her paper ballerina still in her hand, she lulled herself to sleep.

The train came to a squealing halt and she saw food vendors on the platform of a dark train station. She was just about to tell Aayi that she had to go to the bathroom, when three uniformed army men entered the compartment and talked to the people closest to them. There was sudden excitement among the crowd and all at once, everybody was awake and talking loudly. It seemed as if nobody was listening. The important uniformed men must have given them some exciting information.

Eventually the train started and the passengers quieted down and talked to each other in hushed voices. She did not know how much time had passed but it was dark outside. The army people turned on their radio-transistor and they all listened intently in hushed silence. She could hear a distant roar of planes. Rahul started to cry.

"Don't be afraid, *beta*," Aayi said to Rahul, putting her arm around her son. "Nothing will happen to us here, but there is big world news today. America has exploded an atom bomb over a town called Hiroshima in Japan and we're waiting to see what all this means. It seems the American President, President Truman, gave the order, because Japan will not listen to his warnings to stop the war. Perhaps this will end the war, who knows."

"But Aayi, it's my birthday," Ambika said, and began to cry too.

Time went by quickly after that. Everybody in the train compartment talked to each other, passed food to each other, and offered an opinion on the bombing.

Several hours later, the train made its way into the crowded Bombay Central Station by early afternoon. There had been a downpour that morning and the platforms were wet and muddy. Herds of skinny coolies in red shirts and short pants and with red, cloth headgear, proudly exhibiting their government badges, rushed towards the train as it slowed down. Little boys held up newspapers and flashed headlines around for all to see. Rahul read the big print.

"What's Hiroshima?" he asked.

Ambika screamed in his ear, above the din, "I heard them talking. An atom bomb exploded over Hiroshima. It's a town in Japan. Then a big fire broke out and the whole town got covered in dust and mud, Rahul, and people had to breathe bad fumes. Houses collapsed and many people died because they couldn't breathe. Nobody knows more."

Ambika felt important that so much, somewhere, had happened on her birthday, but she was shivering with fright at the same time. She had not forgotten that she wanted to have her birthday party. Maybe, just maybe, her Aayi had remembered to bring her party dress. This was the worst crisis of her entire life, much worse than when Rahul broke her favorite doll's arm by banging it against a wall.

Their aunt's servant of many years was waiting at the train station to receive them. They hired a horse-driven victoria from the railway station to their aunt's house. The rain had started again. Their luggage was loaded and secured at the back of the carriage with rope, and some small items were stashed around their legs. Ambika and Rahul felt crowded. Monsoon winds blew the rain horizontally into the carriage and drenched the children. As the carriage took a curbside turn, the piled-up luggage slid into one corner and the horses lost their balance on the wet road. First one and then the other horse slipped and fell. The carriage overturned, throwing Ambika and Rahul onto the road. Luggage fell around them and their Aayi sat clutching her arm on the cobbled pavement.

Ambika sobbed loudly. First the bomb, and now this. What other misfortune could occur on her birthday. Rahul screamed because the handle of a suitcase caught his arm and he lay twisted under its weight. People came running from all directions to help. A man held his umbrella over Ambika and helped her sit up. She looked at the cuts on her legs as she cried and Rahul supported his swollen arm. Other than a big bump on Aayi's elbow, she remained unscathed. After some time, when the luggage had been collected by the curb and the victoria and horses straightened, somebody lifted Ambika and Rahul with their wet, muddy clothes back into the buggy. Aayi climbed in with her dripping wet sari and the servant perched himself next to the nervous driver for a second time. Soon they arrived at their aunt's house.

In the warmth of this place, which was to be home for the next few weeks, Ambika cleaned up and sat quietly at the dining table. She still carried in her cloth bag the crumpled paper from the train with her drawing on it. Rahul fidgeted on the chair next to her. They did not speak, visibly shaken from their harrowing journey.

"Aayi said we're lucky to be alive," Rahul said.

"Why? Do you think the bomb would have crushed us in Delhi?" Ambika asked. She felt very tired. Even the fact that it was her birthday no longer made her happy.

"No, silly, we could have been smashed from the horses tumbling over us and then it would have been the same as the bomb."

"Do you think children died because of the bomb?"

"I think so," Rahul said. "Papa must have sent us away so we wouldn't die in the war."

Ambika gazed at the paper ballerina she had tried to draw while on the train. The paper was damp and muddy with only a few pencil marks still visible. She tried to straighten out the crumpled folds with her hands. Nothing made sense any more. Not the war, nor the bomb, nor the children dying somewhere far away. She was glad it wasn't Rahul or her. She stared hard, trying to find her ballerina, but the paper just fell apart. Disintegrated like a castle of cards called the town of Hiroshima, far away in Japan, on August 6, 1945.

August 24., A. D. 79, Pompeii
What Padre Roberto knows but won't tell

is that confessions are sacred, he will not tell.
Why, just two Sundays ago,
Senor Giovanni in his swanky broad-rimmed hat
had stopped by the curtained booth.

Padre Roberto knew his voice.
Senor Giovanni confessed: He had slept with
his slave the previous Monday, Tuesday and Thursday.
Given her a gold arm band with engraving.
Won't happen again, he told the priest,
but it did the following Wednesday and Friday.

Senora Giovanni, a black veil over her eyes, knelt too,
Another time, and Padre Roberto knew her voice.

Said the slave had stolen from her husband's pot;
So she wanted to kill her someday, but not just yet.

Then Mount Vesuvius's plinian explosion;
The collapse of Pompeii, August 24. A. D. 79
smothered the windpipes of Senor and Senora Giovanni
and their slave and Padre Roberto.
They found the still slave with her gold arm band on.

The secrets and sins of 20,000 human kind
melted in with bones and rubble.

Sukhatme-Sheth 26

Two Tigers Cannot Share One Hill

My gym teacher yelled at me. "Stand up straight. You! Chung Yung!"

I straightened my back and looked directly ahead. We had been standing at attention for a long time. My thoughts wandered because I was bored, just having to stand. Did my older brother Sam Tai, also practice marching like me? The sun parched my mouth and gradually I slouched again, when I noticed my friend, Kim Yoon, also twelve years old, to my right, smiling. Then we heard our teacher's voice again, and my friend stiffened into a pretend army soldier. This was the beginning of our war drill, the same as every day.

"Left turn, quick march!" said Mr. Pan and we, the sixth graders, obeyed. Above us and around us was the constant drone of flying planes and radio voices. The radio announcers told us the number of people that were killed daily. There was war gossip in the town square and at the dinner table. To obey orders and march, to run and take shelter, even to wear camouflage clothing, were all part of our daily school activity. War enslaved us.

All twenty of us boys in the front row made a ninety degree left turn, and smartly clicked our heels to face the morning sun. Distorted shadows of my fellow classmates appeared in front of me, and our teacher marched us forward, making us feel patriotic. However, it was different for Kim

Yoon. He was behind me as we marched, and within seconds his out-of-step beat, uncoordinated as he always was, broke the rhythmic sound of our marching feet. This time Mr. Pan's voice was even angrier and louder than before.

"Halt! Attention!" Mr. Pan yelled, loud and clear. He walked over to Kim Yoon and looked him straight in the eye. With a quick step forward, he grabbed Kim Yoon's arm and pulled him out of the front line. He spun the boy around like a pole on wheels, so Kim Yoon faced us. Mr. Pan said, "You'll never get to march in a real army, you idiot! You'll be shot before you know it. That's if you're ever permitted to join!"

This was our middle school in Nakahito, Korea, thirty miles south of Seoul. As a twelve-year-old Korean boy growing up under the Japanese regime, I sang patriotic songs for the Land of the Rising Sun. The Emperor of Japan was to be revered; a philosophy ingrained into our psyche. A war was on and we heard repeated messages on behalf of our Emperor. This other man, the Emperor's spokesperson, instilled fear into us, and so we feared this great Emperor who ruled, and whose real voice we never heard. The voice we heard told us this was an important war and it was our duty as the men, women and children of Korea to fight and defeat the enemy.

"We are winning. We will win. We must be victorious at all cost." They pounded these words into us.

A few weeks later, uniformed Japanese came to our house to interview my brother, Sam Tai, who was twenty-two. Peeking from behind the wooden door to the living room, I listened to them talk. I understood very little, but all that talk made me think Sam Tai was privileged and lucky to be asked to join the Air Force. I told my sister, Nene, so. My other brother, Oppa, stood beside me listening. When the uniformed soldiers left, Mother told me Sam Tai would soon be enrolled in the Air Force.

I liked the color of army fatigues better, so to join the army when I grew up and be part of the war mission became important to me, and I paid attention to everything Mr. Pan made us do.

One day, months later, I ran home from school as fast as I could. Sam Tai was home on furlough for five days. His short, dark hair glimmered in the bright sun and his eyes sparkled with excitement when he told us of his training to become a fighter pilot. Sam Tai wore his Air Force cap to one side. Soon, he said, he'd be on a real assignment, and as he spoke, I thought he looked so tall. The next morning he ruffled my hair and playfully told me I'd grown in the four months he'd been away. On his last morning home, Mother called me to the middle room.

"Take this uniform to your brother. It's time for him to get dressed." I carried the laundered, folded uniform over to his room, holding it in my hands like a crown on a decorated platter. I touched the shiny metal buttons on his neatly pressed coat before I entered his room.

Thinking back, I must have been at least ten years old before I understood that we were Korean. I thought of us as a Japanese family living in Korea and either way it didn't matter. Mother had taught us a few Korean words for day-to-day use and I spoke those intermixed with my fluent Japanese.

"You must not let anyone outside the home hear you speak Korean," Mother would say to us. Yet, at home, my mother and father conversed in Korean when they did not want us to understand their talk.

The week after Sam Tai left, my mother said at dinner, "Sam Tai is smart, he'll do us proud. He'll help us win the war." She looked at the rest of us around the table to make sure we understood. Oppa and Nene and I nodded as we continued to eat without looking up, but Father paused between mouthfuls.

"He's fighting the war already, woman." Then he shoved in another spoonful of soup and banged his spoon down on the table. He did that whenever he demanded our attention.

To Oppa and me, he said in a slow, deliberate voice, "Listen carefully to your superiors. Obey their every command. Two tigers cannot stay on one hill."

I didn't know why my father emphasized this sentence to us many times over. Was my Korean father a little afraid of Japanese authority? I wondered.

War continued as the year went by. Father listened to the radio news all the time. I would see him with his head tilted; his lean figure huddled by the radio, and his look distant. He sat in a pensive mood after listening to everything that had happened on a particular day. Then in the evening, he talked to his friends in the village square where they all sat on a bench under the trees and smoked. At times, he and his friends went to the *tabangs* for a drink of ginseng tea or *makoli*.

One day he came home agitated and blew big puffs of smoke even inside the house, something he never did. He sat us down on the bench beside our long dining table after supper and began to talk. He spoke slowly and clearly as if he was trying to believe the words himself. He said, "Bow to the Japanese flag. Be respectful. Remember two tigers cannot stay on the same hill."

All these long, drawn out months, I waited to grow up. My father said I should help my Uncle Kwang in his grocery store on weekends. The store was just a single room with a large front door and a small window next to it. Tins of cabbage and tuna and sweet peas and other vegetables crowded the shelves; all the cans were lined up in neatly formed rows. The tins in the front rows got sold and the ones in the back stayed dusty. Often times, I stood on a wooden bench under the window and looked out onto the street. Strong smells of fish and garlic permeated the air in the far musty corner where the icebox contained fresh fish. Uncle Kwang and my father caught fish on weekends and I went with them, whenever they'd let me. This was 1944. The radio was loud in the shop, and in every home around us, giving us news about our battles at the front and assuring us that we were winning. They told us the Japanese forces were defeating the Allied troops.

Kim Yoon, my slow friend from school, also knew that a big war was on but he did not want to leave his parents and fight like I did. Often he came to the store to buy food. His little sister once said to me, "Kim Yoon can only come to your uncle's store. My mother won't let him go to Mr. K's store because he brings home smelly fish from there. She says you are his friend and you will be kind to him." She said this last sentence in a singsong tone and I liked the sound of her voice.

Our school took us on outings to the pine forests once a week. That's when we kept our books closed for the whole day. Mr. Pan told us we were being given the honor of participating in war activities. We were to collect sap from the pines, which would then be taken to the factories to be purified into oil that they needed to run submarines, airplanes, and Army trucks. We had to work hard to help with the war. I felt important because I was helping win the war, same as Sam Tai.

Collecting sap from the tall pines was a fun game for the first hour or so. We climbed the trees with ease. Then we poked pointed sticks into stubs of the thicker branches that came off the main stem, and sap leaked out. We collected the sap in metal bowls we carried up with us. It took a long time because our arms were not strong, and we couldn't poke the sharp sticks deep enough. Mr. Pan made us stay till we gathered our portions and filled the big vat. My friends became hungry and tired from the heat and cried in pain when their arms and legs hurt, but there were no excuses. I tried to be upbeat and explained to Kim Yoon that we were doing an important job. My brother, Oppa, laughed at my scrawny arms but sometimes he helped me out after school, when his own work was done.

Oppa climbed fast and quickly filled up my allocated bowl, and eventually, our vat. Sitting astride in the tall pines, I'd change my sap-filled bowl with Kim Yoon's almost empty one. This way the teachers wouldn't shout at him for being so slow and uncoordinated. He'd slide down with my filled bowl and empty it into the vat. Eventually he, too, would be caught up. Mr. Pan said the army needed big quantities of sap to get even a little oil, so we needed to work hard.

Kim Yoon and I played together after school. He'd run over to our house after he changed out of his school uniform and put on his play shirt and trousers. My mother gave each of us a bowl of steamed rice and fish and *kimchi*. We'd sit on the doorstep and look toward the snow-clad mountains and shove sticky, white lumps of rice into our mouths with our chopsticks. Then we'd run out and play "soldier, soldier." I'd pretend to be a big general in the Army and he was my assistant.

"Today we'll collect oil from the pine stubs," I'd say to Kim Yoon. "You hold the tumblers, yours and mine, and stay close behind me so the enemy doesn't catch you." I would find a long stick with a sharp end, and marching like the army, we'd walk into the thick woods at the back of the house. Nobody could find us in our secret place, our refuge from the world. As the first evening shadows filtered through the woods, I'd hear my mother call our names. I commanded Kim Yoon to go home right away, although he always wanted to stay longer.

Stabbing the pines is the only war you'll fight, Oppa teased me once. I repeated the same sentence to Kim Yoon when I was angry at him. Kim Yoon always listened to my orders. I spoke to him in a loud, authoritative voice, just like our teacher's.

Several months went by and the summer of 1945 arrived. Sam Tai had not been home for a long time. I wondered if my big brother would find me very grown up and say my arms were strong and that I was ready for war.

"Will Sam Tai come home soon now?" I asked my father at various times. I wanted to hear Sam Tai's voice again.

He nodded without saying much.

Oppa asked Father if he should sign up for the war, since he was seventeen years and two months old.

"They'll call for you soon enough," Father said to both of us. "Sam Tai has a job to do. He'll come home when he's told to, but he'll leave again. He has work to do for our country."

"Father, did you speak Korean when you were growing up, or just Japanese like us?" I said one day.

My father just stared at me, a blank expression masking his face. He did not want to voice his thoughts. I felt foolish.

"We will never be Japanese in our hearts," my mother interjected. "It is forced upon us. The Government will not like it if you do not fight for Japan. They are our rulers."

In a way I was relieved that she could not stop me from joining the Army, or the Navy, or the Air Force. I wanted to be like Sam Tai and come home and tell Kim Yoon many war stories.

On August 6, 1945, the radio was on as usual while Mother cooked us fish for breakfast. My sister, Nene, served hot rice into our bowls and carried them over to the breakfast table. Oppa scurried around trying to find his school tie and scolded me for my mess. He said I was the reason his tie was buried under a heap of paper and unfolded clothes.

"Turn up the radio," Father shouted to Nene, over the noise of sizzling fish.

Oppa and I continued to elbow each other and Nene, in her two-strap rubber slippers, flip-flopped back and forth with the rice bowls. This was our usual morning scene. She ignored the sounds and turned up the radio only after she had served us our breakfast.

Eventually, the music stopped and the news started. The radio sounded too loud all of a sudden because we became silent. The first item was a daily ritual, a list of casualties from the previous day of combat. Then they told us how far our Army had advanced. There was a one-sentence news item about a Japanese fighter plane being shot down over the Pacific. The voice went on to say that another war plane was missing fifty miles from Tokyo. Lastly, there was the usual pep talk, similar to what our teachers told us at school, that we fought valiantly and that our army had advanced and victory would soon be declared. This day, Father made no comment like he sometimes did, and we all went about our business of eating and going to school.

An hour later, at school, we heard the shocking news of the bombing of Hiroshima and it silenced us. Even Kim Yoon seemed to have understood something bad had happened. School closed and we ran home. Father repeated to Mother that the revenge for Pearl Harbor from three years ago was confronting us. A big destructive bomb had been exploded over the city of Hiroshima in Japan. Then he rushed out to the village square to talk to the other elders and find out how bad the destruction was.

A couple of weeks after Hiroshima, when only Mother and I were home, a special announcement came on the radio that for the first time, Emperor Hirohito himself would speak to the nation the next morning. We looked at each other, puzzled.

"Why has he never spoken to us before?" I asked my father that evening.

"His Highness must have an important message to deliver," Father said, trying to be lighthearted. "Perhaps he'll announce that we've won the war. The Emperor is too proud to speak otherwise." I could tell from his face that he was worried and was trying hard not to show it. He must have worried about Sam Tai too. We'd had no word from him since Hiroshima.

At times I wanted the war to end, because once the war was over, Sam Tai would be home and I missed him terribly. I imagined asking him many different questions. Minutes later, I questioned if the Army or Air Force would recruit me if war ended. One has so many problems when one is fourteen, but I was afraid to voice my thoughts.

We crowded around our small radio by the kitchen table the next morning, waiting to hear the Emperor's voice. Perhaps he would say the war would be over in less than a week and then we'd all celebrate a big victory. I imagined my father would let out a big sigh, for he always liked to sigh. Mother would look fondly at Nene and tell her Sam Tai would soon be in our midst.

The Emperor spoke and we all heard the words, deep regret, decided to effect a settlement, the world has turned against her interest, total extinction of human civilization, pains our hearts night and day, etc., etc. Mother sat us down and explained, "We have had to surrender. There is much damage from the Hiroshima bombing. It's like a big fire over the entire city, and the Emperor said the whole world will be destroyed if we don't surrender. The war will end soon."

Our village of Nakahito, Korea, heard the devastating news as did the rest of the world. Oppa and Nene ran out and talked to their friends. Kim Yoon came to our house and wanted me to tell him everything again, and I explained what Mother had told us with my own editorial. Mother said she worried for Sam Tai in case he was flying his aircraft anywhere near that city of Hiroshima. We'd had no news from him for almost a month.

Two days later, an Air Force officer stopped by our house. He told Father that his eldest son was one of the two fighter pilots shot down over the Pacific, a few hours before the Hiroshima bombing. I watched the officer's downtrodden face.

He did not offer any personal consolation for the brother I had just lost. Father said this atomic bomb explosion was horrific.

Within two weeks of the bombing of Hiroshima and Nagasaki, Japan had surrendered. The Emperor had told us so. News that we'd lost the war was a shock clearly seen on the faces of our village elders. My brother Sam Tai's life was just one of many losses.

With Sam Tai's death, war became a monstrous cruelty to me. My dream to share the heroism of war with Sam Tai, (for that is what I thought when I was fourteen) was crushed. Kim Yoon didn't care. All he wanted was to come to my uncle's store to talk and tell me a joke, so I would smile again. I worked long hours after school and on weekends. I kept a shiny button from Sam Tai's uniform in my pocket and ran my fingers over its smooth surface.

From Austria to Germany, Spring, 1939

A separation is
the beginning and the end; starts
across the railway tracks this day.

My little girl Tzipora walks away,
pretends to be unafraid, turns her back to me,
her blue coat flailing in the wind.

My wife has tied matching ribbons
in her neatly combed hair.
Tzipora holds her mother's hand,
now looks at me puzzled across the railway tracks.

I see her clenched teeth, I watch her tears
as she waves her little hand. Then,

uniforms lash out and herd them in.
In, in, faster, faster, and
the train door closes.

Sukhatme-Sheth 38

My Other World

Aunt Natalka and Vasyl Bondarenko were married seven days after they had danced the polka all night long at Vasyl's friend Ivinic's wedding. It had been their first date. She was twenty-three, big-boned and buxom, with a sparkle in her eyes, and she had fallen for Vasyl's tall, handsome figure, his delicate skin, and his tantalizing smile. She loved the music as he held her close when they danced, and she swayed with his deft agility.

"I ask permission to wed your sister, Natalka, next week," Vasyl said to my father.

Father was her eldest brother and head of our household.

"Next year," Father answered in a strong voice, as his way of postponing the event. Talk in the town square suggested that Vasyl was a leech and Father did not like him, but three days of knowing him was long enough for Natalka, and her mind was made up. It left my father no choice but to hold a big family wedding, for appearance sake.

"That roadside beggar, he'll ruin her!" Father whispered to my mother, after he had toasted the bride and bridegroom loudly many times over, and after many more drinks. The older guests sat still with questioning eyes, and the younger ones became boisterous.

I remembered the wedding because of the loud music and dancing and the colorful skirts that twirled around in the small town square. Father's stormy voice and, perhaps, anger, I'm not sure which, echoed in my head. We children ate big scoops of ice cream and ran around between the dancers and yelled 'catch' to each other. Aunt Natalka and Uncle Vasyl pulled me in to dance with them that evening. When I stopped to scratch a big welt behind my left knee with my sticky, ice cream fingers, I looked up at Aunt Natalka's hair with the white flowers in it. She looked so radiant. I also noticed a big, black mark behind Uncle Vasyl's left ear and thought at first it was an insect, similar to the one that had bitten me earlier that evening. They both laughed with me in a good-natured, hearty manner and I liked him just as much.

Then, in years to come, I heard Father comment to my mother, "What does she see in him? He has never done an honest day's work in his life. How long does he think his family money is going to last?"

Ten years later, circumstances changed and my parents sent me to live with Uncle Vasyl and Aunt Natalka. The Russians were infiltrating our small Ukrainian hometown on the Russian border. Newspaper headlines told of soldiers looting private homes, and businesses were closing down. The town changed. At first a few, and then many more, soldiers marched through the streets. Mothers were afraid and told their daughters not to walk home alone. Children had to be indoors before dark.

My parents made that decision almost overnight, and I was sent further away to Odessa where my aunt and uncle lived. I journeyed to the big city with an old farmer, sitting cross-legged in the back of his open truck. Father gave me a note to give to his sister, saying I would be staying with her for a few months and she should get me admitted to the gymnasium for my schooling. Mother sent them a big, homemade rum cake and twelve, fresh farm eggs, packed in a wicker basket, which I guarded.

I remember my Aunt Natalka clearly. I could hear the sound of her weary footsteps climbing all the way to our sixth floor apartment, dragging one and sometimes two metal milk containers behind her. She sold milk from the cows they secretly kept in a far away shed. She walked there every dawn and dusk to milk the cows and bribed the government officers to look the other way. Then she carried the vats home on a wooden cart. I studied at my desk by the window and ran to help her when I heard her coming up the stairs. In the evenings as I looked on, sparkling lights from ships far into the sea shone against the sky. Soon, twilight became night. Street lights came on, delineating city limits and shining over the port. I would stare into the darkness and sometimes see a bright star.

Aunt Natalka washed up and then knocked on my open bedroom door before supper.

"How was your day at the gymnasium, Katerina? They give too much work in school these days. Too many books, I see." She put her heavy, chapped hands on my shoulders and patted them. "Come for supper. It's just the two of us tonight."

I understood. Uncle Vasyl was not available to his family that evening, and there were many such evenings. I had overheard Aunt Natalka talking to the neighbors, "He has a weak heart; it's hard for him to climb the stairs. He stays in that ground floor apartment across town to rest up. The air is fresher there."

I wondered if anybody ever believed her. Old Madame Rabinowitz from next door mumbled away. She kept her door open in the evenings and watched for who came and who left.

Vasyl Bondarenko was a well preserved man, majestic and stiff. He wore a bolero and sported a small goatee. He dressed neatly, most often wearing a white, shiny suit. He must have been at least seven or eight years older than Natalka. She told me repeatedly that he was of delicate health and needed to rest. I tried to look sympathetic and wished I could believe her, but I had reason not to. What happened was the following, and it left a deep impression on me.

Soon after I'd moved in with them, I saw Uncle Vasyl on the other side of the street as I walked home from school across town. I called out to him but he continued walking without hearing me. I turned around and followed him. He walked into a side street and then crossed the road. He knocked on a large, elegantly carved, wooden door that was immediately opened by a young woman with bright red lips. He stepped in and pulled her towards him and then the door closed. I stood aghast on the opposite side of the street clutching my school bag. I felt nauseated by the whole scene and ran all the way home to tell my aunt.

Aunt Natalka's eyes teared up but I could tell she was not surprised. For a while, she remained seated. Then she wiped the corners of her eyes with the end of her apron. As she dug her hands firmly into the wooden arms of the chair she sat on, she said to me in a low, sure voice, "Never think about this again. Just remember that you are not to go there ever, ever, no matter what. I don't want you repeating this to any of your friends, or to any of our neighbors, you understand! For he is a kind man."

They did not talk of love in those days, but she spoke of him in a caring voice, no matter whatever else he did. I slowly realized that Uncle Vasyl spent many of his days and nights in the comforts of this other apartment. My aunt never talked about this other somebody. I never got to know her name. Vasyl Bondarenko came and left as he pleased, but from that day on, I hated him.

There were evenings when my aunt would cook and clean feverishly. Uncle Vasyl would be dining with us, I guessed. I enjoyed the special treats prepared for such days. The taste of my aunt's special lentil soup with bacon comes to mind and I could hardly wait. Aunt Natalka set the table with careful deliberation. I helped her unfold a fresh linen, neatly embroidered tablecloth, with blue and white flowers on it. The aroma of freshly baked bread permeated the apartment. We rolled up matching blue table napkins into napkin rings, and placed these precisely on the right side of the dinner plates. Homemade soup was served first to Vasyl. Then Natalka scooped up a dollop of fresh cream. She stood by his side, scoop in hand, and waited for him to say, "Yes, please." She kept standing till he began to slurp down the soup. Then, with a satisfied look on her face, she'd sit down and say to me, "Help yourself, dear."

The food was always good. My aunt was happy on these occasions. Uncle Vasyl seldom noticed my presence, anyway. Once he asked me if I studied hard and did I still want to go to medical school in Kiev. He didn't wait for my answer. We never talked about my father or my mother.

I helped my aunt clear the table and tidy up the kitchen before I returned to my books. Natalka insisted on doing the dishes because it seemed to me she was ministering to her own needs. To serve food with such elaborate detail was a satisfying experience for her, and putting the washed and dried dishes away completed the evening. In the meantime, Uncle Vasyl sat serenely in his high-back, big wooden chair. He sipped his port and smoked his pipe for the rest of the time. Sometimes, they listened to Mozart on the big, bulky gramophone with its huge horn. It resounded from the square, wooden table in the corner of the living room. Natalka would sit in her usual straight chair opposite him and do her cross-stitch, her eyes focused on the squares and crosses. From time to time, she asked Vasyl if he needed another drink. There never seemed to be any conversation between them. Sometime during the evening, he took out a wad of money and left it by the table lamp. It was our sustenance money. At precisely eleven o'clock, he stood upright and simply walked out. At times, just before eleven, I came out of my room just to be polite and in case he wanted to say something to me, but he never did. My aunt bolted the front door. No one spoke.

The fragrance of fresh acacia flowers from the rows of trees that lined the streets came in to my room with the evening breeze. It made me think of my parents in our hometown, getting ready for bed. Sometimes, I tried to think kindly of Uncle Vasyl. Then I imagined he might be a spy with a secret mission, so he was not allowed to say much. I held a grudge against him as I realized that all along my father had been right. Perhaps my Aunt Natalka realized it as well, but she was a proud woman and would never speak about it, much less admit it to her brother.

Then another big change happened. From our upstairs window, Aunt Natalka and I saw big German army trucks passing through the streets. Young adults, usually many more girls than boys were packed into these. Stories of the German Nazis killing people in our cities abounded.
I did not know then that eventually it was to be my fate too, to be herded away.

A few weeks later, there were loud knocks on our front door. Big, forcible sounds that made Aunt Natalka and I look at each other. Then she gestured for me to go into my room. She opened the front door a little. In a dull haze, I saw myself peeking from behind the wooden door.

"We'll take the girl. Ask her to get her things in five minutes. That's all the time she has!" the Nazi soldier shouted.

Natalka let out a big scream and ran to close my bedroom door. She tried to beat her fists on the young man in his authoritative Nazi uniform, the one who had spoken up and followed her in. Another soldier held her wrists and pushed her down into Uncle Vasyl's special chair. She sobbed helplessly.

I trembled without feeling any pain. I was just numb and my mouth felt dry. I don't think I even looked at my aunt as I was pushed out of the apartment clutching my copy of *The Iliad*, in which I had kept a letter from my father, a letter I read frequently and used as a bookmark. I might have carried out a few more belongings in my shoulder bag, but I don't remember what they were.

Days later in a shoe factory, where I was one number amongst hundreds of other young girls, I hand-sewed soles on leather shoes. I wondered during those times if Uncle Vasyl might at least have tried to rescue me had he been there. Could he have bribed the soldiers into letting me stay? Unjust perhaps, but I was angry with him. As I pushed the long needle in and out of the leather with my calloused fingers, I wondered if my aunt was still alive.

I grew up overnight, but I did not know then that a worse fate might have awaited me in the hands of Nazi-invaded Ukraine.

Several decades later, I stiffened, noticing the name Vasyl Bondarenko on the slides I had just reviewed. The diagnosis beyond doubt was cancer. A patient with a name from my past was admitted on the tenth floor of the hospital. My hands moved back and forth over the goose bumps on my forearms. Here was my possible connection with my long-forgotten past. It was the world I'd left behind when Hitler decided to march his armies southwest to Ukraine. It was my other world; my childhood, my land, and my family. After all these years, I still didn't know what happened to my father. Was he even alive? I knew he had been sent away to some far off place which meant nothing to me.

That was the same name, Bondarenko, which had just crossed my desk. The name was unusual enough. It might just be him. Perhaps he would tell me more about my parents and my aunt? A little part of my youth woke up.

I pushed back my microscope and began to dictate the pathology report on the patient Bondarenko. Halfway through I stopped, thinking of Aunt Natalka and Uncle Vasyl as they looked in their younger days. My office had suddenly suffocatd me as I thought back to the time when I was a sixteen-year-old girl. It was in the early forties when I lived with them in the town of Odessa in Ukraine, more than 50 years ago. Eventually, I had come to America after completing my medical degree in Germany. Little did I know then that a name I knew in my youth would catch up with me in this far away place.

Bondarenko was my Aunt Natalka's married name, so typically Slavic and so unheard of in my present surroundings. My husband, Jeremy, our eight-year-old son, Ivan, and I came to Chicago more than 30 years ago. Many other Eastern European families were also in the area. In our one bedroom apartment on the South side, I invited other little Slavic boys to play with Ivan. He spoke only Ukrainian, same as Jeremy and I. We opened and closed our dog-eared Ukrainian-English dictionary several times a day and got ourselves to English class. We spoke to Ivan in our heavily accented English the best we knew how. His third grade teacher told us it was better for him to hear only English. Then I sent out applications to hospitals that would train me to become a pathologist in the United States. A few months later, we moved forty miles away from the Slavic community and I heard less and less of those names and even fewer spoken Slavic words. The name Bondarenko faded away with more miles and more years.

I'd tried to get information about my parents and my Aunt Natalka and Uncle Vasyl after I'd settled in the United States. The records were just not there. Our son, Ivan, grew up believing he had no other relatives except his father and me.

Standing up behind my desk, I stretched and picked up my bifocals. With long, determined steps, I walked fast to the elevator fearing I might change my mind if I paused to think. On the tenth floor, my legs felt heavy. At the nursing station, I told the nurse that I had come to see Mr. Bondarenko on a social visit since I was also from the Ukraine, and thought from the name that it might be somebody I knew a long time ago.

As she walked in with me, she told me that he'd been in a nursing home for at least ten years in the Chicago area, and had been moved to our hospital for suspected pneumonia.

I knew better. I had just seen his slides.

"He's not listed as an Army man, so he's not a prisoner of war. Somehow he escaped captivity. We don't know how," the nurse told me.

"Did his family visit him in the nursing home? Does the chart say who pays his bills?"

"There is a stepdaughter listed in New York. We've let her know."

The emaciated old man lay quietly curled up in the hospital bed, so different from the Uncle Vasyl of my youth. Only, his eyes were watchful. His fingers picked at his bed sheets. I did not recognize him. He just lay there too weak to speak. I called out his name repeatedly, but he did not respond.

The nurse straightened his pillows and her hand touched a packet of papers. She examined the packet and then handed me the papers because she knew I spoke and read some Ukrainian. Then she left.

I took the small bundle of papers tied up in a dirty, embroidered handkerchief. I sat down on the chair beside the bed and looked at the man who perhaps could be Uncle Vasyl. He had seen me but did he know who I was? From the fixed, expressionless look on his face I wondered for a moment if he thought I might be Natalka. I have the same big bones and energetic eyes.

The feeling of disgust with which I remembered him turned to simple indifference as I faced this dying man. Slowly, I unraveled the cloth knot and saw some German writing. Two photographs and a couple of folded papers fell into my lap. One much handled, faded photo showed a young couple I did not recognize. The second picture was of a woman. I looked closely at it to make sure it wasn't Aunt Natalka. The letters were in German. I read them slowly. One letter talked of Maria working in a clothes factory after the Germans had taken her. The second letter was brief. It said Maria had been sent to a concentration camp. Both letters were addressed to no one.

I knew no Maria, so this was not Uncle Vasyl. Then again, it could still be him. With my charged up memories, I wanted him to talk to me. I wanted him to be my Uncle Vasyl. For him to tell me that they'd all escaped to Germany after the war. Like I had with my husband, Jeremy, and our son, Ivan.

I sat in his room for a long time. The old man kept looking at me, and that look bonded me to him in a strange way. Perhaps, because I'd psyched myself to think that I would be seeing Uncle Vasyl. Now it didn't matter. As I rose to go, I reached out with both hands and grabbed his. He was just another very old man from Ukraine, and Ukraine was the country of my birth.

I kissed him on the forehead and walked towards the door. Another nurse wanting to take his temperature and straighten his sheets walked in as I was leaving. I stopped to talk to her, hoping she would give me more information about this man. When she turned his body halfway up to straighten the sheets under him, I went closer to the bed to give her a hand to support him. There was a black mole behind his left ear and suddenly, the image of that tall, straight man on the dance floor floated before my eyes.

I needed time to think. What should I do next? How should I reenter his life? On what terms?

"I'll return soon," I said to the nurse, but I left without turning back to say goodbye. I didn't want him to see the tears in my eyes until I knew who they were for.

Minutes after

sniper bullets hit public-housing apartments of no great décor,
but home to everyday Bosnians, Aleksander leaves for the steel
factory on his bicycle, and his wife, Emili, takes the baby to her
breast, before she goes to stack boxes in a grocery store. At
home, Grandma starts a pot of *tarhana*, a simple soup for their
noon meal, to be served with one-day-old bread she and the
baby's three-year-old sister will eat. Grandpa died two years ago,
when the fighting first started in Sarajevo. The family believes it
was the Serbs that really gave this Bosnian Muslim grandpa his
heart attack.

Days later
while more bullets strike, Emili returns after dodging the
unruliness outside, and she covers her ears, cowers under the
blanket hugging her baby, asking Grandma, when will this stop,
they're going to kill us, why is Aleksander not home?

Months later
when plastic sheets cover their broken window panes, the curfew
on the streets continues, the baby cries, and Grandma looks for
her knitting needles. Emili sighs – if only I could sleep through
one long night.
The baby's three-year-old sister, oblivious of the bullets, dresses
and undresses her dolls under her mamma's bed.

A Hole in the Wall

War rages on. Johnny Leroy hears bombs exploding, sees balls of light flash across the sky, and then there is silence. No sounds or people around him; the stillness in the air bothers him. He awaits his next order to shoot and wonders if he missed hearing the commander's voice, because he is far behind the rest of them. Had he fallen asleep in that space of eerie silence and now doesn't know how much time has elapsed? On this moonless night, the lights are distant and dim, or nonexistent; whatever happens to streetlights on a small village street in the middle of war.

Johnny knows this feeling from when he was eleven years old. It is a pregnant silence in the middle of the night when he pulls his sheets over his ears and buries his head between his hands. He wants to keep the noises out...his mother's moans, her lover's grunts, and their bed squeaking on the other side of the wall.

Johnny has dropped his helmet. It strangely lifted off his head, as if ghosts of his childhood are pulling at him here in this distant corner of Southern Iraq, and are telling him not to pee in the night. He doesn't understand when voices float around him and yet, say very little. He clutches at his rifle, like it's a solid crutch. Where are Chico and Charlie? They're supposed to back me, he thinks, as he runs under the eaves of the houses, in the shadows, his eyes alert for movement. A dark figure, holding what looks like a pointed spear, is running toward him from the opposite direction. Johnny looks around sharply, wondering what to do, then decides to stand motionless in the shadow under the eaves. He slips into a slightly, ajar doorway. He waits. Waits to see if he is safe, or if he needs to put holes in the approaching figure. He has his instructions not to kill any civilians unless they attack, and his training is for self-protection. Right now, he must wait.

Like his mother's orders. Wait. Her strict regime for him after his father was taken ill. She wants him to be a good boy and not get into fights. She tells him his father was never a fighter.

The figure dressed in black with a turban on his head is almost upon him, but the darkness in the doorway and the angle at which he stands keep him from being seen. John Leroy knows the enemy will find him because there will be more Saddam supporters behind this one. They'll come out like worms from nowhere. He has to hide till the rest of them get past him. In the meantime, he presumes there are many like him in the shadows but he doesn't know where. His concern is for Chico and Charlie who should have been around, but have simply vanished. He doesn't know if it is his fault, although he suspects it might be. Men from his battalion keep disappearing one by one. Finding himself alone, he worries he might be next. He pushes open the doorway, and enters the empty room and moves to the back of the house. A faint groan in the corner makes him point his gun at the old man he sees.

Every Sunday, Mama dresses him in smart clothes and takes him to see his father in the nursing home. First they go to the Sunday Service at St. Xavier's Church round the corner from their house, then for a quick bite at Dog and Suds, where she buys him a small hamburger, fries and a vanilla ice cream cone. Johnny likes the smooth texture of the ice cream when he licks it. Every Sunday, he sees his father's wrinkled body in almost the same static posture. In later years, when he is in high school, he goes alone and observes that his father's face has still not aged. He continues this Sunday ritual for years, till he gets out of school and joins the army. His mama tells him in her letters that she goes when she can; Johnny isn't happy about her infrequent visits, but he doesn't want to tell her.

He looks carefully at the man on the floor, and from what he can discern in the dark, the old man is not hurt. His bent body reminds Johnny of his own father. Johnny thinks he's simply too old to leave his home and walk away in wartime. The back of the room smells of bananas...ripe, rotting bananas. He sees a table, an upturned folding chair, an unmade bed; a mess of clothes and pots and pans and papers are on the floor. A whiff of onions comes his way and he realizes he has just stepped on one.

On the Army application, he writes, "Father dead," for that is how he has thought of his father all these years. It's always been the ghost of his father he visits. He does not tell his mama about this lie, but he's certain she won't care.

Johnny feels nauseous from the mixed smell of onions and blood and the endless hours of filth he has been fighting in. The war noises explode outside but death is in this small house. Johnny slumps against the wall. He's closer to the old man whose eyes seem to look straight through him. Johnny thinks the eyes tell him the man is lonely. The man does not move.

Johnny imagines the eyes to say, "My family abandoned me. They ran away when war came to our village. My three sons, their spouses, and their children gathered up all the belongings, things they could carry on their shoulders, and then they ran to the mountains. My sons tried to make me walk with them but I couldn't burden them."

Johnny remembers snippets of the accident clearly. He was seven years old. He was holding both his father's and his mother's hands and walking between them on the narrow pavement. He was singing a song and watching a big crow fly aimlessly across the sky. Suddenly people were running...chasing each other and screaming as his father's hand went limp. Later, the police said a random bullet went into his father's spine as he pulled Johnny down. He remembers licking his mama's salty tears after they came home from the hospital.

Johnny puts his gun down and talks to the old man.

"Did you say you didn't want to abandon your farm and your home? You have no other place to go, and no other place you'd prefer to die? Well, old man, I'm not going to kill you. So soak in your stench, I'm leaving."

Every time he comes home from the hospital, he thinks he has been to his father's funeral.

Johnny is restless because nobody is coming and nobody is giving him orders. He waits to hear a human sound, but the place is abandoned except for the old man whose eyes are on him.

Johnny can't let go of thoughts about his father. The old man's eyes sparked those thoughts. If he does not go home in a body bag, he decides to make amends to his old man. All he will do is go sit by him once a week. Maybe hold his hand, smile at him, and tell him he'll be back next week.

Johnny slides across the floor toward the old man and touches his hand, but finds it is cold. He is shocked. He lets go and without another thought, quickly walks out into the street, just in time for a bayonet to pierce him straight in his stomach.

Etched Hands of Love and Loss

With her once beautiful hands,
now cracked and sore,
she bathes her baby
on a cold winter day.

She heard him leave last night
ten years of love forsaken.
Her sobs soundless lest the baby awaken,
looks at her once youthful hands.
Next morning, she takes a deep breath, stands up.
The soup needs stirring,
the bread needs to be baked.

Sukhatme-Sheth 56

A Distorted Web

"I should've left hours ago," Halima muttered as she placed her hands on her protruding abdomen and felt the baby inside her tighten into a knot. She rubbed her palms across her overstretched skin in unison, making smooth, circular movements. A vague discomfort descended into her loins. Every few minutes she thrust her fists into her lower back and took a deep breath. She recognized this sensation from before and it no longer alarmed her. It had happened the four times when her healthy children had been born and three times when precipitous labor occurred during the early months of her pregnancies. An episode, a year ago, when her husband, Chima, had kicked her in a violent rage and she miscarried, hurt her the most. The evening light faded fast and Halima hurried through the twilight, tightly holding onto a package of food wrapped in cloth.

"Take the *gulab jamboos* from the fridge when you leave. Too many left over," Mrs Mehta had said. "You said your girl really liked the sweet *jamboos* last time? Tell me the truth, did Chima eat them all?"

"They all got a bite," Halima answered. She tried not to say much about Chima.

Mrs. Mehta, the Indian woman Halima worked for, gave her all the leftovers from their own evening meal. As always, this evening too, despite her discomfort, Halima had waited until the meal was done. She washed the dinner plates that her young helper brought back to the kitchen, and then she emptied the leftover vegetables, the lentil *daal* and rice into her own cheap, tin containers. She packed the remaining flat breads, the *chapatis* she had skillfully rolled out just an hour earlier, from the circular, stainless steel container. Each one of these *chapatis* was individually fluffed up over a hot flame, rubbed with plenty of *ghee* and served hot to the Mehtas as they sat down for their dinner. Mrs. Mehta had taught Halima the basics of Indian cooking over the years and, with time, Halima excelled in making several Indian vegetarian dishes. Now she wrapped these already cold *chapatis* into a large cloth and tied the napkin into a firm knot.

Halima was glad for the food. Being a proud Ugandan from the Moshimi tribe, she made herself believe she was doing Mrs. Mehta a favor by taking the leftovers home. She smiled as she remembered the expectant looks of her young children waiting for her. This day, she carried a special gift for her daughter, Naaz. Mrs. Mehta had cleaned out a chest of drawers earlier that day and found a brooch with a stone missing.

"Here Halima," she had said. "Take this brooch home if you want to. I don't want Vicki to wear it again. Your girl may like it." So saying, she tossed it to Halima.

Halima toyed the brooch with her fingers. Naaz possessed only one other piece of jewelry, a cheap necklace from Vicki's jewelry box. Even with a stone missing from the brooch, Halima could imagine her daughter's happiness. She'd run over to show it to her friend next door, and perhaps to her father, Chima, if he happened to be in the front of their hut. Halima did not want Chima to see it, after what happened last night. She decided to hide the brooch from Chima, at least for a while. She was afraid he'd snatch it from her and sell it for liquor. Before she left for the evening, Halima fixed the clip of the brooch carefully on the inside of her blouse and drew her shawl close across her shoulders.

Halima looked around furtively through the semidarkness. She worried the baby would come too quickly. There was much danger around these days. Lately, many of her friends had bad experiences, but when she asked Chima to come fetch her in the evenings from the Asian family residence, so they could walk home together, he called her names. He might have cared long ago, she thought, when they were first married. In the earlier years, Chima and their eldest boy had farmed their rented plot of land. They grew maize on their hand ploughed property and sold it in the city. A little money came in, and together with what Halima earned doing household work, the family managed to live.

Those were the peaceful times before the Idi Amin takeover of power in 1972. He had declared an economic war on the Asian merchants who owned many of the businesses in Uganda. His Government had taken over the farms, and sent people like Chima to drink. Halima peered into the distorted shadows of small trees that lined the rough country paths. Muddy puddles of water in the middle of the road made strange shapes. She heard no sounds. No whispers. There was no wind and a deep silence surrounded her.

She pulled her headscarf over her ears, and took in a deep breath. She stood still and looked around. The discomfort in her sides quickly changed to periodic spasms. Halima put her hand up to her chest to feel the brooch safely tucked inside her blouse.

She turned the corner and faced the large clearing with which she was familiar. It meant that she had walked almost a third of the way home, although at this point, her path seemed interminable. Across the maidan, she saw the vague outline of a cluster of huts in the far distant corner. Through this eerie haze, just to be able to see her village of Mahuri gave her some comfort. She was afraid her baby would come before she reached home.

It became dark but the oil lamps in the huts had not yet been lit. Chima would normally do it for her every evening before she got home. Chima liked the money Halima brought in. So lately, she told him more lies. Sometimes she said Mrs. Mehta had not paid her for that month. Another time, she said they cut her pay because she broke a precious vase. Things like that, while in reality, she told Mrs. Mehta to hold a portion of her pay back. This way, when she felt the need, she could sneak home some extra grain or firewood or new clothes for one of the children.

Halima remembered Chima from last night and shuddered. Chima, in a state of drunken rage, had shouted at her when she asked about the bruise marks on their eight-year-old son's arm. The child's eye was swollen and he cried a lot, but he was afraid to answer any of her questions. She slept on the mat beside Chima that night but hated his touch. He beat her many nights and she was afraid of his wrath. Especially these days, with a new baby so soon to be born. That brutal kick from last year resurfaced in her mind and she had moved away a little, her eyes still fixed on Chima's back. In the fifteen years since their marriage, things always looked bearable when the sun came up the next morning.

As Halima walked back, she hoped she would find Chima sober that night of all nights. He'd have to get the midwife. She still cared for him, the father of her four children, and the fifth one on the way. She thought about the way things had changed in their simple life. Chima was unable to farm any longer. It was the only thing he had done all these years and knew how to do. Dada Idi Amin's government had imposed severe regulations on the farmers. The government wanted to buy out the land and build big factories on it. There was political turmoil of the worst kind and military soldiers in authority from the Government roamed all over and looted villages, farms and individuals.

Halima thought of her friend, Jessie, whose only fault was that she was born in a Christian family. Jessie, black like Halima, with her children had fled the village after months of harassment. Halima didn't know if there would be as many soldiers in the other villages too, and who would give Jesse and her family a hard time, but she knew the climate was tense all over the country. Jessie had left, but soldiers still kept coming back to harass others in her village. Halima had other friends who worked for Asians and Whites like she did, and some of them had been questioned and mauled. In the meantime, people like Chima drank some more.

Halima's contractions became stronger. She stopped every few yards to take a deep breath. A jeep appeared out of nowhere from behind her and screeched to a halt. It made a noisy U-turn and its head lights glared on her from just a few feet away. An Ugandan soldier jumped out of the jeep and rushed toward her. She could discern one more soldier sitting in the jeep, his gun pointed at her. She peered at the young man who had walked up to her and thought she recognized him as a boy from her village of Mahuri. She couldn't be sure because the military uniform gave all of them, even this young boy of seventeen or eighteen, a look of authority and indifference.

"Do you know the Mehtas?" the soldier in the jeep asked abruptly.

"Yes," she murmured, fiddling with the ends of her scarf, eyes looking down at her big stomach. The pains within her made her shift from one leg to the other. She wondered if she should ask the boy his name, or say she knew who he was, but she was too scared to open her mouth.

"An African working for an Asian. You dog!" the uniformed boy next to her shouted.

She dared to look up but she did not answer. This was the boy from her village whose name was Ali. She was almost sure. Perhaps the other one was also from her neighborhood, she determined. Only they would know where she, wife of Chima, the drunkard, went to work every day.

The soldier standing next to her came even closer. He pulled her shawl down and tore away her head scarf, exposing her short, curly hair. He kept staring at her. He grabbed her breasts as she flinched from his touch. She could smell his hot breath. A hard object, the brooch hidden under her blouse, struck his palm and fell to the ground. His fingers grasped the buttons of her blouse and pulled at them.

Halima saw lust in his eyes. A cramp in her stomach doubled her up in pain and her eyes rested on the cheap metal brooch glittering in the dark. A stronger contraction came on and she winced. She started to say, "Ali, don't..." when he slapped her across the face.

The other soldier from the jeep screamed, "Stop," before he could strike again. He noticed her protuberant abdomen as she let out a muffled gasp. "You slut, you thief!" the first man shouted. Then he paused for just a brief second as he saw the brooch. He looked around as if wondering who to impress with the loot he had found.

"She's stolen some jewelry, this no-good mama," he yelled out to the driver and the other officer who had shouted at him for hitting her. "Let's take her in. She'll look good locked up."

A man in uniform jumped out of the jeep. He circled around her as if wanting to see her from all angles. Halima jerked forward as she felt her knees buckle. She stood rigid, face to the ground, arms across her chest trying to hide her exposed breasts. Her bundle of food, still neatly knotted inside a cloth, lay in a dirt puddle. Halima kept her focus on the food till her vision blurred and she could see nothing. She could not move. The jeep started up and seconds later, the two officers pulled her in and pushed her into a far corner. She cried out in pain and then she was numb. Inside of her, she could feel the contractions coming on stronger, and then suddenly a warm release, as she sat huddled in a pool of water and blood.

The wet warmth penetrated the seats in the jeep. The officer sitting next to her looked around him. Alarmed by the wetness and stench of blood, he turned to Halima. Her breath was labored.

"My baby! My baby! Coming, coming!" Halima screamed as the cramps came on stronger. Then she sighed heavily and relaxed before the next contraction started.

"Move man, move," the soldier Ali shouted. "The bitch's about to have baby!"

"What bother! You picked the wrong kind, you stupid asshole! What to do? What if she dies on us!" The two men in uniform started to whisper.

"Faster, faster, move," Ali shouted to the driver.

"They're all the same. Dirt. Just dirt!"

"Who are you? Mere boys who have now become important soldiers. Even your skin is the same color as mine," she screamed.

"She has to be in jail, we have our orders. These bastards that work for the Asians, and she's a thief besides. At least we could have some fun, if she weren't this way," the soldier she did not know said.

"Let's just dump her. Do something, man. She's trouble in the jeep!" Ali shouted to the others. The jeep roared on. She wondered if the boy Ali really cared.

"Yes, dump her, quick. We won't have to explain anything to the boss man." It was again the voice of the soldier Ali, the boy from her own village who had torn open her blouse.

She felt the jeep swerve and change directions. They must have traveled for another two or three minutes before the jeep lurched to a stop.

Halima found herself being pulled like a shapeless mass and set on the road side in the shadows of some huts. Somebody threw a hard object next to her but she was too weak to stretch out her arm and retrieve the brooch. She heard heavy boots walk toward the jeep. Then the jeep roared away. She was just too weak even to cry out for help.

Halima did not know how long she had been by the roadside. When she opened her eyes she saw a shadow walking toward her with a lantern in hand. She shrank back and turned her face away. A faint cry that sounded like her name made her look again, and in time, she recognized Chima's silhouette, his sure step, as he came forward with the lantern through the darkness. Somebody must have seen her being dumped. Somebody must have told Chima. Maybe they heard the jeep come into the village and heard the soldiers bragging.

Halima's first thoughts were that Chima would beat her instantly for starting the baby on the street. He'd ask her many questions. Then she heard Chima's steady voice, a voice without anger and without the drunken drawl. She heard him tell a child to get the village midwife. She felt his strong arms around her as he picked her up, mess and all, and moved her to the side of the street.

The tap still drips all night long

Standing at the doorway of his big stone house,
I imagine an echo of my daddy's voice.
Then sitting on the bed where he fell asleep,
I rub my fingers against the faded embroidered bedspread,
silencing death in my mind.

I brush off the cobwebs, open a jammed window,
and welcome the scent of jasmine.
The tap in the bathroom nearby drips noisily.

The gigantic maroon velvet couch looks forlorn
in the living room
Once, Mummy served tea and biscuits in there.

Photos, without viewers, stand dusty on the mantel,
as life dribbles through our adult days.

Today, years later, in their big stone house,
the same tap drips all night long,
echoing other forgotten sounds.

Namaste

A small paragraph on the fourth page of the Chicago Tribune has caught my husband, Janak's attention this Sunday morning.

"Listen, Meena," he calls out to me, as he stands up from the sofa in the family room.

I'm used to hearing his continuous rustle of newspaper pages and this has suddenly stopped.

"Guess who's in the paper," he says.

He comes beside me by the kitchen stove, where I'm boiling *masala* chai, our first morning drink. It's only on Sundays that I've time to boil the milk and water and spices and tea, together with plenty of sugar. We enjoy our routine of dipping buttered toast in it, as we read the newspaper and talk of current political upheavals.

He reads out loud, "Mr. Satish Lodhia, a renowned lawyer, has given up his practice of fifteen years and earns his living playing sitar at the well established Khyber Indian restaurant in Boston. This change of profession has led to a substantial reduction in his alimony payments to his ex-wife, Diana, a fashion model. She will take him to court for the third time next Monday." Without comment, Janak hands me that section of the paper and returns to his sofa.

Through the lacy curtains of our French windows, I see a sheet of white glimmer on the lake beyond. The first snow of the season is settling over the icy glaze. I wonder where the geese have flown to, the ones I'd seen bobbing up and down on the partly frozen lake just two days earlier. They come back year after year, but I marvel all the same when they are gone.

I have the urge to know more about what life has dealt this man, Satish. Some vague idea wants him to reenter my life. The next day doubt sets in, and I wonder if he even remembers me, my face, or my handicapped arm. He married perfection, a fashion model. My artificial arm, my cross, why did I even imagine he cared for me in those days! I hadn't even known that Satish was in the United States, the same as us, thousands of miles away from where we were born and where we spent our youth.

Two days later, I tell Janak I plan to write to him and Janak simply nods. I address the letter to the restaurant where Satish plays. I tell him we have a family trip planned to India the following month leaving from Boston. I ask him to come to the airport if he has time, so he could meet my husband and me. We can talk of old times, I say. Then I write the exact flight number and our departure time.

I say to Janak, "Will you please read my letter and mail it for me." I trust his judgment. He'd tell me if I wrote something that sounds fake.

Days later, I say to him with feigned indifference, "Do you think he'll come?" I continue to wipe my already spotless, graphite kitchen counter top, trying to hide my emotions behind a blank expression. My tone is apologetic and there is a slight tremor in my voice. I'm afraid Janak may notice the tremor and I don't want him to. He's sure to ask me more questions, just from curiosity or perhaps with a tinge of jealousy. After so many years of marriage, Janak understands my body language far too well; sometimes, even my thoughts.

Janak walks away without a word, as if he has not heard me. Minutes later, I hear his heavy step on the wooden stairs leading up from the basement. I spin around and walk up to open the basement door wider. Janak sets the empty, Naugahyde suitcases down with a thud, their dust laden surfaces releasing a fountain of particles in the air. He picks up the brown hand towel I've left on the back of a chair as he waves his hand in front of his nose to clear the aerosol he has just created.

"You bet he'll be there," says Janak, with a little tease in his voice. "He couldn't have forgotten your big brown eyes now, could he?"

The beginning. I'm seventeen.

We live in the small town of Morvi in Western India. The center of the town is a single, main street with a clock tower at the end. The main attraction is a swinging bridge across the narrow river that passes on the outskirts, where young and old gather after their evening walk. Little shops lining the streets get crowded at dusk. A cobbler squats on his shop floor and stitches handmade *chappals*. He keeps several pairs ready for when customers stop by. The shop next to him sells ready-made clothes. On the opposite side, next to the bookstore, is a tailor, and then the grocery store overflowing with goods. Just about everything can be obtained along this busy street, but there is nothing for a young person like me to do along these dirt roads. Except perhaps, to long to travel on the road beyond the bridge; the road that disappears into the dusty horizon.

Most young boys leave for college or get jobs in bigger cities. Girls my age get married off and move away, hopefully to seek better fortunes. When I complete high school, my parents want me to stay home or, if I really must, send me to the local 'Girls Only' college. They tell each other in my presence that my immediate marriage prospects are dim because of my handicap. I'm angry with them for wanting to keep me at home. I argue and am persistent that I want to see the big city of Bombay, to know for myself that I can survive in spite of my right prosthetic arm. Finally with their blessings, I'm sent to a college in Bombay.

I do not remember the exact facts, events, or circumstances but that memory of being young and seventeen gives me ecstatic happiness. At such times, I even forget I've one prosthetic arm. Small memories trigger images, like that peacock green barrette in my ponytail, the one I thought made me attractive, and then, the laughing fits we girls went through in our get-togethers at the ice cream parlors. Our noisy conversations when everybody talked and nobody listened. Through all this, I always knew when his eyes were on me, even in the midst of a crowd of friends. My legs trembled when I saw him approach, but I never found the right words to speak to him.

He and I are classmates since our freshman year of college. We cross each other in the corridors on our way back and forth from class, but I don't have the nerve to look his way. He always comes in late to class and finds a place next to me. I like to lurk in the back rows where I think fewer of my classmates will notice me. He is a tall, thin, very upright young man with a bush of curly, black hair. I see his aquiline nose through the corner of my eyes as I take left-handed notes in class. In my own mind, I decide he's good looking. At first we seldom talk, and at best it's usually an exchange of a few monosyllables. Then one day he surprises me.

"Can you come to my sitar recital tonight?" Satish asks.

I'm astonished, not knowing if he really means this as a special invitation. I'm fond of instrumental music, more so the sitar. I can't hold the string instruments in their slanting positions, nor use my right hand fingers for the bow. One tends to like what one cannot have. I enjoy the sounds and content myself to listening.

I sense he wants to know me. I'm pleased and flattered, but my birth defect looms large before me and my heart is pounding.

We sit cross-legged on straw mats in somebody's two-room flat on the second floor. Cool evening air blows in through the open windows, and brings with it a delicate resonance of sitar sounds and a mild fragrance of jasmine. His melody rings into the quiet of the night. I sit entranced. They serve coffee after the performance has ended. It's midnight and I escape unnoticed when he's talking and laughing in the midst of all his friends. The fragrance of jasmine remains with me.

After that, we talk. There are times when he offers me potato chips during class. I smile and politely decline. We have pleasant exchanges of conversation in the classroom. Then one day on our way out, he asks if I want to go for ice cream that evening. I'm pleased and nod.

Many evenings we stand in ice cream parlors, most often in groups of four or five. The college crowd is always there and every seat is taken. There is standing room only, but it never bothers us. We laugh at silly things around us, like somebody's fancy hairdo or another person's peculiar gait. We talk of trivial matters. We settle nothing.

"Write to me soon."

"You must, you must."

We scream in each other's ears when college years are over and all twenty of us friends part our different ways.

He does. He writes often at first, three or maybe four times in the first few months, but then the intervals get longer. I do not write to him, not for twenty-five years, not till this year, because Janak and I are married a couple of months after we graduated and all of us have gone our separate ways.

At night, hazy moonlight filters into our bedroom and I lay awake looking at Janak beside me. I move closer, afraid my touch will wake him up. I'm still in love with him, twenty-five years after we first met. Janak, with his parents, came to our house for the bride-viewing session. There had been other bride-viewing sessions before I finished college, and each time the family had rejected me because of my arm. What he saw in me I do not know to this day, but he made up his mind very quickly. Adjustments come faster in an arranged marriage when one tries and knows there are no alternatives. Somewhere in these years, I've told Janak about my first crush, one-sided on my part, I say to him. He laughs and says all young girls go through that.

"Remember this when it's your daughter's turn to fall for the guy next door," he says, looking at me with affectionate eyes. I look up at our daughter's picture on the mantel. She's away at college and I wonder who sits next to her in class.

Satish sits in a remote corner on one of the fixed seats opposite the airline counter. The counter is empty at that hour in the afternoon; it is still too early for check-in. I see him glance up, the distant look, then the sudden recognition. He stands a little hesitant, a little bent. I see the same smile, and the aquiline nose, the face I once thought I admired. My youth has resurfaced.

He seems not as tall I remember. Maybe because this is the United States, I'm used to taller people. Perhaps he's stockier, I think. His mass of curly black hair is totally gray. He's so different from the person I knew. There is still some distance between us and as we approach him, I pull on Janak's arm as if to say, "Let's not go on," but Janak ignores the tug and we keep walking.

"Namaste," Satish says to me, standing up. He does the traditional Indian greeting by joining two hands in front and bowing his head, that leads Janak to do the same. I simply bow my head. I never do a *namaste* because my right arm is awkward.

"My husband, Janak." I introduce them, and they shake hands. His glance moves sideways and his eyes rest on my prosthesis for a fleeting second, but I've noticed it. It bothers him still, I imagine.

"I'm so happy you wrote, Meena," he says. "It's been a very, long time."

"Yes, I know," I say, slowly and deliberately. Memories from long ago parade swiftly in my mind.

"You haven't changed much," he says.

"Only older," I reply.

We laugh as if we werewaiting all three of us. Then we sit down in awkward silence. Janak starts up some trivial conversation about Boston's traffic and congestion and our own life in the quiet midwest. After a while, Janak announces he needs a drink and walks away.

"Tell me about you," I say suddenly, looking at him square in the face. "Is the divorce still painful?"

"No, not any more," he answers with care, weighing every word he speaks in a slow, deliberate, very Bostonian accent. We sit in silence for a few more seconds. Perhaps he doesn't like it that I was so blunt. I'm a little ashamed that I was so brash.

"I did the two most important things in my life for the wrong reasons," he continues, looking in the distance. "You know about that."

"I've heard a little about it," I say.

"Diana, my ex, was a beauty. I married her perfection only to find out how far apart we were in our chemistry. She loved our lifestyle, our parties, our superfluous evenings of drinking and dining. I hated it all the more. I practiced law only so we could live the way we had both become accustomed. Our daughter was growing up a spoiled child but I loved her dearly.

"Divorce was inevitable. I'm surprised we even stayed married for twelve years. Then my beautiful Diana turned bitter.

First the divorce settlements, then custody battles. After that, what you read in the papers. Alimony payments. I tried to continue my work in the law firm, but I'm tired now. There is a consuming desire within me to turn to my music. I play the sitar. It's always been there, dormant, burning, and ready to explode."

"How old is your daughter?" I ask.

"Ten," he says. "By the way, I named her Meena."

Janak has joined us now. He listens to us talk without saying a word. Then Satish addresses him, "My Meena is a lovely girl, Janak. Just like yours."

"I'm a lucky person, Satish. I realized it the very first time I saw Meena's brown eyes," Janak says without looking my way.

They shake hands. Satish nods his head in my direction without really seeing me and walks away without another word.

I feel seventeen again; shy, awkward, and speechless. He called his daughter Meena. Our friendship mattered. I must have blushed as Janak puts his arm around me, and gives me the same curious, amused look; the one he gave me a few weeks ago when we were between dusting the luggage and the cleanup of the kitchen counters. I think of my frozen snow-blown lake where the geese and the ducks will come back to life next year.

We sit on the hard airport seats, waiting for the counter to open. Janak asks if I'm thirsty. An hour later, an airline officer turns the 'Closed' sign around. We walk forward with Janak wheeling our heavy luggage, and hoisting them onto the weighing platform. I dig out our airline tickets from my large travel purse, still feeling a glow on my cheeks.

Together we stand in the line for the security clearance.

The Village Perimeter in 1930

Ranga returns to his village after ten years of learning poetry and city sounds. Thinking of the London he's left behind, he feels anxious as he steps out of the local train. His once-starched shirt and neatly creased khakis are limp in the noon heat. His lonesome eyes search the distance for his soft-spoken mother and his emotionless father.

The elders greet him at the village perimeter. Saffron-clothed pundits join them. "Come no further. We need to purify you. A three-day cleansing ceremony. You're an outcast because you've crossed waters to reach foreign lands." Holding in their hands incense, fire, camphor, and water, they stand firm, leaning on their walking sticks. He sees his father stands next to them.

Shocked, Ranga says, "I'm not a believer. Please let me pass. I must bow in reverence to my parents. I will touch their feet and receive their blessings. I was born in this village; this is where I choose to return."

The pundits do not budge. The elders do not move. Word gets around that Ranga is an outcast because he has foreign water in his blood. He had crossed the oceans.

Four hours later, still at an impasse, with the afternoon sun strong, and the dusty winds high, Ranga vows out loud that he will never cross the village perimeter.

The outcast never returned to the playground of his youth. He married a city girl, became a well-known playwright, and together they mocked man-made boundaries and fences. Accolades and awards came his way. The cynicism in his heart never died; the noon heat had snapped his soul.

He never saw his parents again. His simple mother could not write; she was never taught. Girls had their boundaries. His father continued to side with the pundits.

Posthumously, the village named a school after him, and invited his daughter to cut the ribbon. The whole village came to applaud. Prancing around, the village idiot sang, "The outcast will haunt your souls."

The Pipe-Man

On a dark street in Mumbai, India, I happen to see a pipe-man. He sits semi-crouched by a glowing fire, just inside the open end of a large sewer pipe lying by the roadside. A child sleeps in the shadows abutted against him. The fire is a stack of broken twigs and crumpled newspaper, the flames contained within a few smoldering bricks. Mounds of dirt, stones, and old cement surround the dug-up pavement, waiting to be hauled away. Headlights from moving cars cast crisp shadows on people near him. They are huddled in small groups, some sleeping with only a tattered rag for a covering. Others sit, perhaps waiting to lie down after someone wakes up. Their outstretched arms reach out for warmth. These strange contours give me goose bumps, for I do not know if they are sleeping or simply dead.

It's three o'clock in the morning; a cool, moonlit night in the big city of Mumbai, and I recognize this main street. It seemed wider years ago when the huts with the squatters had not crowded it. My hosts, Rajesh and Sonali, have come to the airport to receive me even at this unearthly hour.

"All our relatives arrive from the United States at night and often times, the flights are delayed. We're used to our late-night airport trips," Sonali says.

"Fewer people wandering in front of my car and less cars at night," Rajesh adds. He's sitting next to the driver. He speaks with his eyes intent on the road. His look tells me he'd rather drive.

Sonali gets an orange drink from the small ice box near her feet. She wipes the bottle mouth with a tissue she gently pulls out from a box of Kleenex sitting in the back ledge of the curtained car window. The curtains seem to shut the world out. Sonali hands me the bottle. It's the end of December and the temperature late at night is cool, even in the tropics. Sonali has a light wool Nepali shawl loosely thrown across her back and shoulders. Still, my cheeks are flushed and I feel warm and thirsty, perhaps from just having to face a big jump in the temperature. When I left home twenty-four hours ago, my backyard was covered with snow and the weather man pointed his wand towards Chicago, saying the wind chill factor was minus ten degrees. I gulp down another large mouthful of the cold, orange Fanta. It feels so good, as does the air blowing through the air-conditioning vent.

At night there are fewer noises in the dark city streets. No bicycles, no street hawkers chewing *paan*, and no motor rickshaws spewing out diesel fumes. An occasional heavy truck rolls down the center of the desolate street, and random cars let out a shrill honk. I stare into the darkness trying to find space within this chaos. Several feet away are outlines of small huts set against dense bushes, casting oblique shadows in the moonlight.

"The street people," Rajesh says. "Too many thriving in big cities all the time! It's like New York these days. These people rule our lives."

"Perhaps," I say quietly. I have not forgotten the homeless in New York and Chicago, but they seem to have increased so much more here; but then, it could be just my perception.

I think of the pipe-man's life and mine; of my husband far away at home. Sonali's diamond earrings glitter and the world of contrasts hits me at this dark hour. With time, I have chosen to remember only happy memories of friends, of family, and of people I knew in my younger days. Twenty-four hours is not enough time to take in a forgotten truth; the stark reality just outside my window.

Rajesh begins to tell me there have been riots in the city.

"Some strike or the other," he says. "Last week it was the *taxiwallas*, and next week it's supposed to be the airlines. Always, there's a struggle over something."

Sonali says she was worried about my journey because of the danger of war.

"One never knows with Iraq, and what else may happen there. We worried about suicide bombers turning up anywhere; attacking which target where, who knows!" she continues.

War talk! More war talk, with the same keywords in India too! That's all I heard over the daily news. How odd that the ugliness of people affects all corners of the world. Foolish, perhaps, but I did not want to think that war would cross my path. A certain obstinacy filled me, an unspoken feeling that I needed to keep my plans and visit my aging mother, no matter what wars and enemies existed in the world around me.

My mother's letter said she wished to see me one more time before she had her eye surgery. It's a simple cataract operation, and it bothers me that she makes a fuss about wanting me to come. It's her way of being in control even now. Perhaps she's afraid; I'd kind of overlooked that. When I was ten years old, I argued with her because, according to me, she stitched my dresses one size too big. She never listened to my objections.

Rajesh, Sonali and I talk of other matters; my daughter in college, their teenage son, and the rising cost of gasoline and food. The conversation keeps drifting back to war politics. All three of us express ourselves assertively. It has been five years since we saw each other last and there is much to say. The field of war, the human act of giving and receiving, the drama of the victor and the vanquished, all are a struggle to survive.

Rajesh is my classmate from medical school. My husband and he did their medical residencies together in Chicago in the same hospital almost twenty years ago. We lived in hospital-provided doctor's quarters. In small, one bedroom apartments, we cooked basmati rice and *daal* and chicken curry on Saturday nights and reveled in rented Indian movies with plenty of love songs. Subsequently, Rajesh and Sonali moved back to India, to this crowded city of millions, Mumbai, and we stayed on. We argue about politics, both Indian and American. We talk with zest, and we remain friends.

This evening, too, there is a lot to be said, but my mind is dazed after the long journey. My eyelids are heavy from lost sleep, and now, somewhere in the middle of this turmoil, I am acutely aware of the pipe-man with a boy sleeping beside him. I have seen the two distinctly separate from the rest of their people. Somewhere in the hierarchy of living, the pipe-man has won the right to this shelter.

He is a lean man, perhaps in his mid-forties, perhaps older, I can't say. He has dark, shaggy hair and an unkempt beard. A light cloth, the mere semblance of a shawl covers his shoulders that seem otherwise bare. Some shapeless piece of material drapes his knees. His semi-crouched position gives him body warmth, I think. He had looked straight at our car and beyond us.

The next day is a warm, tropical afternoon and from the guest room of my hosts' bungalow, which is now my room on the second floor, I see clusters of red bougainvillea along the fence of their large yard. The sun adds richness to the bright color of the flowers, and together with the green foliage, the bougainvillea form a dense wall protecting us from the outside road. I'm to stay with my friends for two days and rest up before Sonali takes me by car to visit my mother a hundred miles away.

Sonali knocks on my door and asks if I'm ready to go to the bazaar. I love shopping and I want new Indian clothes, the latest fashions in cotton *salwar-khamiz*. I grew up wearing these baggy *salwars* or pants, with long shirts or *khamiz* to go over them. Going back to the country of my birth makes me want to fit in right away. Sonali says we'll take a taxi because parking is difficult.

This day, the pavement is thick with people walking back and forth, talking, laughing, arguing in voices loud enough to be heard above the din of radio music booming from every shop.

Our taxi takes us past the site where I've seen the pipe-man the previous night. His image haunts me. Sonali rattles on about a shop she's acquainted with, oblivious of my interest in looking for the pipe-man again. She asks the taxi to stop around the corner and let us out. She pays the driver a hundred plus rupees, about two dollars for a good twenty minute ride. We cross the road at a traffic light. A child in rags holds out his hand for money. I feel a deep hurt inside of me as I see his deep-set eyes that seem too big for his small face. His hair is a dull, dusty brown, somewhat crinkled, brittle looking, and under his shirt hides a large, protruding tummy. His legs are spindly as is his stretched arm. He must be eight or nine years old, I surmise; only he looks much smaller.

"*Paisa deo*," he demands in Hindi.

Sonali gestures for me to move on. "We'll give him something on our way back," she says. "Perhaps some fruit." She gently guides me on saying we'll collect a crowd if we stop to open our purses.

I watch the boy as I walk away. He continues to follow us. Has he seen my hesitation? He demands more money. I find myself moving sideways to get out of his way. An uncomfortable feeling suffocates me as he corrals me into a corner. There are just too many street people in this city, each with a need to survive. With difficulty, I manage to extract myself and notice a look of amusement on Sonali's face.

"Just ignore him. Walk straight on. *Chalo, chalo*," she says to me.

We enter a shop, one amongst a row of many single-story shops with the entrance doors two steps above street level. The doorways are partly obstructed by displayed merchandise, mostly ready-made outfits. Some are faded from the strong sun and show discounted prices pinned over the fronts. Sonali pushes a hanging shawl aside as she enters.

We look at colorful pieces of clothing on several different racks. Sonali points out the newer designs. I like a few but several appall me. There's even a singing Madonna on one of the *khamiz* dresses, and the two look mismatched to my eyes. The stagnant air inside the shop is stirred by our arrival and leaves a musty odor as we pull clothes off the racks and take them to the front of the store. We want to see them in bright daylight. I find a few traditional styles and like those better. The number of clothes and variety stacked in such a small shop amazes me. One can do a lot with just a little. I choose two cotton outfits, a delicate pink and a pastel green, but I've lost the art of bargaining. Sonali is good at it and an hour later, we leave with more packages.

The same boy with his spindly legs comes running up and wants to carry our packages for us. We ignore him and move on, making our way through crowds of shoppers. He follows. We look into several other shops. I sense him observing our moves.

A street vendor roasting corn on a charcoal grill calls out to us. We look at each other and nod. I stand there salivating as the aroma of roasted corn-on-the-cob with lemon and spice hits my nostrils. The boy holds out his hand, and looking me in the eye, says, "I need ten *rupees. Deo, deo*." (Give, give.)

He rubs his other hand over his big stomach in slow, circular movements. Then he says in a low voice, "*Bhuka hu*." (I'm hungry.)

This time, Sonali opens her purse and quickly gives him a *rupee*. She waves her hand, asking him to go away. She does not want him to stare at us with his hungry eyes. The boy takes the money but does not move. His face is expressionless, not even a hint of gratitude. Soon he'll demand more, I can see that.

"Let's buy him a corn," Sonali says. She asks for one more, and holds it out for the boy. Quickly, he puts both his hands behind his back and shakes his head.

"*Na, do chahiye*." (No, I want two.) He puts two fingers up.

I'm about to bite into mine, but seeing the boy's action, I stop. His rudeness and his demands, like my mother's, annoy me. I hold out my corn and he grabs it. He runs across the narrow street holding the two corns and disappears behind the crowd, but my eyes are on him. I see him talk to a pipe-man, still holding a cob in each hand. Then he pushes one corn into the older man's hand. The pipe-man doesn't move. In the daylight I see that the pipe-man is younger. He also has strange eyes. A second later, I realize that he cannot see. I don't know if he is the same one or not. My images of the pipe-man and his sleeping child from the moonlit night come back with clarity.

"Is he the same child I saw sleeping in the pipe last night? He's the same man, isn't he?" I ask Sonali.

"It doesn't matter," she says. "There are many. There are many children too."

As I go to bed that night, I think of war. I'm to travel to my mother's house the next day. I imagine her in a hospital bed with her eyes bandaged. Could I have come sooner when her eyes were not so bad? When she had not stumbled in the park and bruised her face and forehead? She said her eyes had not been affected by the fall, but I keep wondering. How much longer will my mother fight for her survival? Wars will end, perhaps next month or next year, and newer conflicts will begin. My man, the pipe-man, and his boy will still be there, fighting for their daily bread. Then one day he will not be able to light his own fire.

I suspect the boy will then become the pipe-man.

News from an Australian Newspaper, circa 1931

Three young half-aborigines escape from a military-like school,
where they are pumped with English and made pretend white,
so they learn etiquette when required to serve the white masters.

The sisters, thirteen, ten and eight hide in bush country, run,
limp, cry some more; shiver and starve for love as they flee
toward home six hundred miles along the rabbit-proof fence.

Six hundred miles away, mother and grandmother circle the fire,
beat the drums and ask the gods to bring the girls home safe.

Nine weeks later, two arrive.

Miracles happen like when I found my runaway dog in the heart
of the city.
scampering on three legs.

"Doodh, doodh"

Mr. Dwight Marks, a Harvard School business major, had risen to the top at Bingham and Marks within five years of starting his career there because, not only did he have the brains and the right smile, but he was the grandson of the original Martha Marks who founded "Exotic Orchids" in New York. The company had offices in five other countries and was looking for further expansion. Dwight, named after his quiet grandfather, was asked to look into its expansion in Asia. Dwight was not a traveler, but he took pride in the fact that he could negotiate his way through any situation and achieve his goals with ease and charm. His company was to send him to meet some hardcore business people in India, where negotiations had not been entirely successful on the last two attempts when a senior member had come for the task. This was Dwight's second visit, the last one for this year, he hoped.

On a bright, sunny morning Mr. Dwight Marks, dressed in business attire, stepped out of the luxurious Taj Hotel in Mumbai, India, and looked around for that scrawny child.

He'd noticed the girl with her outstretched palm several times before, but he never stopped. Eventually, her hungry eyes had got to him, for this day he decided to give the beggar something. He brown-bagged his leftover breakfast, much to the chagrin of the restaurant manager.

"Take this," Dwight said, shoving the bag of leftover toast, jam and rice cakes into the face of nine-year-old Leila, a street urchin with skinny arms.

Leila grabbed the bag and ran away without a word. Mr. Marks hailed a taxi and went about his day. He attended his business meetings and sat in air-conditioned boardrooms in high rise buildings all day long. Mr. Marks didn't care for all the modern furniture and the new architecture of the highrises along the waterfront. The old Taj Hotel with its stone facade and domed roof had become a habit with him. India to him meant exotic and ordinary extremes and he lavished in the luxury.

The next morning, he saw Leila with four others like her in almost the same place. Leila was bolder. She tugged at his elbow even after he gave her food this morning. The other little girls just looked at him. They were all begging for something more.

"Give me *doodh, doodh*, there, there," Leila said, pointing to a corner grocery store.

He feigned not to understand because he had no time for beggars, but a passerby who stood to gape at the American in his business suit, came to his rescue and helpfully told him *doodh* meant milk. Dwight had been in Mumbai several times over the years and he knew how pesky beggars could get. So this time, he simply walked away. His thoughts drifted to the big meals they were served at their own executive luncheons and evening banquets. He began to think of this intense luxury as a waste, and he felt the desire to brown bag more food from the dinner table. Something related to etiquette warned him not to, and so he didn't.

The following day, alone in the hotel at breakfast, he asked the restaurant manager to give him leftovers from other people's plates. A five star hotel does not pride itself on having a business man walk out with ten bags of leftover food from breakfast, but the manager had seen eccentrics before, and who was he to question a guest he had seen on the premises several other times? Dwight waited for the manager to bring him the bagged food and then stepped out. To his surprise, he was met by twenty little children, all with extended hands pulling at his neatly tailored suit coat.

They called out, "*Doodh, doodh, doodh*," in unison and surrounded him. He figured the food he had given them was not enough, and for a while, he felt cheap. Then guilt followed cheap.

"Damn!" Mr. Marks said under his breath. He looked around to see if any of his business colleagues were in the area. He saw nobody he recognized. After a moment's hesitation, he signaled for the little children to follow him to the grocer's. It was his last day in Mumbai. Suddenly he was pleased with himself for he was about to perform one big altruistic deed, perhaps the first in his life.

Strange, he thought, how awkwardly the children behaved when they got their much hankered-after milk cartons. He bought two cartons for each of them in his sudden bolt of magnanimity. Why were the hungry weaklings not drinking the *doodh* in hand? Not one of them opened their cartons. Not one smiled or even nodded or said a thank you. They just demanded. Is it that they wanted more?

"Rude, simply rude!" Dwight Marks said to himself, and walked away to find a taxi across the street.

Late that afternoon, before he checked out, he told the manager his story from the morning. The manager was a placid, non-excitable man, who went about his job almost unnoticed.

"Always open the carton yourself and make them drink the milk," the manager said. "Otherwise they sell the milk cartons to the street vendors, and their fathers drink up the money."

Color drained from Mr. Marks' face. The weak had manipulated him.

Harry runs a Marathon

Harry sits in a reclining chair by the picture-window, watches
joggers panting,
dogs on leash, doing whatever they do, and lovers walking arm-
in-arm.
Harry dreams he'll run a marathon someday.

Six feet tall, three hundred and thirty-two pounds to the exact
detail, Harry waits. At
lunch time, wife Henrietta brings him four hamburgers, ketchup,
mayo, mustard, with
two cans of soda.
Where's my French fries? he barks.

He eats, drinks, imagines he'll run a marathon. Someday.

At Harry's memorial service, his son, so like his father says,
"My dad was a good man, never demanded much, except French
fries."
His only regret was not training for a marathon.

Dad, I'll do it for you, someday.

Nana, Throw Me a Ball

My husband, Geza, once an active gardener and an avid deer-hunter, camps out on the sofa, and between snores, watches the afternoon cooking show. On Saturdays, he watches old movies. Always the Green Bay Packers on Sunday. When the phone rings, he makes no attempt to move. He hasn't heard it, he says, when I ask why, or so he makes me believe. This cold Saturday in January when I'm in the middle of mixing the pie dough, the phone rings. I dust flour off my hands and reach for it. Anna's high-pitched voice comes across. It's two o'clock in the afternoon and she wants to know, "Can you come shopping with me? Please do." She's never bossy; simply insistent.

"The bargains are great today. Kohls and Penneys have great sales." She talks loud and quick, mostly with high-pitched energy. "The morning papers say these are the best bargains of the year. We must go. Besides, there's something special I have to buy."

Anna flips through the weekend papers and fills her closet with bargains she says she'll use someday. She grew up in the old country of Yugoslavia, where food and money were scarce. She and I possessed two sets of school uniforms when we were young; to be washed and worn on alternate days. Often over morning coffee, Anna tells me she enjoys the luxury of hoarding things for, as she says, "When the time comes" and "Just in case!"

I'm hesitant about the shopping because Anton, my eight-year-old grandson, will be visiting with us, as he does most Saturday afternoons. That's when I try to play ball with him even if I'm tired. Yet, going shopping with Anna, and her wanting to get something special, arouses my curiosity.

I tell Anna I'll call back in half an hour, because I like getting out of the house; but I've to wait and see what kind of mood Anton brings in when he rings the door bell.

This afternoon I say to him, "Anton, I'm an old lady. I can't run like you."

Anton is not one to give up on me. Anton's mother is my daughter, Iris; she lives on the next block. Just as well, because she is our only daughter, and there's nobody else for Geza and me to lean on. These days it's she who depends on us, what with two little kids to take care of. I think she likes it that we're near by, because her children, Anton and Cathy, can walk over to our house after school.

"Nana! No, no, Nana. Don't ever say you're old again!" Anton screams at the top of his lungs.

I tell him I can't stand up that fast or bend over to catch the ball when it is not thrown directly at me. Anton looks up at my face. Then in a softer, pleading voice the very next minute, he adds, "Please, please, Nana, throw me a ball."

I can never resist Anton's smile, placed so perfect between his two, deep, dimpled cheeks, or the cajoling tone of his voice. I wave for him to follow me to the basement. With the stove turned down to a simmer, I leave the kitchen. The aroma of beef broth and mixed vegetables trails us to the basement. I walk downstairs holding on to the railing, placing my right foot sideways before bringing down my left. It's an old habit from when I injured my knee, which still gets stiff when the temperature drops. I'm petrified of falling again. Several of my friends have had their knees and hips replaced.

Anton overtakes me and runs ahead with thumping steps, shaking the unpolished, wooden railing Geza put up several years ago, but never found the energy to anchor down with extra brackets. He has not stripped and varnished the steps to a finish even now. Geza sees us go down and gives me that look, as if to say, you've got sucked into it again! Serves you right for spoiling him so. Geza, my husband of forty-five years, is a couch potato. I give him a big grin to tell him it's really okay. My old self can handle this much wear.

Not Anton, not Cathy, certainly not me; not one of us can get Geza to move unless he wants to. I keep the children busy to maintain the peace till Iris comes home. Cathy, like Geza, simply wants to settle down on the sofa with a bag of potato chips by her side.

After fifteen minutes of throwing ball, I tell Anton we need to break. We'll play again in a little while, I tell him. I sit down on the old basement sofa and think. I must call Anna right away.

No matter what he calls me, he's learned some of his words from Geza. I can never be angry with him. When we are together, Anton cuddles up to me. He talks and laughs and throws me flying kisses. Cathy says Anton is such a baby. It almost seems like there is a pact between Geza and Anton, the two teases in my life.

"Mind if we go a little later, like four o'clock," I say to Anna. "I'd love to go." By now I know I'm ready.

"Okay," is all Anna says, and drops the phone down, as if the receiver burnt her hand.

I don't know what to make of this. Perhaps she's baking a cake and the timer just went off, or maybe the doorbell rang and she felt hurried. Better still, I imagine their dog, Tolstoy, bumping her husband Arman's books off the dining table and I smile to myself. Anna will tell me if she's annoyed about something. I'm her old Slavic friend from when we were ten years old, and if only Geza and Arman were not so different, Anna and I would be living in each other's houses. Geza can't stand dogs and messes and exercise, and Arman, amongst other things, won't stop fixating on his prostate. He really wants to stay young.

Geza says to me, "Don't we all?"

Anton amazes me with the little notes he leaves me from time to time. Always so respectful, so even-keeled, so loving.

"Dear Nana, I hope you have a wonderful birthday," the note I found last week under the cookie jar said. Then again, the one from last month when I was out doing the groceries. "Wish I could have hugged you today just because. Mom's here and I must go home. Love, Anton."

Dear Anton! He knows I'm partial to his Slavic name! The kids call him Tony at school and he always reminds me, "It's our family secret, Nana, you can call me Anton at home."

Cathy has confided to her mother that she will be teased if the other girls find out she has a real Slavic name the girls haven't heard. So we keep our promise to our grandchildren, sometimes wondering if it really is so difficult for our kids to accept that we are from the old country. Somehow, even after thirty-five years in America, we still cherish our old customs of preparing dumplings, celebrating family traditions on Christmas Eve, and hand painting Easter eggs. I am delighted that the children call me Nana.

This week, Anton's messy scribble said, "You old, old lady, why don't you like to play ball with me? Love, A."

Anna drives us to Brookshire Mall. She looks at the big sizes in women's pantsuits and picks out three bright colored sets; a red with delicate stripes, a plain sea green and a cerulean blue with bright flowers. I try on two petite sized pants, a plain gray and a navy blue. In the fitting rooms, we talk across closed cafe-style doors that do not lock.

"Let's go to Penneys after this," she says. "I saw a magnifying mirror advertised in the paper. It's a great deal. I must buy one today."

"What do you need a magnifying mirror for?" I say, thinking to myself, here goes the hoarding again. Anna and Arman are one of those families who have a need to buy three pressure cookers or four knives or two dozen glasses all at once. Either because they have found a cheap deal or, as Arman says to me, "The rubber ring on the cooker can come loose anytime and then we'd have the spare cooker right away." Arman's habits date back to World War II. He forgets we can buy what we need now.

The top of Anna's dining table is covered with books. For the last six months, Arman has had plans to sort them out! He thinks they'll need to buy a large shelf to categorize the books by subject, or vintage, whatever, because he's bought his books at second hand stores. Then he gets busy trying out different natural remedies that will cure his slightly high blood sugar. He has been told it might lead to diabetes one day and he wants to delay the event. Every now and then, even Tolstoy helps with the sorting of books and the boxes and drops them to the floor. There are bottles of herbal pills that sit on the dining table.

I like the pants I try on and Anna likes two of the pantsuits, after she makes sure I approve of them. We walk out with our packages and then head out to Penneys to find the magnifying mirrors.

"My wrinkles," Anna says, as she turns her face to the right and then slightly to the left. She looks with piercing intensity into the magnifying mirror. "These deep lines in my skin have been bothering me lately. I need to find my wrinkles up close and, you know, to see that one stiff hair that pokes off my chin sometimes."

Cathy can hardly wait to grow up. I, on the other hand, won't admit to my furrows or my tiring strength, because I want to play ball with Anton. So unlike Geza, who won't move. When I look close up over Anna's shoulder and see her face in the magnifying mirror, the crow's feet at the corners of her eyes look like deep mountain crevices. I want to deny those crevices on my own face. I hate those outlines on her face but by now, I'm curious. It's time that I, too, buy a looking glass. I justify it to myself by saying I'll use it to put on my make-up and pencil my eyebrows with more care. To look prettier, to defy age.

Perhaps.

Speaking of wrinkles, Anton's wrinkle-free face stands out for me.

Anton is slighter than most eight-year-olds, born with a birth weight of four pounds. His bronchi spasm when he runs hard, so it's difficult for him to keep up with the other boys. He has to slow down and search his backpack for his inhaler. He cries when the other boys tell him to grow up. That's how our Saturday ritual of throwing ball started. My daughter Iris, a nurse, knows Anton's limitations. Anton enjoys giving me orders. He instructs me on the many rules that make up our game. The bigger boys at school won't listen to him, he says.

Playtime on Saturday afternoons also gives Iris time to shop without having to worry if Anton will tire himself running around like a wild animal racing through the woods. Sometimes the way Iris talks of him to her father worries me. It seems to me she fixates on her superior nursing knowledge and believes he'll stop breathing any minute. Being an Emergency Room nurse has its wearisome moments. She doesn't talk about her worries to me, because she thinks I'm too stoic.

Then Anna confides in me.

"I was trying to pluck the hair off my upper lip," she says, "when you called. I just can't see them properly any more.

I want to be sure not a single one is left, and the magnifying mirror will help."

Anna likes the magnifying mirror at J. C. Penneys. The stand is sturdier than the one she had seen at another shop a few weeks ago. She says she has obsessed about getting one for several weeks but wanted to bring me along to make sure she is not being foolish. So I know she'll buy it. She never buys anything that's not on sale, a leftover habit from childhood.

Anna buys two mirrors, on sale for $9.95 from $14.95. She tells me the second one is a birthday present for her daughter-in-law. I wonder what message Anna is sending to her son's wife; she has griped about her only daughter-in-law, Margie, for several years. Lately it's been about the style of clothes Margie wears. "Miniskirts don't become a thirty-eight-year-old with three children," Anna has said firmly. "Who's to tell her? Jimmy won't say a word."

I listen because I have the same gripe against Iris. These days mothers can't tell their daughters anything either and it starts young, I've noticed. Anna and I wished many years ago that when our children were grown up, Iris would marry her only son, but Jimmy married Margie from high school and that put a stop to our old country dreams. We are free Americans now.

I buy one magnifying mirror. I plan to sneak it into my bedroom, so in the quiet behind closed doors, I can scrutinize my face and hope not to see too many wrinkles. I might even find more energy to play with Anton. Anna and I saunter out of the store, balancing our packages. Both of us always talk to each other in our Slavic language, just a habit of sorts. We like it that nobody in the shopping malls can understand us. We window shop as we talk. Then I wander across to The Chocolate Swan and buy some mint candy for my two grandchildren and a separate little package for Geza. It's white chocolate, the only kind he'll eat; because that is the kind he remembers eating when he was young. Once war started, there was no more chocolate.

It is dark by the time we get home. Iris is late and the children are hungry while I'm out. Geza is angry because he has to think about supper. He has made them grilled cheese sandwiches and dished out freshly made soup from the stove. He announces it to me as I enter the doorway to chaos. What a fuss Geza makes over little things!

Anton wants to know what all the packages are. Cathy is happy with her candy. Anton opens the one item I have placed on the table because it is fragile, without even asking me. He's intrigued by the magnifying mirror. By that time I join them over dinner and start to explain why Anna wants to see her face magnified. Then I change my line of talk and tell them Anna bought two mirrors to see the two sides of her face. I decide to leave out details about the hair, or to tell them my reasons for getting one. This way I don't have to explain too much.

I'm done talking when Anton says he wants the looking glass for himself.

"Why, Anton? Do you have wrinkles?" I ask with a smile.

Anton keeps a very serious face.

"I need it so I can see my first moustache hair, Nana. I'm getting big, you know."

"That first hair is very important, Anton," says Geza. "These women will never understand."

Geza and I look at each other and we know. This is a serious matter.

"Maybe I've one already but I haven't seen it because I don't have a mirror that makes my face look big. When I see it, it means I'm grown and can go to bed when I want to," Anton says. I nod agreement. I should have bought two mirrors like Anna.

"You keep the candy, Nana," Anton says, pleased with the mirror in his hand. He's trying it out at various angles, searching. "Nana, you can share my chocolate, so you'll have more energy to play ball with me next Saturday."

I'll call Anna tomorrow and ask her to go with me to the store again. I'll buy one more magnifying mirror, but maybe she'll buy three more, for just in case. They are a good price.

Later that evening our house is quiet again, and I'm seated in my favorite chair doing needlepoint, when Geza decides to share his chocolate with me. The same as he did when we were wrinkle-free in the old country.

Black and White

Black for darkness; black for screams, black when hiding under
blankets;
I hear stealthy steps in the attic.
Black for rattling pipes, a toilet flushing, a child bereft of sleep.

White for daytime, white for clouds;
for the fluff in his speech, the plumes in her Ascot hat.
White for parfait, tea parties; my packed-away wedding gown,
white flowers in my hair.

Black for a movie that rolls time. White for memories.
Black is the locked-up box in the cellar.
White for the letters,

my great-grandchildren's children will find inside.

Neon lights in Vietnam

You straighten the bold sign, Moonstruck Tattoos, in the shop window. Good price, it reads, all in one line. You like it, the way the name rolls off your tongue. You adjust your light blue, silk *aoi daai*, your long Vietnamese dress with its high collar and baggy pants, and feel fluffed up like a peacock, because you've managed to hold your job for three weeks.

The owner, Mrs. Tran, has entrusted your dainty hands with a key which unlocks the aluminum shutters rolled down over the front door. You take charge at 8pm, which is when you roll up the shutters, then sneak way back to hide your cloth purse under the metal table with the rickety chair. You come back up front into the main room, and sit on a low wooden bench. For a few minutes, you look at the neon lights flashing over the narrow shop windows across the street. Crowds of people walk on the footpath, their faces shimmering and bodies discoing under the bright neon lights, and you imagine their comings and goings. You feel quarantined in this long, narrow room with its whitewashed walls. The lights inside are dim; but the bright light from outside shines into the front of the room, filtering in through the large front window. A flowery plastic curtain is gathered across the other side from where you sit. You always remember to draw it when you ask your customers to sit on the inside bench, or at other times, to lie down, depending on where they want their tattoo positioned. You like the money Mrs. Tran gives you. It buys you extra fish to take home from the big market on Sunday nights.

You recognize the men in uniform, now in jeans and T-shirts, who go over to Angelo's next door. Later at night, on their way out, perhaps, dizzy from dancing under the strobe lights and having imbibed whatever pleases their fancy, you think they get sentimental because they come into your tattoo shop and ask for a tattoo. You notice how young and muscular and good-looking they are, awkward sometimes, as if stuck in a pair of shoes too big for them to walk in. You have heard Mrs. Tran say these young American boys would never have to come to Vietnam unless they had to, whatever their reasons.

You feel sorry for yourself because you're born here, and now that you're grown-up, your mother says, "You big. You need to earn money to pay me some rent, and help me buy food."

You snap back at her, but she is right. Her rice paddies need more water, your father is old and drunk, and you are just a lazy daughter, who has dreams.

She shouts at you another time, "Get to the city. Go! More money there. A war is going on."

You yell back, "Me, Me, listen to me. You'll get your damn money when I'm ready." Next day, you get on the bus to go far away to Saigon, like she said you should, and find yourself this job in Moonstruck Tattoos.

You've seen the young soldiers stare in the window and read the sign. Sometimes they hesitate, walk past, and then come back and step inside. You've tidied up the tattoo designs on the small table over and over. Butterflies, hearts, arrows, and simple names like Mary, Betty, and Susan come up. Your choice for them would be different, like those of your friends, ones like Laughing Dragon and Sweet Pea and Passion Fruit, but Mrs. Tran says we must give them what they want.

"Americans are different, you not understand their mind," she says.

Anyway, you don't have any friends anymore. War changes life for young girls like you. Nobody stays at home to milk the cows and help with the farm and go to school. Mothers and fathers have to do work on their own. Your mother even let you go to Saigon.

This evening, a white military man, still in uniform, comes in, holding hands with a sweet little miss with eyes like yours and a smooth skin. She's a petite woman, about your height, and you longingly think you'd like to be in her place, holding this husky's hand. You like her and you decide they look so comfortable together. Maybe, just maybe, you hope he'll want her name on his forearm, but then, he, maybe, is just like the rest of them. They never do. They never want a Vietnamese name for their tattoos. He knows and you know that tattoos are for real. Too permanent, you suspect. The young men will go home and they'll want to show their tattoos to the Marys and the Bettys in their lives when and if the damn war ends, and if they ever get back. They will tell their women in sweet whispering nothings how much they missed them when they were in battle. You eye Passion Princess standing next to him, while he goes through the designs. She's just a tag along for the evening, a vapor that will not exist the next day. Like Vietnam. Like you. A nothing, a nobody.

The soldier wants Harry, short for Harriet, you suspect but really don't know, on his upper arm. He wants a red arrow and a green heart to go with it. You think he chooses the upper arm because he has something to hide. They decide on the forearm when they want to display the tattoo to the world. Passion Princess rubs his back gently as he moves his biceps toward you, for you to pierce the needle with the green dye first, and make him a neat-looking heart. You have to remember the arrow has to be red. He doesn't wince. They leave arm in arm, her head leaning into his shoulder.

It is quiet inside the shop again, and you sit in your cell, away from the crowd and noise outside. You imagine your mother yelling for you to fetch water from the tap in the courtyard. You hear her curses at the other end, while you wait for the bucket to fill. Your water buffalo keeps his head down and munches at his straw, making strange noises. You hate the work your mother makes you do, but you are an obedient Vietnamese daughter and every morning, you cook *pho*, the soup for your family breakfast. At night, your family eats by the street kiosk. You used to work in the rice paddies too, but the Americans coming to Vietnam changed everything.

Suddenly he walks in. Alone. You've never seen him before this, but you like his smile, and you like his eyes and when he tells you to needle a tattoo to the right of his deep cleft and just below the dimple in his back, your knees shake and your face goes red. He drops his pants and points to the place. You feel hot and uncomfortable, and feel lucky he can't see you. Then you remember he hasn't told you what he wants embroidered in his skin.

You ask, "What you like for your tattoo?"

He remains silent.

You ask again, thinking he doesn't understand your Vietnamese English.

He says, "Honey, tell me your name first. Let me see if I like it."

It's your turn to say nothing. Why is he asking? You are afraid. Not his business.

He's still lying flat on his stomach. He says, turning his head toward you, "Fine, don't tell me. Just tattoo a name you like. Nobody is waiting for me back home."

You feel sad for him. He's in the wrong part of the world, and in a war that is not his own. "Get out, America," a voice inside you screams. You decide he has no business being in your country, your town, your space. You're lonely too. With meticulous care, you tattoo your own name. You place red innards inside a green heart you have tattooed in the middle of your name. When you are almost finished, you are nervous and happy at the same time. You want your last needle in and out before Mrs. Tran comes in and questions you on the perfect tattoo you have just made.

She'll want to know, you're sure of that. You are also determined to explain nothing, as a part of you finally escapes to America.

A Mother's Advice to a Twenty Year Old in Army Fatigues

Don't blink, don't daydream of Amy, don't look at your feet,
when you're poised through a skylight in your tanker.

Just point, look right, look left, just point.
Don't shoot, don't you dare die,
when the sky fills up with thunderous sounds.

Sit like your father, the ice-fisherman, squinting across blank
horizons,
feeling the dark hole in the ice for a tug. Be focused, be patient,
Don't shun peace times because there is war.
You learn plenty in peace times too.

Just don't let sand-dust prickle your eyes.
Your father taught you to discern a piranha from a goldfish,
Do watch out for that one shot.
Be alert, don't blink, don't daydream of Amy.

The Girl

At dawn, the girl observes notices a bare-chested Japanese in his tai-chi stance and sees his distorted shadow in the sand behind him changing with meditative ease. In his black tights, he stands with his legs apart, his knees slightly bent and his feet planted firmly in the sand. He makes smooth, circular movements with his outstretched arms, changing direction with slow, purposeful intent.

.   She wants to stand and stare at him, but that would be rude, so she simply continues on with her bare -foot jog. The sand on this side of Waikiki, further away from the crowds, is coarse and slides between her toes and hurts her feet. It reminds her of another sharp insult that stays within her and rules her life. She has come to Waikiki to escape that pain. Tangled thoughts erode the very fabric of her brain with, "Why me? Why me?" but it had happened. She brushes back the hair blowing into her face and runs on. She wants to forget Richard, although she loves him. She feels inadequate, like she'd never be able to give him all he deserves. The bare-chested Sumo man, in black tights stands with his legs apart, his knees slightly bent and his feet implanted firmly in the sand. He makes smooth, circular movements with his outstretched arms, changing direction with slow, purposeful intent.

A man so strong and yet so gentle with such graceful movements. She wonders if he argues with his wife and wants to win every time. That is exactly how Richard would want it.

When she and Richard went for a drive, he'd be the one to pick the spot. In fancy restaurants, he'd order for her. He approved of her clothes or didn't, so she never again, wore the clothes he did not like when she was with him. She dared not tell him that her choice was different. She doubted herself. On one of her bolder days, she said to him, "You're treating me like a pet, maybe a dog or a gerbil."

He laughed.

He bought her flowers and offered them to her with tenderness. With time, she saw something gentledeep she loved about him, a softness that grew on her when she saw how he talked to her mother, who was in a wheel chair after an early stroke. After six months of knowing each other, he kissed her with passion and she, feeling like a prude, told him she wanted to wait... until her wedding day. Her honesty angered him and he said she'd be the only virgin left in town, and continuing his wrath, said "You've done it before, haven't you?"

She remained silent that evening; then tried to talk of something else but the mood had changed. She thought that was the end of their courtship, but she was saddened by it. She had come to love Richard, and was struggling to overcome the ghosts of her past. He did not call her for two weeks, but months later, they were still together. He had a need for her, and she for him. That must be love, she said to herself. Yet, she could not talk of the past.

She wonders now, a year later, how she found the courage to come to Hawaii on her own, but she had done it, after she had broken her engagement with Richard.

She runs another long mile and decides to catch her breath and look at the rising sun. A bright yellow glow spreads across the horizon. Clear blue water stretches for miles beyond her vision. She notices man-made garbage strewn behind her and a stale smell coming from some hamburger wrappers and French fries pressed in the sand. A sweeper, some distance away, picks up yesterday's remains and stuffs them into an overfilled garbage bag he carries. She sees the huge dumpster nearby, smelly and untidy all around. On the other side of the dumpster and toward the front, is a rumpled blanket spread on the sand, and as she looks on, she sees movement under the blanket. A jogger, engrossed in his own world, listening to his i-pod, runs close to the blanket when a startled face of a young man, unshaven with sleepy eyes, pops up from under the covers. The young man looks around as if unsure of his surroundings, then adjusts the blanket to cover himself and the body of a semi-naked woman next to him, He's asleep again, or so it seems. She wonders at the ease with which these two people sleep together.

She and Richard had dated for over two years before their engagement. She was twenty-five years old when finally he proposed and she eagerly said yes. After all, he had been a gentleman and kept his distance. She knew he was enamored by her. After their engagement, the talk of setting a wedding date came up every few months. It made her nervous., and she told him she needed time. He said he understood, but she doubted if he really did. She did not want to explain anything to him, but her dark secret frightened her.

Ten years ago, it is a rainy cold day. This was the mid-nineties and there were taboos. The sensation of wetness, bloody smells and pain enters her head like it happened just the night before. The drunk hiding behind the garage door had grabbed her as she parked her bike, and he dragged her to the alley behind their house. She remembers her own screaming as he punched her down, and then just feeling numb. She doesn't know how long she lay under him, just knows that she felt empty. She cried for endless hours and hid her face even from her father for several days. They did not report it to the police, they did not talk about the episode, then or later.

Six weeks later, her mother took her to an unknown doctor, not their usual grandfatherly medic. The new doctor examined her and performed a small operation on her two days later. He told her, "You're good as new."

Her naive mother believed this would be the end of the stigma. She said to her, "You start your life from here on. Your classmate Peter loves you. You should go out with him, and some of your other friends. All of you deserve a carefree childhood. You're fifteen, damn it. Be free."

The girl has never been free of that nightmare. Not even when she was dating Richard. She doesn't have the courage to tell him what happened; she thinks, he'd never understand. Richard never had time for getting to know her innermost feelings. How often in the dark of the night, she wants to scratch that drunk's eyeballs out. She could even twist his neck. She feels guilty that she did none of this when he attacked. Too shocked and couldn't move. She could have done something. She should've done something. Could've and should've have become part of her psyche. Until that one thing she did for herself. She did not want to ruin Richard's life. Two years after her engagement, she met Richard for lunch and in the midst of tears and anguish, gave him back his ring. He didn't ask why. He said he understood. She knew he didn't. He said he was sorry. He wanted to remain friends, and she nodded and left before her lunch order came.

She continues sitting on the beach and finds her fingers digging in the sand. She makes slow circles and figures of eight without consciously thinking of what she is doing. An irregular soft object with a fleshy feel comes into her hand. Maybe it's just a jellyfish. She drops it quickly, as if it were a reminder of her guilt from years ago. She stands up. The sand under her feet feels mushy and coarse. She tries to cover the fleshy lifeless object by throwing the sand on it with her feet. She had tried to blot out the nightmare from her brain when she was with

Richard, hidden her thoughts in a dark corner, but it occupied space.

The sun is high and it is warm. She starts back and sees many more people basking in the sun on the beach, some doing their daily stretches and rituals in many different ways. The big Japanese is not there

Her thoughts zoom back to that night. Her hand feels dirty. Shaking with fear and a sense of helplessness, she starts running toward the street and finds herself in the middle of a crowd standing by a hotel entrance. She thinks there's been a robbery, but people are looking at something in the sand, some object that must have floated in from the sea. Then she sees the object. A bird is laying limp in the sand, with its head down. There is blood around his neck. She hears someone say that the bird flew into the window and broke its neck. It needs to be taken out of its misery. Like her.

There are many "uhs" and "ahs" and "what's to become of the poor bird!" Some stop to stare, some linger on, others ask if there is something one can do for the bird. The girl sees the bird on the ground, is about to run on but changes her mind. She finds her way through the crowd and picks the bird by its tail feathers, soothes her fingers over the head and neck that are limp in her hand. She looks carefully at it struggling and she has conflicting thoughts. She needs to kill the bird and rid her mind of guilt from what she knows is not her fault.

With a swift twist of her own wrist, she slings the bird over a nearby stone. Then she lays the lifeless bird in the sand, and slowly pours sand over it, as if to say, lie buried here, the good and the evil, rest in peace. Rest in peace with the demons that have tortured her all this time.

She walks to the nearest telephone booth and calls Richard.

A One-Way Street

I'm eighty-nine, living on the fourth floor
of an assisted living facility.
My window faces a college dorm and
in that room across from me,
is where I want to be.

My eyes distort figures. Perhaps
that woman's room has a man in there,
could it really be?
I paint an image from my brain's desire
when she was eighteen, and
I was twenty.

I want to dance
with her in my arms.
I'd like to roll on bails of hay,
and together we'd laugh.

I see our innocent smiles
smooth the wrinkles away.

I want to climb over that
wall of age, and
be in that room across from me.

Red and Green Jello

The nurses' aides want me to help with changing the linen. I assist with this task most days, because beds need to be made frequently in a hospice. Patients die and newer ones are brought in, just as sick as the previous ones. After the clean sheets are tucked under, the aides leave and I'm alone in the room, left to sanitize off the surfaces and clean out the trash. Tons of Kleenex, thrown in by relatives with wet eyes, fills the cans.

This evening the large nurse, who is forever trying to corner me into doing something nobody else likes to do, orders me, "Susan, please feed the patient in Room 229."

"The name is Brian," she says, "You don't need to know more." She keeps her stern countenance. "He likes jello," she adds, as an afterthought.

I adjust my red streaked hair in a bathroom mirror. Then I push open the door to Room 229, and step inside. I don't want to disturb the old man. After many such gentle entries into closed rooms where the doors are opened just enough to let one in, my nostrils are sensitized to the stagnant odor of phlegm and Lysol. I stand for a moment to get my bearing. In the dimly lit room, my eyes focus on a young man, not the shriveled up old man I had expected to see. Why hadn't the husky nurse said something? I go near to his bed.

Brian seems long, at least six feet tall, perhaps even more. It's hard to judge when he's lying on his back on a raised narrow bed, almost like a stretcher that takes patients to the operating room. His body is flat on this pedestal, and his face is turned towards the door. His dark eyes sparkle; he even smiles at me, in an odd sort of way.

"Hello," I say, trying to sound cheerful, but I'm nervous inside and afraid he will hear the tremor in my voice. "I'm here to feed you."

So far, he hasn't said anything. I extend my hand to take his. He attempts to pull out his right hand from under the covers but doesn't quite make it. His right eyelid blinks incessantly. He makes a garbled sound, acknowledging my greeting.

Then I nod to an older woman in an armchair on the other side of the bed. Two photo frames stand upright on Brian's bedside stand and I see the woman's photo in one of them. The mother! She continues to sit and gives me a bored look, but I see her vigilant eyes. I sense she has seen color drain from my face. Then quickly, I take charge and adjust the food tray already set beside him. I reach out for the bowl of orange jelly and spoon it.

Brian opens his lips, but struggles to swallow, and most of the soft jelly drips down the corner of his mouth.

I wipe the side of his chin and neck with great delicacy, as if a firmer touch could hurt him any more. I curse the nurses for giving me this task, which I am not able to master. I'm in a horrible situation. I blame that horrible judge who sent me to do this volunteer work. I'm angry at my father as always.

It happened like this several months ago. I had not told my dad, but the round, flat nail in the center of my tongue is my vengeance against him for being so square. He'll hate this tongue piercing, but then, he never understands the objects college kids can lay their hands on. Dad and I fight on just about everything and finally he gives me an ultimatum. He wants me to find a job and a place to live.

This is the pits for any young woman. If Dad had not found those damned cigarettes I left in the front hall five months ago when I was late for my hair appointment, it would not have come to this. That's when I was obsessed with getting the latest straight hair and red highlights. I wanted to tease Dad, "Maybe you'll love me more as a Goth!"

"So this is how you spend my money! What else do you do?" Dad thundered as I walked in three hours later with my red-streaked hair and a new nose-ring. He shook the cigarettes at me, his face ugly with anger. He stared at my triple pierced ears and my face, but did not comment on it. He glossed over my new hairdo, when I really wanted him to say he liked it. Just once, he could be happy for me.

"Just because you can't smoke any more," I shout back at him.

I have the memory of sitting in his lap when I was a little girl and even then, I hated the smell of smoke on his breath. Mom and he argued about his smoking often. Now he was acting big, he who only gave it up when he developed that horrible cough and the doctors told him his lungs would kill him if he didn't stop.

Mom sits next to me in the courthouse when the judge announces my punishment.
"You almost ran over a little boy and you didn't even know it." He says I was lucky to get away without a jail sentence because the boy miraculously escaped, but if this were to happen a second time, "You'll be ruined for life." From a side glance I can see Mom's exaggerated tick, the way she twitches the left side of her neck and raises her shoulder repeatedly. She does that when she's nervous. She's never been in a courtroom before, not even to defend herself against the one traffic violation she got for parking too near a fire hydrant.

Last night, I told her about the speeding tickets I haven't paid for in the past, but she had chosen not to comment. She'll never know the delight of flying along the freeways.

The social worker talks to us at great length after the judge makes his pronouncement in court. I think the judge knows the sentences he speaks by heart, and I sense he has delivered this exact message before.

He says, "I've worked with young people like you for many years. I've dealt with drug offenders, alcoholics and the like, usually good kids gone wrong." He stares at me through his bifocals as he speaks, and goes on and on, and when he's done, I yawn.

The social worker is a boring young woman just doing her job; she doesn't seem to really care about me.

Nobody does, I think to myself. They may just pretend to sometimes, perhaps like Mom and Dad. Why can't everybody leave me alone? As it is, I know very little about a hospice, although I'm twenty-one. Simply that old people are taken there to die, people with terminal illness, nothing that concerns me. I don't have time to ponder on life; there is so much else to do. So, to be given this punishment of volunteering at the hospice is a very inconvenient episode, but the judge has made it amply clear that I have no choice. Only after I've served the two months will I get my driver's license back. St. Anthony's Hospice is the place he has chosen for me to volunteer.

On our way home, Mom and I remain silent when the traffic lights are red, and she looks at me. She does not speak even when the lights turn green. We just move on.

I say to Mom, "Lets not tell Dad about how I got my new job in the hospice."

She says nothing.

I notice a change in Dad's attitude toward me. Dad says for a young woman like me to work in a hospice shows integrity. He's chosen not to mention the cigarette episode again or to comment on my hair or the pierced body parts, the ones he knows about. To him working means I've started to improve my ways. Like working this entire summer. No partying till the late hours. He believes eventually I will make it to medical school, although he and I never discuss that either. I just hear him say so to Mom, in tones loud enough that even our neighbors can hear. Dad likes the sound of his own voice. He rarely has time to hear me out, and so I let it be. It's best Dad not know that a judge is involved. He doesn't need to know the finer aspects of my new job, as he calls it.

So for the summer, I get myself to the hospice five times a week on the bus. The nurses there seem to know the real story of why a young woman like me is at the hospice on such a regular basis, four hours at a time. They must have seen it happen before, but I don't care.

The chief nurse's eyes are on me at times. Maybe her daughter wants to have red hair or piercings. Once she asked me if my bus came on time, so she must know I don't drive. I wonder if she worries that I might steal some of their syringes. I feel out of place when I walk those endless hospital corridors, and feel tired of my life this summer. I want to smoke, but I'm on a leash and don't dare. Frankly, it all stinks! When I get my driver's license back in the fall, I'll be done. I'll pretend to go for a vacation, perhaps to Costa del Sol to bask in the Spanish sun. Not a chance until I work and earn some money.

All through the weekend I wonder if Brian will still be there when I take the bus back to St. Anthony's Hospice on Monday. Will his mother be in the room? I want to not think of that sight in Room 229, but it continues to haunt me. When the nurse on duty decides to send me to another room the following week, I ask for Brian.

This time around, Brian's mother introduces herself to me as Mrs. Lang. I start to feed Brian and she sees me struggling with the Jello.

She says, "Most people can't stand to come back." Then, quickly, she snatches the empty spoon from my hand. She stabs it in the bowl of green Jello. Then with the gentleness of how one would prop up a baby, she lifts Brian's head and angles the jelly straight into his mouth. He manages to swallow it.

"Here, you try," she says, handing the spoon to me after just one bite. "That way you'll feel you've done something. I do this everyday."

I wonder at her being so matter-of-fact, so businesslike, so cold and so efficient. I don't want her to judge me, but I know she will.

In my orientation hour for hospice where I sit and frown, they tell me I'm to talk to patients. I'm supposed to take the lead. A few patients will want to say plenty. They'll talk of unfinished issues that have plagued their lives. Some relatives will speak for hours, while others may want to be quiet. Everybody is hurting.

"Mostly it'll be family relationships, childhood trauma and undelivered love," the orientation volunteer says.

I look around the room and see so many older people who have retired from their careers and volunteer because they want to. I'm different; young, not yet embarked on a career and simply here because I got stoned. Otherwise, I'm an average woman with a mom and a dad and a middle class suburban home with a neat front yard and colorful petunias. Also, a dog named Russ. The problem is my father never talks to me, never really, really talks; like, that's the way it's always been in our house. I blame him for many things, like the empty bottles of beer I used to find on our neat lawn in the mornings when I was in high school. These days, I'm afraid I'm like him. He drinks and I won't quit smoking or drinking and we both hate the world. Now I have to walk five blocks to catch a bus to get myself to St. Anthony's. I'm not to smoke or drink, so the judge ordered, and I'm required to obey.

Four weeks of my ten weeks of hospice work are already over. I'm getting used to the circumstance. Even the smell of cooked cabbage in the hospital cafeteria and the stagnant smell of Lysol spray and death in the hospice become routine. On the bus over, and often in the shower, I wonder if Brian will still be there. I want him to be because I tell myself, he's just two months older than I am; he can't die. I've seen his birth date in his hospital chart.

Mrs. Lang and I greet each other when I enter Brian's room. Every day she tells me a little more about their family. I'm getting good with the jelly and the custard, she says. I like the way he rests his head in the fold of my arm when I prop him up. I remind myself, this is hospice care. Terminal comfort. Why should Brian need that? He's so young. So like me. We could be friends under different circumstances. He might have been in my school or we could have met at a bar some evening when a group of us went out drinking.

I don't talk about my circumstance to Mrs. Lang, although she has asked me how many hours of work I put in every week, and I've had to answer that. Then I change the subject. She tells me more about Brian. I've looked at his chart and know some of the facts. I think my mom would have lost it if she were in Mrs. Lang's shoes. Would Dad care? I don't know. I listen to Mrs. Lang's words.

"...but that dreadful Christmas Eve, his jeep struck a tree on his way home. Driving too fast, the police said."

I dare to suggest, "Perhaps the roads were icy that night."

"Perhaps," she says softly.

The next time she talks about the redhead in the photo.

"Dido," she says, as she looks at the picture of the girl with her long, red hair flying in the air, standing next to a good-looking Brian in a polo shirt. I notice his soft, gentle eyes. Then she pauses. "They were in the Peace Corps in Somalia together. He'd just come home last summer. Dido and he were both headed for law school. He was to give her a ring in two weeks."

"Does she come to visit?" I ask with some hesitation, and then I look at Brian. I want to meet her, this redhead; Brian's love. I feel alone for no good reason.

I can tell that Brian is listening with his eyes. He cannot turn his head unless it's turned for him, but he can hear us. His eyes change when we talk of Dido. They wander off toward the picture of Dido with her wavy, red hair.

Mrs. Lang stands on the opposite side of the bed from me. She is standing where Brian can't quite see her. She seems thoughtful when I ask if Dido will visit. After a while, she shakes her head which I understand to mean no. I watch Brian's face. A tear drips from his incessantly blinking eye and falls on the white sheet next to his pillow. Instinctively, I move forward to help but then hold back. Let him think I haven't noticed.

I lived out-of-state when in college. Even when I was home last summer, I ate and went out before Dad came home. Then I rolled in late at night and slept off the party toxins until midmorning. This summer, I don't have time to worry about my life at home. Both Mom and Dad wait up for me and we sit together for a late dinner.

Dad asks about my hospice work. Mom wants to know if I want second helpings. Dad offers me a beer, which I decline. My counselor has told me to stay off beer completely. Dad goes ahead and opens his own. He wants to know if I ever drank in college. Girls never do, I hear him tell Mom. Who's he kidding? Which planet does he live on? I change the topic to the Green Bay Packers and Dad is off discussing their quarterback. I'm tired but I've Brian on my mind. In an odd sort of way, I want to make a difference in his life.

Next evening I say to my father, "It's interesting work at the hospice, Dad." It's my response to his question about hospice work, the way he starts dinner conversation every evening. I tell them about Charles, a seventy plus-year-old who, the nurses whisper to me, will be dead within the week, but who tells me his detailed plans for a fishing trip in the fall.

"Mom, the man really believes he'll make the trip," I say.

"At least in his mind, that's good enough!" Dad says, soberly for a change.

Mom adds, "His planning keeps him alert and thinking."

I don't say anything about Brian. They would surely have words of wisdom about his mother and him. What do they know!

Brian's mother? Is it anger or pity that I feel toward her. She has told me Dido will not be back. She has that angry look on her face, same as Dad always has. She is blaming somebody somewhere.

Four weeks later on a Monday, Brian's room is empty. The nurses turn the blankets down, and strip the sheets, preparing for the next patient. I just stand in a dark corner of the room, unable to move, realizing I'll never come back here again. I'm accustomed to Brian's eyes, and I wait to hear the gurgling sound of his swallowing the Jello. There is nothing else left of him.

I go with several of the hospice nurses to the memorial service; I'm surprised to see Mrs. Lang with red lipstick. She wears a bright red dress, and I notice a sense of quiet through her peaceful eyes, as she stands by the closed casket receiving condolences. She must have worn red to uplift her own mood as she remembers her son's spirit. She has to go on living through the memories of Brian's life. I look around for Dido, but do not recognize the redhead I've seen in the photo frame. There is a long line of people and when my turn comes, I walk up to Mrs. Lang and hug her.

"I'll never eat Jello again," she says, holding my hands.

"Me neither," I say, as I walk away.

That evening, Mom is in the kitchen setting the table and Dad is settled on his favorite chair, beer in hand, when I confide to him that I will get my driver's license back in a few weeks. Mom looks up at me sharply and Dad doesn't quite get it. Quickly, I add that I'm going to apply to medical school. Then I tell Mom I will not be having any supper that evening.

In the quiet that follows, I hear Dad slurp his soup. I look at myself in the front hall mirror, adjust my tinted hair, and take Russ for a long walk.

I try to remember the judge's name, but can't.

My First Day at Work

On the mortuary table
sleeps a cold body.
Be it a homeless man
once swearing under the bridge,
or the lady, who strutted in diamonds,
and died in her sleep.

Next to the table,
new at it, seeking the science
of the living, I stand poised.
My hands, the table,
all arctic, all cold.

A motionless mortuary table, a body marble cold.

With warm breath, an anxious sigh,
I gently raise my scalpel.

A Snake On An Icy Patch Of Green

The minute I entered her small room at St. Augustina's, she said, "They gave me fried chicken feathers and gravy for supper tonight."

I raised my eyebrows for a split second before realizing that such a statement was typical for my ninety-two year old mother with her sparse, neatly combed, gray hair and that smirk on her face. She seemed pleased with what she had said, and maybe more so, as she watched the reaction on my face. It was perhaps her way of telling me that this is what happens when you no longer command your own kitchen. I stood beside her bed, trying to put meaning into her words. Then she clasped her bony fingers over my wrist, but turned her face away from me. This was her second day in the nursing home and she was still angry at me.

I bent over and gently pecked her on the cheek and then, very tentatively, asked her in a low tone of voice, "Did you like it then, the supper, I mean?" I could not mask the twinkle in my eyes but I tried my best to keep a serious countenance. Chicken feathers indeed for supper!

She answered me in a slow, monotonous voice, "They were crisp all right." Then as if in mockery, she raised her neck high and added, "I ate nothing."

I snapped back at her, "Mama, they would never...!" but there I stopped. Feathers they stayed. I convinced myself that the corridor buzz may have made it difficult for her to hear. Truthfully though, as I sat down on the chair beside her, I knew my mother had lapsed back to her own farm in Usingen, Germany from sixty years ago.

As a little girl, I cleaned the chicken coop with my father on cold winter days. The chickens flapped around and I ran behind them to catch them one by one. Their flapping raised clouds of dust, and the feathers flew all over. I gathered the feathers in one hand as I rubbed my nose; it twitched so badly from the dust. When I began to sneeze, my father would tell me to go inside. My fingers turned blue with the cold. I ran into the kitchen and brushed feathers off my little dress with my tiny hands. I remember how I leaned my head forward and let my long hair fall over my face. I shook my head from side to side to get dust out of my hair. My mama looked gigantic to me in those days. She was nearly six feet tall and stood by the big coal-burning stove, stirring a pot of stew. I loved the way she tied her auburn hair with a red flowery bandana.

The juicy aroma from the stew that simmered on the stove filtered into my mouth as I entered the kitchen. When Mama saw me come into the house, she poured hot water from the stove into a metal bucket sitting on the kitchen floor. She carried the bucket over to the far end by the kitchen sink. Filling a large steel jug with cold water from a big container standing beside the stove, she poured it into the hot water bucket to cool it down. She felt the temperature of the water with her fingertips, and when it was just right, she called for me.

I walked slowly over to her, singing my own tuneless song, and deliberately passed close to the hot stove. Then I'd stick a finger in the ladle that had been used to stir the stew, lick it, and quickly run over to the sink. She soaped me and sponged me down with her big, strong, hands, the roughness of her palms making me grimace. I made faces that said I was not enjoying the wash but I'd no choice. The breeze blowing in through the wooden door felt cold against my tiny frame, but I was clean when the hour was past.

Decades later, my mama lived not too far from us, so I was able to visit her two or three times a week. Sometimes my children stopped at their oma's after school and she would always make them wash their hands and faces, and then offer them milk and fresh baked cookies. I'd stop by on my way to work, or more often in the evenings, and we'd enjoy a cup of tea. Over the last two or three years, we talked about our farm, her childhood, the church they got married in, her wedding dress. I challenged her gently from time to time, but her facts were always the same and I enjoyed listening to her. She seemed happy and unconcerned. She kept a meticulously clean house even at this age. I figured that as long as she was content about whatever she wanted to talk about, there was no need for me to be concerned.

Then the pattern had changed, for now she wanted action. She said she wanted to walk to the corner store to see the butcher about the veal she planned to cook for dinner. She said she was expecting three guests from Heidelberg. One day she told me she had waited for the milk bottle to be delivered to her door step that morning, but the milk man had become very unreliable. One spring morning on a Saturday, on our returning from our morning walk, Jim and I found her sitting on the doorstep. It was only with forceful persuasion from Jim that she came inside, still very upset with the milk man.

On a cold day last February, I stopped by her house just a few blocks away to see if she needed anything. In reality, it was my excuse to find out if she'd had an uneventful night. There she was in the front yard in her checkered flannel housecoat with only her red house-slippers. No socks. She was busy throwing things on the curb, searching for something at the bottom of the dumpster I'd carried to the curbside the previous evening. When I confronted her, she snapped, "You threw out my new black blouse, Trudy. I was to wear it this afternoon for your Aunt Ruth's funeral." Aunt Ruth had passed on more than twenty years ago. Angry as I was, I brushed her hand off and looked around to see if any of the neighbors were watching. Had they seen my mother in her flannel housecoat trashing the yard in the middle of winter?

After that incident, I just could not let her live alone.

Can a mother and a daughter share their lives forever? It took me years to shake off that shell of comfort and emerge on my own. Although she was never far, I had my space and she had hers, and I did not need to lean on her. For the last several years, my children mowed her small front lawn and cleared the snow off her driveway, till at last they sprinted off to college. I continued to plant flowers in her yard, listening to her choice of plants and her sermon on colors. A strong, stoic woman that she was, she trimmed her own roses and cooked her own food, and always told me I never learned to make apple strudel quite the way she had taught me. I disappointed her when I married a man with no German blood in his veins. His being Irish simply did not cut it for her. They were civil to one another and held some very polite conversations, but that was the extent of their relationship. So, although I worried about it, the question of her coming to live with us never came up.

Lately, she and I had talked about old age as a slow motion picture shown in rundown movie houses where the film breaks and has to be glued together several times before the reel can move on. I brought up the talk of her moving to a retirement home but each time she pouted and we made no headway. As months went by, I knew it might have to be a nursing home. She told me it would be a prison to her if I ever made her leave her own yard.

The next afternoon was a different experience. She wasn't in her room. A flat-breasted aide in the corridor said, "I saw Tony wheeling your mother into the dining room." In fact, she remembered there was some commotion because she said, "Mrs. Frieman was being stubborn. She insisted on walking and Tony thought she needed a wheelchair. They argued. Mrs. Frieman started walking, but after a bit, she started to lose her balance and shouted at Tony for not giving her a wheelchair."

"These old people are always right," the aide had added whimsically.

My mama gave in to a wheelchair! She'd started to recognize her limits, I thought, as I walked into the dining room where there were fifteen or so other wheelchairs. I peeked in but didn't see her. Then, I quickened my pace and looked in several of the other rooms when someone told me to go to the sun room. They'd seen her in there. I wondered if she'd started to make friends.

She sat in a wheelchair by herself facing an open French window, which overlooked a large patch of green. Her hunched back and flat hair made her look small. A square blanket meant to cover her legs was lying on the floor. Her shift-gown was partly open, and with her fingers, she was picking at the rest of the buttons trying to undo them.

"Mama, you're half naked," I said aghast, pulling her gown together and laying the soft blanket across her lap.

"I'm looking at the green grass," she said without turning her head. "Your papa is buried there."

"It looks so peaceful, Mama, with the sun shining on it," I said, as I kneeled beside her and buttoned her up.

"Don't fuss, Gertrude," she said, pushing my hand away. "Let go of me. I want my freedom. That cloth is too heavy." She shunned my touch.

I pulled up a chair next to her. I told her that my son, George, was finishing college and would be home for the summer before he joined law school. I told her that Gretchen was bringing her boyfriend home to meet the family. "They'll come to visit you, Mama," I said.

She did not answer and I suspected that she was not listening. At first, I thought she was pouting again, angry with me for having brought her to this place. However, this time she did not turn her face away.

She must have felt smothered in her own world. "I want my freedom," she said. "I want to be free." That night I went home with a heavy burden.

Someone from St. Augustina's called me a week later at two in the morning and said they were taking my mother to the Emergency room. She had fallen trying to get out of bed.

The doctor at the hospital assured me it was a minor mishap. "She has a crack in the bone above her right wrist; she'll need to have her arm in plaster for at least six weeks. Old people heal slower. It'll be a while before the discomfort goes away. She'll need some pain pills."

"Mama, what happened? How did you fall?" I asked her a couple of days later, when I felt she was rested and not in pain.

"Oh, Trudy. Your papa came to visit and we were going for a walk. It was so icy and slippery."

"Mama," I said. "Why didn't you ring the call bell? It's hard getting up from sleep."

"I don't know what you mean," she said in a haughty voice.

I showed her the wire under her pillow and the call button pinned to the side of the bed.

"Oh, that's the snake I'm afraid of," she said, panic stricken. "Take it away, Trudy, it's been running on my patch of green."

"Okay, okay," I said. "But Mama, why didn't you hold Papa's hand? He would have helped you across the icy patch of green."

"I know he would have, Gertrude, but I'm too proud. I wasn't about to ask."

A secretive look of trust came across her face.

"At least you understand, Trudy," she whispered. "Daughters always do."

I left her in a happy mood, wondering to myself what Jim and I would have for dinner that night. Surely not chicken feathers!

Last night she died. Complications from the fall, they told me. At age ninety-two, she'd earned her walk on the icy patch of green.

My Daughter's Shopping on a Cold Day

She bought a trench coat
from the Salvation Army Store,
three sizes too big.
Wore it in the house,
strutted around,
asked if I liked it. Without waiting for my answer,
said, "Meg's bought one too.
Only hers is camouflage green.

Out of the same shopping bag
came khaki pantaloons
with pockets,
and flaps and a camouflage belt.
On went the pants,
meant for a six-foot three.
Then came a warm scarf, not dainty,
but masculine-like.

Another beret? I asked, how many do you have?
Eyes rolled up as she said, Mom! and left the room.
Too much of a soldier in her, I thought,
She doesn't know to be sixteen and pretty.
Sturdy and so un-woman-like,
I said to my husband when we were in bed.
Let her be, he said, she saves us money.

Only Voices

In a small village in Kerala, South India, there is an abundance of tall coconut trees, and in this peaceful place of three hundred or so people, a thousand birds, like a thousand thoughts, chatter at dusk. Tree shadows reflect into stagnant, narrow backwater canals. Small houses pocket themselves between trees, their side steps sinking into the muddy, green waters. Wooden rice boats are anchored by the side of the steps. The hot sun of the tropics has begun its descent into the folds of the Indian Ocean beyond the village. After the birds make their noisy debut to the whole village, both birds and people settle down for the night. There is not much else to do, other than hear a stray dog bark.

At dusk, Grandma Sophie hears this noisy babble in the air and senses that in a few minutes, street lights will go on. Then, fifteen-year-old Rachel, a neighbor from the house next door, will walk over to ask Sophie if she requires anything for the evening. Sophie gropes along the wall, finds her white cane and places it by her chair, so she can reach for it with ease. She stretches her other arm and feels for the small tape recorder on the table. With her middle finger feeling for the record button, she decides to add more to what she recorded for her granddaughter two days earlier.

Sophie has kept the tape recorder in the same spot for the last two years, ever since her daughter, Miriam, sent it to her from America. Sophie hates to disrupt the order of things around it. She is the only one in the neighborhood to possess a tape recorder, and with a big smile on her face, she points to it with pride when friends come to visit.

"Amma, I want our little Becky to hear her grandma's voice till such time as she meets you," Miriam had written. "You're her only grandparent and she is your only granddaughter. One day, although God only knows when, for it may be quite a while, we'll come visit you. Until then, Amma, you must record all your stories for Becky. Tell her everything about our home in Kerala, our family, and my childhood. Describe the small home I grew up in. How even without brothers or sisters, I never felt alone because we had friends around us. Tell her about the coconut trees children play around. Teach her some songs too, Amma, perhaps the same songs you taught me, if you still remember them. I still know the song about the smell of fresh rain when the monsoons come. When I hear birds twittering, even now my mind goes to the backwaters where we children swam for long hours."

"I'm here, Rachel," Sophie calls out from the inner room when she hears the front door squeak.

Rachel, a big girl for her age with short, curly hair and a flat nose, sits cross-legged on the straw mat next to Sophie's chair. She wraps her flowery, cotton frock over her legs and hugs her knees and says, "What are you going to say today?"

She listens attentively to everything Sophie dictates into the tape recorder for her two-old granddaughter, Becky, over in America.

This dusk, it rains heavily. Sophie sings into the tape recorder, and asks Rachel to join her. She wants Becky to hear Rachel's voice too. Then, she thinks, far away in her daughter, Miriam's house, Becky will know her grandma has someone with her. Sophie hears the sound of rain through the open windows.

Rachel gets up to close the windows when Sophie says, "Let the child hear the rain too. Its soothing, warm rhythm will help her stay calm, perhaps help her sleep." Rachel shrugs her shoulders and again, straightens her flowery skirt and sits down.

The tape will carry all the sounds, but the earthy smell of fresh rain will not carry on to America. Nor the fragrance of the coconut curry Sophie makes for herself that evening, nor the smell of wet mud and grass. On the other hand, Becky will also not get a whiff of the unpleasant fish odor that permeates the air when the wind blows in a certain direction off the canal waters. Every day and each place sets its own pattern.

"Do you want me to sleep in your house tonight? My mother said to ask you,"
Rachel asks after Sophie had stopped the recording.

"Tomorrow will be fine. Don't spoil me so much, Rachel. Tell your mother even though every day is dark, I'm not afraid of the dark any more."

Sophie has had a new problem in the four years since Miriam left for America. It happened even before the tape recorder arrived, but Sophie will give her daughter that news. She needs time to think, so she says at first. A dark curtain has fallen across her eyes, first the left, in which she was seeing lightning-like flashes, and then a few dark spots, which quickly became very big, appeared in the right eye, but enough sight remained. The nearest eye hospital was miles away, but by the time Rachel's father took her there, the doctor said it was too late for surgery. A few weeks later, a dark curtain blinded her right eye also. Retinal detachment, the doctors told her, "Only in big cities with the latest technology might this condition be cured."

At times Sophie gets anxious for the day when Miriam will visit, and bring baby Becky with her. In her letters to her daughter, always written by Rachel, (for although Sophie speaks English, she never learned to write), Sophie does not mention her blindness. Miriam is a young mother, and alone in a foreign country. Why add to her problems? So Sophie thinks.

In the beginning, the whole village has many questions, a loving curiosity, some nosiness, maybe even a sense of responsibility, about how Sophie will handle her new problem. Friends her age advise her to call Miriam back. Others tell her to pack up and go to America, but this is the only home Sophie has ever known and her whole life is jammed in it. She will never leave; she knows that much.

Sophie tells her neighbors it makes no difference whether her daughter knows about her eyesight or not, because Miriam can't travel so far with a small baby. So she'll tell her everything the following year. After all, nothing can change the darkness that has befallen her. So, two years go by; little Becky is walking and talking and singing songs she's heard her grandma sing in a quivering voice on tape.

Miriam met Dan, a young pharmacy student, at the hospital when she had first started her radiology residency in America. Since then, Dan graduated and works long hours at his father's pharmacy. Now, ten thousand miles away from Sophie, Miriam and her husband, Dan, are ecstatic, anticipating the arrival of their first born. Miriam wants to work till the real labor pains start, not the false ones her friends talk about. She plans to spend all her maternity leave looking after her baby. Miriam says to Dan, "I'll make sure the baby recognizes me before I go back to work. Would be so good if Amma lived nearer and helped us care for our baby."

Miriam's water gushes out when she is just over six months pregnant, and little Becky is barely two pounds at birth. She makes feeble noises when she takes deep breaths on her own; the latest machines purr around her in the neonatal intensive care and they give her blood exchanges to purify her blood. She needs tubes to help her lungs breathe air. They give her extra oxygen and she needs two surgeries to correct complications that have arisen from her prematurity.

Eventually, after more than eight weeks in the hospital, doctors tell Miriam and Dan that she is progressing well, and has put on weight and she'll be ready for home in another two weeks. She has fewer tubes in her, but they'd test her frequently for problems from prematurity, such as abnormal brain activity, hearing, or sight problems. At a follow-up appointment weeks later, they are told she has no vision. Dan and Miriam have suspected this all along.

Becky is two years old and Miriam does not have the heart to write to her mother that her only grandchild has a handicap. She sends a tape recorder to her mother saying she wants Becky to recognize her grandma's voice. So she writes cheerful letters and answers all her mother's questions, often on tape.

Miriam plays the tapes her mother sends to Becky. Becky is happy to hear her grandma's voice, and she coos at the foreign accent and musical sounds. She wants to hear the sounds all the time, so she reaches up to the tape deck. Like any other child, she knows where it is placed. She has a certain path of walking around in the room, so she won't bang into anything as she reaches out to the tapes and brings them to her mother. She says, "Amma, Amma," as she hears Sophie speak. Then, Miriam notices Becky sings the same songs in the same tones and the Kerala accent as Amma does.

Miriam writes to her mother and tells her she'll enjoy playing with Becky. She doesn't know how her mother will face this challenge of a blind grandchild. She postpones her visit to India by one more year.

"You'll like her looks, Amma, a proper mix of Dan's fair skin and high cheek bones and my dark, straight hair and black eyes." Her heart is heavy when she imagines the scene of her mother greeting her only grandchild.

"Come when you've saved enough money. Dan will like our country. You must show him around," Sophie tells Rachel to write. "I'm not going anywhere, I can wait."

Another dusk and again, a thousand birds crowd the trees along the canals, causing their cacophony to fill the air.

Grandma Sophie has enough time to think. She suspects it's not money holding her daughter back. She senses there is something else. The thought comes to her from some casual remark young Rachel makes. It's Becky's first birthday before Miriam finally sends Becky's photos to her mother. She remembers Rachel saying Becky has a bewildered look, and a lovable smile in her photos, but what a petite little girl she is, dressed in a pink, frilly dress. Sophie holds the photos in her hands for a long time, moving her fingers up and down over their shiny surfaces, suspecting something may be wrong. She says nothing.

"I manage well enough, what difference will it make to my faraway daughter," is how Sophie justifies her own news. At other times she thinks Miriam will be upset. Perhaps angry, perhaps disappointed and with feelings of guilt, all tied up in knots of confusion. There is never a right time to give bad news. Would it be different had her daughter stayed home and never left for America? It's too late to ponder over circumstances that cannot be altered. Sophie is happy for her daughter's love and for her granddaughter's friendship through her voice.

Sophie does not want Miriam to blame herself. So she makes her decision never to tell her that she has lost her vision. She's not going to ask Miriam to visit, but encourage her to stay in America. If she writes she's coming, she'll say she wants to go on a religious pilgrimage that month, so to come another time. She'll encourage Miriam to pursue her career, enjoy life with Dan and her baby girl, and see America. Tape talk suffices to bring her joy. Their voices bring her all the love she needs. Besides, she has Rachel to keep her company.

Rachel is eager to meet Becky before she goes away to college in a couple of months. The tapes work well and Sophie does not need for Rachel to scribe her letters that often. For the last four years, Rachel has the more important job of mailing the tapes once or twice a month. She also opens the mail for Sophie when letters and tapes come from America.

The next time will be the last time Rachel will go to the local post office and mail Grandma Sophie's tapes. She decides to include a note to Miriam and Becky before she seals the parcel. Rachel takes her younger sister with her to the post office, so she can learn the procedure of sending tapes abroad.

They're playing in the family room before supper when Dan brings in the mail. Miriam recognizes Rachel's handwriting on the little parcel and rips it open right away. Miriam is surprised to see a letter enclosed in the parcel. She places the just opened tape in the recorder and asks Becky to listen. Little Becky is delighted. Her mother sits back on the sofa, puts her feet up on the coffee table, and reads Rachel's letter.

"Dear Miriam,

Thanks for the lovely sweater you sent my mother, and for the earrings you sent me. I'll take them to college and think of your Becky, although I haven't seen her yet. I told Grandma Sophie about your gifts and she said they must be beautiful. She's okay, cheerful and kind, and has fun recording her stories and songs for Becky. She loves hearing your voices because it makes her feel you are close by.

"Soon I'll be leaving for college, so your mother will be lonely. Maybe in a few more years when Becky is older, she can keep her grandma company. It's a dark world for your mother, but there is much joy in her soul. Her great source of happiness is hearing Becky's voice. Sometimes she tells me she's getting old and she'll never get a chance to hug her little Becky. Bring her a new tape recorder when you come; this one's getting old. Not that she wants a new one, it's my own idea. I'd love to meet Dan, too, but when you come, I may be away at college. Love, Rachel."

Becky wants to listen to Amma's tape again and cries obstinately when they press stop and tell her it's time for supper. Dan and Miriam indulge her needs, and Becky wants to start the recorder herself. She feels for the rewind button, and then finds the play button, and it pleases her when the sound starts. She sits on the carpet by the recorder, caressing her Bitty Baby, and sings along with Amma.

Miriam thinks of her mother. She senses her mother getting old, but trying to appear content. She can envision the disappointment on Amma's face for she could never have imagined a blind grandchild. Miriam's thoughts are riled up, restless, and flow through a dark maze. She hasn't heard a word of what her mother says to Becky on tape.

What has happened in the many years since she has been away from home? Her mother must have aged. Old age is sad when one is alone. What depressing, dark thoughts. Miriam lies awake all night long, staring at a distant street light she sees through a narrow slit in the drapes. Perhaps she should visit; at least talk it over with Dan.

Becky is four. She makes plenty of conversation; she imagines a lot. She, too, wants to send a message to her Grandma Sophie everyday and she does. She tells her about the pet frog she'd kept in a shoe box, but he hopped into the flower beds making a grunting noise, and she doesn't know what happened to it. The next time it's about their neighbor's cat that sat on the fence and jumped into their yard.

"My Dad let me touch its fur. He said it's big and black. We don't know the cat's name but she meows so loud," Becky squeals into the tape recorder.

When Sophie hears the child's voice, her happiness exudes warmth that has no limits. Their emotions cross technological boundaries.

A time comes when Miriam decides they should visit her lonely mother. She's tired of hiding in a distance. She tells Dan she can face their beloved daughter's handicap with equanimity and will tell Amma calmly that Becky is different from any other grandchild. Face to face, her mother will be happy to see Becky, and accept the problems.

The flight over is long and tiresome. Miriam is nervous in the taxi after they arrive. She wishes she had told her mother four years ago when Becky was born. She feels afraid she's letting her mother down. Afraid Amma will be disappointed when she sees Becky is blind. Finally they arrive.

Miriam knocks on the heavy wooden door that's left open during the day. "Amma, Amma, we're here," she calls out and enters. She looks around the dim, front parlor where many of the family photos she has sent over the years are tacked on the far wall with scotch tape. Sophie, hearing the knock and Miriam's call, stands up, cane in hand, and walks towards the entrance.

"What happened? Amma, Amma? Did you fall?" Miriam asks automatically looking at her mother who appears older and so different. Amma's straight gaze reminds her of Becky. Then the white cane in her hand and groping gait tells her all. Miriam lets out a scream, checks herself, and then she cries loudly. Perhaps tears from the joy of hugging her mother, at hearing her Amma's voice; perhaps tears from grief at seeing her mother is blind. A tangled emotional web tightens around her; she can't say a word. The subject of Becky's eyes is left untouched. This is so different from the homecoming she had expected.

"Come, come, my darling," Sophie says feeling Miriam's face. "Bring my baby near me. Where's Dan?"

After a pause, Miriam says, "Amma, Dan is making sure the luggage is all here. Becky and he will be here in a few minutes."

Rachel's sister, her friends, and other neighbors spot Dan and Becky as he gathers the luggage. They crowd around them with questions. Nobody in the village is shy. They have waited a long time to greet Sophie's American son-in-law, and their own Miriam and her daughter.

Miriam takes Becky in her arms and brings Dan's attention to Amma with her gestures. Dan understands.

Becky says, "I thought we're coming to Amma's house. Did she go away? Why isn't Amma talking to me?"

Then she hears Amma calling her name and Becky has known that voice all her life. They hug each other and talk and laugh as tears stream down Sophie's face. Together they start to sing the song about the pitter-patter of rain on earth.

Later, Miriam and Dan discuss Amma's blindness when they are alone on the front porch. It has numbed her sensibilities and Dan tries to say it is what it is, nothing can change fate. They watch the sun go down and hear the chirping of a thousand birds, the voices of Miriam's childhood. The sun sets, the birds perform their high-pitched symphony and tell the world there is order to chaos, and thus they herald the dusk.

Street lights go on in the next few minutes. Becky clings to Grandma Sophie, hides her face in her lap when she hears the cacophony, not seeing how far away the birds really are. She tells her grandma she loves her. She's not afraid of the sounds anymore.

Amma strokes her hair and sings her another song. Then Miriam calls her to bed saying its dark outside.

Cricket in my yard

Our cricket field was but a
small patch of cement,
but at age ten,
it was real to me.
Let me play cricket,
I said to my brothers.
No, you're a girl,
you don't know how.
Our friends will laugh you off the field.

I'll stand here anyway,
I'll be a pest.
I'll pout and sit here,
in the middle of the field.
Oh, come on then,
at last someone would say,
hold the bat like this and swing.

So I played cricket
my brothers and I.

That day we learned to be friends.

Sukhatme-Sheth 144

A Hard Seat

Savi sits herself down on one of several hard seats at Frankfurt International airport. She has a four-hour wait before her next flight to Chicago. There's hardly an empty place and she feels lucky to find a seat. Most of the seats are occupied by travelers holding bulky hand luggage and appear to be weary like her. She sits there, afraid to move. There is a continuous exchange of someone sitting down, another getting up, and an occasional chair being left empty for a few seconds. She sits in her chair for almost two hours, listening to the announcement of arrivals and departures of planes over the airport intercom. There is also the noise of people speaking, bags rolling by, and tired children screaming as they are dragged along by their parents. Savi yawns and rubs her eyes, closes them, but each time a plane is announced, she opens them and wonders how long it will be before her AI 216 departing for Chicago is announced. She clutches a huge travel purse on her lap close to her, and periodically feels for her hand luggage by her feet.

Savi is twenty-two years old and is traveling abroad on a Ford Foundation Scholarship to Chicago. It's her first time in a plane and her first time out of India. Her uncle, who lives in the big city of Chicago, has warned her to be careful of her belongings when she travels and when she arrives in America. He writes that he and his wife will come to receive her at the airport. Savi has not understood how exactly she's supposed to guard her luggage, except that she knows not to leave it unattended. From her perch, she has seen men in uniform walking around holding guns and dogs sniffing the luggage.

Savi left her hometown of Bilaspur in Northern India two days ago for the first time. She has made brief trips to Delhi and Lucknow for family weddings prior to this big outing, but she has always traveled with her father, her mother, her little sister, and at times, her grandparents. Savi had imagined herself in places other than her small hometown since she was a young girl. When a distant cousin who had returned to Bilaspur after finishing her education in America stopped by their house, Savi had asked many questions about the foreign land.

She wonders what awaits her at the end of the next eight-hour journey to Chicago. How is she to spend her time in the airplane? She has not talked to anyone. She looks out of the airport windows and notes that it's a gloomy day in Frankfurt. Around her, the cheerless buzz of the busy airport continues. She misses her younger sister with her endless questions, and her grandmother's monotonous chanting. A few words like "yes, please," or "no, thank you," to the airhostess who brought her breakfast and dinner is all she has uttered. Yet she is surrounded by people and chaos.

She realizes she's dressed differently. She wonders how the people around her perceive her. Smiling to herself, she imagines they might see her as in a fancy dress party, although nobody has really stared at her, so it must be okay. It's all in her mind. Savi begins to observe other individuals walking by; looks at faces like hers and different from hers. An African woman wearing a colorful headgear and an ankle-length bright skirt walks past her. An Italian looking couple in black, a lean man and a large woman stroll along, talking animatedly and gesturing with their hands. Then she sees an Indian couple with two children trudging behind them. She feels happy to see them; perhaps she could walk up to them and introduce herself, call them uncle and aunty, as she might in India, but they don't even smile at her. She sees the woman's sari, what normally would have been elegant attire, is messed up, perhaps from a long plane journey. Savi is comfortable in her *salwar-kurta*, the dress her ammi and she had so carefully selected. Would cotton wrinkle? Her ammi had worried about it. Savi straightens her shirt, the *kurta*, with her hands and brushes her long hair back from her face. She likes the pink and green colors in her attire. It reminds her of sunshine and home.

The big boned woman sitting next to her had been sleeping most of the time. She suddenly leaves with her luggage. Savi hopes that whoever sits next to her will talk to her. She has grown up in a large extended family and is comfortable with people. The Americans are friendly, she's been told; it's the Europeans you watch. The airport is everybody...Americans and the rest. She sees a young man with a punk hairstyle, kind of like an oblique mohawk that has a tinge of green on the right side of his head. He's holding on to his skinny girlfriend wearing a black leather miniskirt. This is so different from my world, she thinks. I never even saw my older sister and her husband hold hands, leave aside leaning into each other like this.

In the meantime, a small built woman in a black dress, with a mass of gray, curly hair, has placed her hand luggage on the hard seat next to Savi and stands there looking around.

"Is *toilette* that way?" she asks Savi in a heavy European accent.

"Yes," says Savi, "just round the corner. I saw it as I came."

"Please, you watch my bag. I come back quick. You go to Chicago also?"

Savi nods, eager to please. She decides she'll take her turn next, and ask the woman to look after her luggage. After all, the old woman has smiling eyes. She's bent and can't walk straight. Friendly, perhaps a little eccentric, she thinks. The woman reminds her of her own grandmother. She can't imagine her grandmother traveling alone like this. People outside India are so brave, she decides. She feels timid, because she is young and traveling for the first time. She will not let the woman see through her façade, in case she decides to talk to her some more.

The woman comes back after a while, grumbling how crowded the airports are, and that she couldn't even reach the hand dryers. Savi sees her wet hands and wonders what is expected of her.

"We on same plane to Chicago," she says as she unzips her packed-to-capacity carry-on bag and begins rummaging through it. She removes some clothes, a chocolate box, and two gift boxes wrapped in fancy paper onto the seat, pulls out a hand towel, and wipes her hands. A button from the woman's black cardigan catches in the handle of her luggage, breaks loose, and falls to the ground. The woman appears not to have noticed it, but Savi is hesitant to lean under the woman to retrieve it. She thinks she'll do it later, once the woman settles down on her seat. The woman puts all her items back in a hurry, and sits poised at the front of her seat, waiting for her plane to be announced.

Savi is reminded of the crowded bus stations in Delhi, where one must rush to get in.

"Oh, Denis, there you are at last," the woman exclaims, sounding relieved. "My grandson, we travel together," she turns her head and tells Savi. Then abruptly, she stands up erect and walks away fast, as if someone is chasing her.

Savi is surprised and looks in the direction of the man the old woman has called Denis, but there are many people around, and she is not sure which one is Denis. After the woman has walked away, Savi notices one of the gift wrapped packages the woman seems to have forgotten on her seat.

"Your grandmother was sure in a hurry," says another young man who has come to occupy the empty seat. He picks up the package and hands it to Savi. She assumes he must have seen them talk.

"Yes," says Savi, hesitant, because she doesn't want to explain everything to a stranger sitting next to her. In her own mind, she thinks, "We'll be on the same flight. I'll give it to her then. Also, this button from her cardigan." So she picks up the button and puts it in her purse and the package in her hand luggage.

Savi has gone up and down the aisle of the Boeing 747 several times looking for the gray-haired grandmotherly woman. Some passengers are beginning to notice her. Self-conscious, she returns to her seat. Maybe she misunderstood the woman; maybe the woman made a mistake. She doesn't even know the woman's name, otherwise she could have asked the airhostess for help. Savi keeps looking as passengers walk through the aisles and stand in line for the restrooms.

Later, standing in the passport checking-in line after the plane has landed, Savi spots the woman with the gray hair again.

"Silly me," she thinks, "why didn't I find her on the plane?" The woman is a little ways ahead of her. Savi wants to call out to her but she's in the line ahead of her and Savi is too well brought up to shout in public. "What would I call her anyway? I'll just wait until after passport check, and meet her in the customs area."

Savi tries to walk fast in to Customs after passport check. She doesn't want to miss the old woman. After passport check-in, she gathers her luggage and sees the woman in the adjacent line, opening her bag for the customs officer. Savi smiles at her but the woman looks past her.

"That's strange," Savi thinks. "She doesn't even recognize me? She'll be thankful when I give her the package."

The Customs Officer asks Savi, "Do you have anything to declare?"

"No, sir."

"May I see your hand luggage?" he asks.

Savi unzips her carry-on for the officer. Instantly his hand reaches for the old woman's package.

"What's in this?" he asks as he turns it around and sniffs it.

"Oh, it's not mine. I don't know what's in it. I found it on the......'

"You shouldn't be carrying packages for strangers. I've got to call you inside for more questions, Ma'am."

Savi is in tears and her hands tremble. She looks around desperately to see if she can locate the old woman with the curly gray hair. She spots her disappearing through the automatic doors at the end of the enclosed area. A sense of doom, of being cheated, descends upon her. The woman has taken advantage of her naivity. Savi maintains a bland look to keep from crying. A scant second goes by.

"Quick, officer," she screams. "The parcel belongs to that gray haired woman in the black dress."

The officer has also seen that woman. He picks up the phone and talks frantically into it. There is a long moment of waiting when Savi hopes the woman is stopped. The officer must have believed her. Savi sees another official and the woman coming back toward them.

"Do you know this young lady from India?" the officer asks the woman.

"No sir, never set eyes on her." The woman replies very properly in a British accent, barely glancing at Savi.

"She left that package on the seat next to me. We'd been talking before that, so I thought I'd return it to her on the plane. Only I couldn't..." She feels foolish even saying she couldn't find her.

The officer examines her baggage tag. "Same flight, I see. Why didn't you return it?"

Savi doesn't know why she couldn't find her and gives no answer. She just stands there looking at the woman in total dismay.

"I'm afraid we have to take you in for more detailed questioning. That package could be illegal, or so we suspect, or may be nothing. Such transactions can mean big money for somebody. Students from India are always in need of money." Turning to the woman, he continued, "I'm sorry to have detained you. I apologize for the inconvenience. You may go to your destination. Welcome to our country."

Savi sees the woman bow ever so slightly, and walk away very upright and very elegant, so different from when they were at Frankfurt International airport.

"Officer, sir, can you ask the woman to show you the black cardigan in her hand luggage? I've something that belongs to her."

The officer looks puzzled but does the needful. "Excuse me, ma'am," the officer calls out after the woman; then runs up to her, talks to her and takes her hand luggage. He opens it to find a black cardigan in it. Savi shows him the spot where the button is missing, then digs in her purse to retrieve the button she has so casually dropped in it. The woman begins to twitch her neck and starts to walk off, but the officer is quicker. They stand facing each other. Then Savi throws the button into the woman's opened hand luggage in the midst of a false nose and a mass of black hair.

Savi is relieved to get out of this mess. She feels like an alien in these new surroundings but at the same time, this is her freedom to take charge of her life. She'll buy the food she wants, she'll eat flavored yogurt of her own choice, and she'll sleep for as long as she wishes to in the mornings. She has a new awakening.

At the same time, she hopes her uncle and aunt have come to receive her. She needs a soft shoulder to buffer her entry into a new land.

The Konkan Coast

Sunburnt fishermen bare-chested,
with bandanas and loincloth,
push their wooden dinghies
early morn, into the open sea.
Rhythm in their gait and voices,
they jump in.

The boats disappear
beyond the Konkan coastline.
It was so long ago but,
barren images still cling on,
for me sitting in silence,
watching people
waiting for a strike.
I see a speedboat zoom by,
then a water-skier hurry past.
Noise, action, turmoil all here within me.

Sea-washed images come back,
nostalgic for a homeland faraway.
I ponder long, trying to remember,
the once familiar rhythms
and old faces.

Strange Fragrances

It was strange, almost whimsical, how the whole incident got put together. One April morning, between a bite of toast and tea, Senator David Brookston, Ingrid's husband of thirty-five years, announced that they were to entertain twenty-some guests the following week.

"Catered at home, perhaps," he said casually, seated at his usual place in their breakfast nook, his head buried behind the *Washington Post*. He said it was to honor a Sanji Rastogi, an Indian politician who was coming to Washington.

Ingrid, stunned, walked out from behind their cafe doors; shocked as if a strand of electricity had just passed through her body. She steadied herself.

"A restaurant will do fine. Our usual?" she said demurely, as she continued to water her wilting jade. She tried not to remember the man David had so casually mentioned. Had he said the name on purpose? Did he want to see how she reacted? Is that why he had mentioned he would like a catered affair at their home? Giving it some thought, she walked back to the kitchen with her empty can in hand. She doubted all of the above, because David was too fickle with names, especially foreign names, and thirty-some years ago is a long time.

Ingrid was restless the whole afternoon, the entire evening, and for that matter, the whole week. Her daughter, Sonya, with a degree in home economics, started to plan a German menu for this party. Sauerkraut, brats, buns, baked beans, perhaps some grilled chicken with a mixed salad sprinkled with walnuts and pine nuts and oven-toasted garlic bread, hand-crumpled and tossed in, Italian style. To finish it off, Sonya decided on a Black Forest *torte*.

"Too casual," David said, when she told him.

Ingrid couldn't recall his exact words from almost thirty-five years ago, but she was certain her impression of the day was accurate; and on her own final analysis, she felt hurt.

Ingrid had taken him to visit her parents on Thanksgiving Day at their home in the country in Virginia. One thing she knew: Sanjivan Rastogi, called Sanji by everyone who knew him (not likely that there was another Sanji, but still she wondered), did not mince his words.

"Too rich, too bland, too much cream," was what Sanji had likely said on their way home in the car. A psychology major herself, she wondered at this man with whom she was so hopelessly in love, in spite of his ruthlessness about her German heritage. She puzzled over the happenings of years ago and hated him all over.

After discussing many options with Sonya, Ingrid decided she preferred they serve Indian food in honor of their guest. No matter what kind of spread she decided on, it should not be, "too rich, too bland." Sonya wanted candles for a center piece and Ingrid okayed that. She knew he was allergic to a certain kind of lily, or maybe any lily, so she approved the candles idea. Much as she wanted to, she did not bring up lilies of any kind or talk of the past with Sonya.

Sonya said she'd manage the caterer, and told her mother to be a good host and keep the guests entertained.

The day before the event, Sonya, with the help of Marcella, their kitchen help, polished the candlesticks and got the table linen ironed. On the day of the big event, Ingrid told Sonya she'd buy the candles on her way home from the wine merchant's at noon, because Sonya would be hard pressed for time; she had too many chores planned for the day. The evening guests were to arrive around 7pm, and with the caterers arriving with thousands of questions, the layout of the outdoor tables, the positioning of the buffet and warming of the chafing dishes, and the setting out of the party plates, napkins, linen, and silverware, Sonya would be overwhelmed, so Ingrid thought. Ingrid said they'd discuss the seating arrangements in the afternoon, after she came home with the candles and the wine.

With a little trepidation, Ingrid looked left and right and then stepped down from the pavement onto the road. Cars zoomed by, for the traffic in this Georgetown street was always heavy. She had come to love the noises of the trucks and the buses and the cars with loud radios; it all meant people and life. It meant nothing would change for her in this ever-vibrant world.

It was thirty-five years ago that she had moved here with David. The oak in her yard had grown to maturity and majestic as it was, it spat leaves in the fall. She liked the creeping ivy that hankered high against the red brick next to the garage. Every day, she had wished Mrs. Cramer next door, "Good morning," and "Good evening," for that was the extent of their friendship, until Mrs. Cramer died quietly one fall day, a year ago. So her son Ben, visiting from New York, had told Sonya from across the porch.

These happenings gave Mrs. Brookston a sense of belonging. David, her Senator husband, was always busy with his own agenda, and Ingrid kind of liked that. She savored the time to herself, to think and ponder on life. To wonder how different her life might have been. In fact, almost had been, had she stayed married to Sanji.

"Good morning, Mrs. Brookston," a voice called out to her from behind, as she waited at the island to cross the road. Startled, she looked around, forcing herself out of her reverie.

"Good morning, Ben," Ingrid acknowledged him. "What brings you home so often these days?"

"Settling Mother's property. The lawyers. Plenty of work involved." Ben was brief. "Besides, I like it around here. How's Sonya?"

Ben was a young man with pleasing eyes and a subtle smile. Quite suitable for her dark-eyed Sonya. How was she to influence these young people? What right did she have when she had so much to arbitrate in her own life? Well, after so long, her life was settled; it was her mind that needed an anchor.

Her association with Sanji flashed before her. Sanji was that bright young graduate student from India when she was an undergraduate in college. They talked for hours, and a longing for each other blossomed as they spent time in each other's company. Sanji had said he was almost sure his mother and father would not approve of their getting married. After that, they never discussed the matter further. She remembered a sentence he had mumbled one evening, "Not because it's you, but what you stand for."

She had asked him what he meant, and he said, "White skin."

She wondered if her pale skin had made her stand out in that Indian crowd. Surely, there was depth to their friendship and love for one another. She felt the pain of his words.

Now, years later, crossing the street, she wondered what it was like when she walked next to him, perhaps crossing this very street, as she did with Sonya for years. They had parted, it seemed to her, a hundred years ago...she and Sanji. If he, Sanji, were standing next to her now, would he be humming? He liked to hum. Would he say anything? Would he even speak? She was not bitter all the time; neither remorseful nor sad, but such thoughts did come back to her, more so this week. She wondered with slight amusement if this evening Sanji would talk about the weather, or change of seasons, and change of years, or a change in her? She knew that no matter what the hour or the season, the younger Sanji never noticed the red sky or the flowering trees, and it would not matter to him if they were in Georgetown or Timbuktu. He never saw clouds or rain, or even people passing by. She talked of poetry and feelings, when he puzzled over bricks and cement and mortar. That's what engineering students did. Yet, he said he liked his time with her, and wanted to marry her, but couldn't find a way.

One day, she had said to him, "I'd love to go to India someday." At twenty, one is so gullible, yet unafraid.

She went with him to his parents' house in a small village somewhere in Eastern India...Orissa, Bihar, she remembered the names of a few states. She had tried to look up the name of the village on the map, but the place was not named. Thinking now, she'd argued with herself many times that she had done the right thing in returning to America. She had listened to his family's threats.

His family, the Zamindars, the landowners of that village, held a prestigious position. They were the law. She had not yelled, or screamed or created a scene. She had not threatened them with police action. She felt a coward now, not to have protested more strongly, not to have made a bigger fuss. What choice did she have when she was all alone over there and not even allowed to see him? The way she was brought up would make her have Sanji as an equal partner, to discuss, to argue, to negotiate their terms, and that could never be. His family was the ruling force; they had made him disappear, and to her mind, there were evil forces at play here. It hurt her to imagine that all young Indians may be like him...kowtowing to their elders.

"Just a few hundred people in my village," Sanji had told her, when they talked of his home. "One school, up to the eighth standard, one main dusty street with shops on either side, and the neighbors nosy into what you have for lunch or dinner. My family runs the show."

She had wanted to go there. "You'll take me there one day," she'd prodded him on. "Unless you don't care." For years, she blamed herself for how things turned out. There was a time she berated herself.

Sanji was quiet on the subject most times. She waited for him to bring up the topic. Months later, by which time they had become inseparable, he told her they should go to India next month and they would get married there. He'd written to his parents and given them no choice.

Ingrid wrote to her parents immediately, but they sent their apology and said India was too far for them to travel. Ingrid felt sad, but relieved in a way. Her parents had not taken to Sanji, or he to them. It would all fall into place once they were married and happily settled, she decided.

Weeks later, after she had returned, Sanji wrote her and apologized. Their marriage had been annulled. It meant nothing to her because by then, her mind, her face, her body had become one stiff piece of wood, or perhaps, like a stone that could not be pierced. With tears and nausea and having lost more weight, she arrived back in D.C. and married David on the rebound, two months after she was back from India.

Her friend Petra was to join the dinner party. Years ago, they had sat on the living room carpet of Petra's apartment. She had confided in her friend that she was in love with this simple dressed, wide-eyed, dark-skinned man from India and Petra had said, and she recapped the words even now, "Your Indian man is not to be trusted. He doesn't understand women."

Ingrid understood her to mean he would be fickle. She didn't care if it meant he was not up on his American etiquette, like shaking hands and saying several hundred thank-yous, when what he was really comfortable with was a "namaste," done by folding both hands together and a giving a smile and a nod that expressed all his gratitude. But, she didn't think that's what Petra meant. After all, what did Petra understand of the opposite sex and that, too, of a foreign man whose culture and beliefs were unknown to her? All she cared about were her Vislas, the hunting dogs for which she had such a passion. To train them, show them, and breed them, and win a few blue ribbons. Sanji hated dogs and that may have been the reason he never considered Petra a friend. Their meeting again would be interesting. Ingrid felt good that Petra would be by her side when she faced Sanji, a kind of bodyguard, a hunting dog to give her emotional support through the evening.

After picking out the wines, medium sweet, whites and reds, and two bottles of champagne, and having them sent home, Ingrid entered the candle shop. Tall, white candles were what she wanted for a centerpiece. The shop fragrances overwhelmed her, like they did in India. The same ethereal feeling came back. Incense, frankincense, smoke, flower fragrances, all mixed in one. Another strange smell was in the air; somebody told her it was camphor. Why had Sanji not warned her of this? Then she realized he grew up in the midst of all this confusion; it was not foreign to him, just a part of his daily existence.

Their wedding ceremony seemed to have taken hours. Men, mostly in safari suits, their hair well-oiled and neatly combed, sat on one side of the flowered canopy, the *mandap*, where the ceremony was taking place. Women in colorful saris wearing heavy, gold necklaces beset with precious stones, dangling earrings, and scores of colorful bangles sat around the stage on folding wooden chairs, and ogled at her beauty, but more so, because she was a foreigner. A *firangi*, a foreigner, that's what she was referred to as. It seemed like the entire population of the village came to witness the goings-on in the home of the most important family in the village. Women stared at her blatantly, especially when she looked at Sanji, trying to find that glint of happiness, that connection she desperately needed from him. Amidst all the commotion, people socialized, the priest chanted his mantras in a loud monotonous voice, and she sat there, suffered, as she prefers to think now, all because she was so much in love with Sanji. Sanji was, after all, that absent-minded guy who didn't comprehend details other than what involved a civil engineer's pad and paper. It was a language nobody else understood. She had imagined from almost the beginning that she would be his eyes and ears to the world, but this was such a foreign world to her. She thought she'd take charge once they were settled back home. Remembering that they would be home in Washington D.C. in ten days made her feel better. In the meantime, she tried to participate in the most important event of her life.

She failed to understand why the whole village had to know what happened on their wedding night; it humiliated her. It was their custom, a female cousin of Sanji's explained to her. Embarrassed, she had tried to hide under the sheets of their wedding bed with its four wooden carved posts and the canopy overhead, decked with red roses and white carnations. The servant-in-waiting had smiled at her, and then made her own assessment public to all the women relatives gathered in the kitchen the next morning. They gave her knowing smiles when she walked into the women's sitting quarters later for breakfast. She saw little of Sanji the rest of the day, only fleeting glances, and he was accompanied by his relatives all the time.

The next night, she felt sick to her stomach; something she ate, she decided. The maid-in-waiting took her to another room, where the commanding presence of her mother-in-law, who spoke only a few words of English, overwhelmed her. This woman's eyes and hand gestures did all the talking. Ingrid was in a daze the next two days and nights, sicker still, and when she asked for Sanji, the same mother-in-law who visited her three times a day with potions of strange medicines, said he was busy and not to be disturbed. Ingrid had cried like never before and never since. She cried all the way home, alone, ten days later, when her maid handed her an air-ticket back to America. No family member came to explain or say good-bye.

Ingrid told Sonya she should place the guest of honor next to her; actually between David and her. Over the years, she had vacillated from feelings of vengeance to wonderment to even feelings of affection, but lately, a certain calm had settled in her psyche. After all, she has nothing to complain about in her own life. She was ready to face him. She still read the Indian newspapers in the public library, and she had followed Sanji's climb in the political circles. For years, she didn't know why she bothered to follow his career, but quietly, she suspected she might still be in love with him in a distant sort of way. One time, she bought *The Statesman*, a newspaper from Delhi, which gave the story that Mr. and Mrs. Sanji Rastogi and their two children had been in a car accident, but had escaped major injury. She had kept that newspaper clipping for many years, but then had thrown it out one morning while rummaging through her desk. Why should she care, she asked herself all the time, looking at Sonya, but somehow, she did think about him often, and lately not with anger.

The day moved along. Everything seemed in place; the timing was perfect. She felt good he was coming to her home. David's and hers, she reminded herself. Yes, she wanted to see him desperately, to sit at the table close to him, to smell his after-shave, to hear his voice. She was in a frenzy about what to wear, and had gone through her options many times. Then David came home that day and said, "I say, Ingrid, you'd look rather attractive in a sari for our Indian guest's dinner. Like the one you wore to the Indian Embassy party."

She stroked David's arm very calmly as she said, "I've put on a few pounds and a sari just would not look attractive. Some other time."

He shrugged and went upstairs to shower and change for the evening. Men didn't really care; she knew that, especially not David.

An hour later, Sonya said the table was ready. The caterers were settled and the curries looked enticing. Sonya told her mother that the candles made for an attractive center piece, but asked why she hadn't got flowers for the house, like always. "I thought you said Indians loved flowers, and India is full of fresh flowers," Sonya asked.

Years ago, she had told Sonya about her brief sojourn in India, but she had omitted the harrowing details of her experience. Today, all Ingrid thought of when she remembered Sanji was fresh flowers from the wedding canopy...red roses, white carnations, and perhaps one or two marigold for good luck. A faded picture but it did not matter; it was still a definite vision. There would be no flower fragrances in the house.

As Ingrid entered their large living room, she heard David say, "Our honored guest, Sanji Rastogi," to Petra, standing to his left. Ingrid was wearing a soft, beige dress with a little embroidery around the neck. She had filed her nails for longer than she needed to. Then she had rummaged through her jewelry box, selecting and rejecting bracelets until she found an old one, one with red and gold beads, interspersed with some sandalwood beads. It even smelled a little musty, but she didn't care. Where she had acquired it, she couldn't quite think at this last minute, and it bothered her that she didn't remember. It matched her embroidered dress and the red barrette she wore to keep her hair tied back. Her perfume, a light one, what if Sanji was allergic to it, she mused, but she'd already rubbed it in. A rigid hair spray and high heeled sandals to go. She was late coming down the stairs, but there nothing she wanted to do about it.

"We've met a long time ago," Petra was saying to Sanji, as Ingrid went toward them. "Remember me, the lady who loves dogs. One of Ingrid's friends from way back when? You used to think I was a Russian spy."

"Yes, of course," Sanji said. "I wouldn't have known without your telling me." His voice was very polished, very affected, as if trained to say just the right things. A politician! He didn't want to say more, that much was clear to Ingrid. She'd play along when her turn came.

David put his arm around Ingrid and said fondly, "My wife, Ingrid." She could tell that David had not understood Sanji's, "Yes, of course," to Petra. If he did, he showed no signs of it. Then, without any inflection in his voice, Sanji spoke, "My pleasure to see you again, Mrs. Brookston."

David said, "I didn't realize you two had met before, perhaps it was at an Embassy party. Of course, Ingrid's told me about her numerous Indian admirers in the past. I'm sure you'll find a few common friends and acquaintances, plenty to catch up."

He looked at Ingrid casually, just as a waitress stationed herself in front of them with a smile and a heavy tray of wine glasses. David picked up two glasses and handed one each to Petra and Ingrid. Then he got one for himself just as Sanji nodded to another waiter with soft drinks on his tray. Sonya beckoned Ingrid aside with a question. Other guests mingled in and Ingrid tried to look pleasant and make small talk. She watched Sanji and noticed that he didn't even give a furtive glance in her direction. She judged that to mean he was indifferent to her, and this angered her. She realized David had no idea of the depth of her feelings, but she wasn't sure herself. Her ambivalent thoughts ran a wild gamut; her legs felt a little shaky as she poured down half a glass of wine into the potted jade. She felt relief. This guest would be no different from the many political dignitaries they hosted. Dignitaries connected with other governments, why was she so riled? Did she think she was to have a showdown with the chief guest?

David was talking to Sanji on India's need for urgent relief money, after the earthquake. After a while, he moved to a guest on the other side of the room, and suddenly, Sanji moved in her direction.

He stood close to her. "You never answered my letters. I wrote three before I gave up, but I could not forget you. I wanted to tell you so many things, like how sorry I was for the way my family treated you and got you to leave India. I apologize. Everyday in my thoughts, I wish you happiness."

He remembered!

She said to him, "There isn't much to say now. You've done well in life, and as you see, I didn't do too badly either." She fingered her gold and sandalwood beads from nervousness. Her eyes moved across the room to see David and feel secure. Then she noticed Sonya next to her, offering a guest Pinot Noir, and making some light conversation. She looked at Sanji and smiled.

"I want to explain everything to you," he said instantly. "It won't take long."

She knew Sonya had heard him say that, the way Sonya looked at him, and then her mother.

Ingrid tried to keep her equilibrium, but all of a sudden, that distance of thirty-five years dissolved. She thought she'd faint, but managed to sit down. She didn't care what Sonya heard.

"My life is here in Georgetown with David. It is wonderful to feel the security of a warm fireplace and to kiss under the holly at Christmas. I need no explanations, no memories." Her voice quivered as she lied.

"Mother," Sonya whispered with a sense of urgency. "Are you not well? Is something wrong?"

Sanji talked as if in a daze. The guests were being summoned to sit down, and David was busy getting a drink as the crowd thinned out. Sanji said, "Food poisoning just about killed me," he said. "The village elders kept giving me potions to make me better, so they claimed, but I believe I was poisoned. I was locked in a dark room for two months, thinking of you every second. Then they told me you had asked for a divorce and left. Why didn't you fight them?"

"So you blame me? So be it, I don't need to hear more."

"One more minute while we can," Sanji said. "Listen. I tried to argue with my family. My mother said she'd commit suicide if I so much as wrote to you; that you were a bad person, trying to kill me, hence I was sick. She believed it. The truth is, and I came to know this much later, that a few months before we went to India, my parents were in debt. A gang was blackmailing them and they agreed to accept the daughter of a rich gang leader as a bride for me. One who would bring in a big dowry. Their plans were spoiled when you showed up next to me. Being important people in the village, they made a show of a big wedding. After that, the gang got into action, and the village blamed you for leaving. I refused to marry the rich gangster's daughter. I haven't talked to my parents since that day."

"Too bad for you, Sanji," Ingrid said. "You were left alone. I came back with Sonya. Maybe the gang should have killed you."

She felt free. As if her inner self had just been liberated. She looked around. The waiters were busy herding the dinner guests outdoors to be seated at their grand table with candles and china and polished silverware. At dinner, she heard Sanji's sniffles as the fragrance of cherry blossoms floated in the air. He talked continuously to the guest on the opposite side of the table. She had seen Sonya's face pale as she left the room.

It was a pleasant evening overall, and Ingrid knew Sonya would survive the trauma. She'd cross the street carefully with Sonya beside her the next morning. She'd wish Ben "good morning" if she were to run into him, and maybe invite him for a cup of coffee. She'd want to explain everything to Sonya, including her choice of the wine and the candles. She'd have a long chat with Petra, on the phone like always. She'd try to explain more to David, but she knew he wouldn't care.

Attrition

You! Man of no significance.
Years of youth,
Hours of age,
I know the touch
of an aching heart
on white sheets.

I once knew the feel
of wind in my sails.

Leather Soles

I notice blood on my underpants for the first time the day my *ba*, my mother, died. I come out of the secret room looking around stealthily, my face ridden with guilt, as if an ugly demon has exploded from inside my body and everybody is looking at me. Perhaps a kind of penitence for thinking I will have more time to play, now that my mother is no longer sick. This must be punishment for my sins, it has to be.

We live in a big *chaalee*, a kind of old-fashioned five-story building that houses twenty small, two-room flats on each floor. Common bathrooms and toilets are located at the two ends of the building. I find several neighbors, the men who live on our floor, seated in our front room with my papa. Many neighbor women squat on our worn-out carpet in the inner room and weep noisily. I stand to one side because I don't care for most of them. I hear their wailing, "Hai, hai, why did she have to leave us. So young too, and she has two young ones left behind! Who will take care of the little brats!"

I run up to my *masi*, my ba's youngest sister, Renuka, who has come to help us with my mother's illness. In tears, I try to say something, but she brushes past me, to the inner room where my mother's body is lain out on the floor. My *masi's* arms are loaded with white sheets and *Ba's* white sari with a blue border. She has a small, copper container on top of the folded sheets.

"Holy water from the River Ganga to anoint my sister," she says to one of her children, as she tells the boy to be careful and not bump into her.

From where I stand, I hear a woman whisper, "He's not capable of much, is he? He's out all the time. These musicians always keep such late nights."

"Mediocre music in a small restaurant, who listens! What can he do in the house? After all, a man?"

"Cook?"

I hear a contemptuous sound.

"He'll get married again, I tell you. All children need a mother to discipline them."

I see their blatant stares. I hate what they just said. Is it sympathy, I wonder, as they look at my younger brother, Manish, and me, we children who have just lost our mother? In this big city of Mumbai, in the early days of June, there is a pregnant wait for the monsoons to arrive. The temperature is high, the air sultry, intermixed with whiffs of fried food coming from the flats downstairs, and so humid, it wrenches water out of my body. Having so many people in the house only makes it worse for us.

My mind focuses back on my other "problem." It's all happening at the wrong time. I stand there biting my nails when a sharp thump on the back of my hand shakes me up. Vasanti-masi has no right to slap me just because I'm biting my nails, but she is our friendly neighbor and at a time such as this, she and all the other neighbor *masis* must want to take charge and discipline us. I take my fingers out of my mouth but stand defiant, my eyes looking straight ahead. I will not look at her or lower my gaze. Manish clings to me in tears, seemingly afraid he'll be yelled at if he makes a noise. I clasp my hand in his. I notice my father's stern, emotionless face in the front room. He's in a corner seat by the narrow window with the vertical bars, the window that overlooks a row of four-story buildings across the street. There is no place for sunshine to enter our two-room flat, even on a sunny day. I wonder if Papa will ever talk to me, have long conversations—like the way *Ba* talked, before she became ill. Will he give Manish a hug? My baby brother is only eight. He needs to be cared for, to be loved, like *Ba* used to. I miss *Ba* already.

No one seems to have time. Besides, there is no one I trust, except perhaps that one masi who seems to have so much to do. I need answers to a kind of delicate question. I can't even talk to my Lord Ganesh, the Elephant God, because I'm too embarrassed. I look around and decide to walk over to the kitchen to sneak a cloth from the shelf and shove it between my legs, so it will take care of things. I hope they won't notice my bulky underpants under my threadbare, flowery dress. Threadbare, simply because we are not exactly poor but I have only four dresses at any one time and two sets of underclothes.

A hand on my shoulder stops me from leaving the room.

"Swamini, sit down with the ladies and cry loudly if you want to," the woman says. "Even a pretense will do." I glare at the well-endowed woman wearing a bright green sari, her long hair bundled at the nape. She wears a big red dot, the *kumkum*, on her forehead and plastic pearl studs.

I sit down on the cement floor. Our worn-out carpet falls short of where I sit, and the floor feels cold and hard. Sitting cross-legged with my face cupped between my hands, I let out a few loud sobs. I cry for many different reasons.

My mother's name is Ganga. She is the fourth daughter in a family of eight children. I know her parents found a match for her very easily, because my masi told me so. *Masi* said my mother is the prettiest of all the sisters, but she is also the frailest.

"Your mother has a leaky valve in her heart. Don't upset her," Papa shouts at us when we make a fuss. "Help her by rolling the dough and cooking the chapatis. Take responsibility, Mini."

That's all he ever says!

I have a habit of listening to my parents' talk while pretending to be fast asleep at night on my mattress on the floor, next to my mother's. Papa, a tall man with dark, serious eyes and a small moustache, lounges on his cot by the wall. Manish sleeps on the other side of me. I hear Ba tell him that the doctor wants her to have surgery. Papa murmurs that surgery will cost money. Where are they to get it? Whispering, *Ba* says she could ask her middle sister, the only one married into a rich family. That *masi* of mine is rich because they own two houses and they have no children on whom they can spend their money.

I tell Manish secretively the next day, when the two of us sit on a cloth mat in the kitchen, eating soft bread dipped in tea. "Our mother will be going to the hospital soon. She needs surgery on her heart." I feel important because I have this grown-up knowledge, but I'm a little scared.

All Manish says is, "Minididi, will you help me pour hot water for my bucket bath when *Ba's* not home? The bucket is too heavy for me."

He's not afraid for *Ba* like I am. He doesn't seem to understand. Maybe because I am there for him, but Papa is there for both of us, I think. Then in a few days, she'll be home from the hospital to wash and cook and braid my long hair.

I hate that rich uncle of ours because he never misses an opportunity to say Papa is a moody musician and doesn't work hard enough to be a good provider for his family. Maybe he is right because Papa is never in the house, and even when he is, he doesn't know what we need or what we do. There's an instance I remember. I am ready for school and at the door I look at my *chappals* with their very worn-out soles. All of a sudden, I tell Papa I need a new pair of leather *chappals* because I can feel the hard road when I walk in mine. Papa looks at me like I'm asking for his right foot. *Ba* hears me and says, in a soft voice, heaving up from the bottom of her chest, "Soon, Mini, I'll ask your Papa to buy you some. Wear mine in the meantime. They have strong leather soles. I don't go out much these days anyway."

I am instantly gratified. I take down her *chappals* from the shoe rack by the door. Black leather straps and worn-in soles, and they feel big, but comfortable on my small feet. I am glad I'm becoming her size.

Ba has not left the flat for months now. She can barely walk from one room to the next. When she does move, it is with slow, deliberate steps, her puffy legs making her gait unsteady. With her breath loud and heaving, she leans her weak body against the wall and rests every few minutes, and then she resumes walking.

One evening, my middle *masi* and her rich husband come to visit and stay for a long time while Papa is at work. He orders Manish and me to go downstairs to play. I know he doesn't want us to hear the conversation. Next morning, I hear *Ba* tell Papa that her sister's husband will not be able to loan us the large sum of money needed for her surgery, because there is no hope of getting any of it back.

"He is eager to help us in other ways," she says, "but I said no. I don't want to separate Manish from Mini. He did say he will help us out with medicines and doctor's bills."

I hope medicines will help my mother. I believe they will, too, with all my heart.

The last two weeks have just been a daze. *Ba* takes to her *charpoy*...it used to be Papa's cot. It is the only proper bed in our home and it belongs to Papa, who now sleeps in the front room. The rest of us sleep on mattresses on the floor which we roll up every morning and stack neatly in a corner. Renukamasi, who lives in our town, has been summoned and she sleeps on a mattress next to my mother's bed, and helps her through the night. During the day, she goes home to bathe and cook for her family. She brings food back for the three of us. *Ba* hardly eats anything.

"Mini, while I'm away, boil those herbs in water for at least thirty minutes, then decant them, add lemon juice and honey, and feed the concoction to your mother, a few drops at a time." She gives me many other precise minute-to-minute instructions besides. I stay home from school most days and run between the kitchen and my mother's room, trying to catch up with my chores during the four or five hours that my *masi* is away.

I stand with my "problem," awkward and bulky, not daring to move. My fists are tight by my side, my teeth clenched; I watch from the corner of the room as they prepare my mother for her last journey. Her sisters and the neighbor ladies wash and dry her. They unscrew her earrings and take off her gold bangles. Her arm seems heavy and shapeless as they pull the bangles from her wrists and replace them with glass ones. Instinctively, I look at her face to see if she winces, but her pale face is serene. Her long eyelashes look protective over her soft, closed, angelic eyes. They part her hair neatly and even braid the long strands. I hand my braid band to the lady who combs my mother's hair. They drape my ba in her cotton white sari, the sari with the small blue border that I really like. As they turn and twist her, I see how stiff she is, like a log around which the cloth is rolled over.

"Come into the inner room," a neighbor lady calls out to Papa after *Ba* is fully prepared and laid flat.

He walks in, robot-like. He stares at her, and then puts a big *kumkum* on her forehead, as he is told to do. It signifies she is married at the time of her death. Later, they tell me my mother is blessed because she predeceases her husband. Then my eldest *masi*, the not-so-rich, plump one, puts drops of holy water in my mother's rigid hard-to-open mouth and covers my mother's body with a white sheet. All the women bow their heads as they walk past, look at her peaceful face, and try to contain their sobs in the folds of their soft cotton *palloo*, the sari end. Then all her sisters and brothers put marigold garlands around her neck. Her whole chest looks a field of bright yellow. Like the bright color of sun emanates from within her. I sense her strong presence within my barely teenage body.

Then the rest of the men, who have been waiting by the door, go through the procession. My father and brother and I are the last ones left in the room. I lead my brother up to stand beside her. I tell Manish to do exactly what I have seen my uncles and aunts do, because I look at Papa but he doesn't even see me. So Manish and I touch her feet and bow our heads. I want her to hold me but her arms are all wrapped up. Seconds later, we walk out, leaving my father alone in the room with her. That is when I really want to cry, but somebody orders me to close the door to her room, so I do. When Papa finally emerges after what seems like a long time, he makes a sign to one of the uncles. I see them carry a wooden plank in and raise my mother on it. Several more marigold garlands are placed around her neck. A procession of men leave the house, walking through the streets chanting God's name, "Hey Ram, Hey Ram" in rhythmic unison. I look from our window, but the city noises merge into the chanting and I can't see them.

All the women just sit anywhere and everywhere in our three rooms for a while, and then gradually they leave. Manish and I huddle together. Renukamasi, comes to where Manish and I stand. She puts her arms around us, and I feel her warmth. She reminds me of my *ba*, the same odor of sandalwood paste coming from her skin, the kind my mother always rubbed on her wrists. I wish for Papa to come back soon, so he will say something to us, console us in some way, but he does not, even when he returns home hours later after the cremation. With *Ba* gone, perhaps he doesn't want us.

I sit in the front room for a long time. I have plenty of time to think. Suddenly it occurs to me that "it" must be the curse my mother had when, for those five days every month, she sat to one side in a corner all day long and was not allowed to touch anything. She did not cook either and I had to get Manish ready for school. I never questioned *Ba* and she never explained. A friend I visited after school had the same routine when her mother "sat out," as they called it. *Ba* said it was my chance to run a household for the time when I got married. Every girl needed to learn these things at a young age. A girl has to grow up, she had said to me.

Why had Ba not said this curse would come to me? Why me? Had I cut myself? Maybe I'd die too. I see Ba's leather *chappals* in the corner of the room. My rich *masi*, trying to be helpful, is about to pick them up, saying something like, "I'll give these to the beggar downstairs."

I scream at her. "Mine," I say. "Ba said I'm to have them." I stand opposite her, stubborn-faced, my hand extended for them. Then I put my feet, one by one, into the little-too-big, comfortable, black-strapped *chappals* with the well-worn soles.

I walk back next to Manish. It is a cloudy evening, but the few marigold flowers scattered on the floor from earlier on, when *Ba* was there, are still bright yellow. I pick one up and crush the petals until the yellow juices get ingrained into my fingertips.

Much later, Manish whispers to me, "I'm hungry, Minididi."

So I climb on a chair and reach up on the shelf for the biscuit tin. He eats the last two biscuits I give him. There is nothing left for me to eat.

Years later, I realized I became a woman the day my mother died.

I want to be a Belly Dancer

I want to be a belly dancer.
I hate South Beach,
Jenny Craig and Weight Watchers.
I'll wear bells and veils
and backless blouses,
wiggle my hips and jiggle,
the plenty of, you know.

I want to be a belly dancer,
I'll drizzle away the pounds.
He will wonder,
What's her secret, what does she do?
I won't tell a soul.
He'll think I have a new boyfriend,
He'll be jealous, maybe love me more.

Won't it be fun and fancy
to have a dollar or two,
Tucked in here, tucked in there.
I want to be a belly dancer
Zumba and grow.
and
learn to smile again.

The Kokopelli flute

In a spacious hall with high ceilings, the society women of New York sipped their wine and indulged in delicate cucumber sandwiches. They continued to smile and nod as whispers of gossip floated through the air. They couldn't understand why Patrick, a wandering artist, son of their own Mrs. Lily Anderson, and his young Navajo girlfriend, Yazhi, should think of a church wedding after they had lived together for four years. Apparently, they planned to return to New York.

Mrs. Dorothy Smith, a close friend of Mrs. Lily Anderson, wearing a flapper hat and bright lipstick remarked, "He wants his girl to fit in with his mother's lifestyle, don't you see? He wants to legitimize his choice, for inheritance sake, mind you. Make a decent woman out of her."

"Keep the old woman happy," a not-so-close friend remarked.

Later, the elegant Mrs. Anderson was heard to say, "I'm ecstatic Patrick is coming back. He says she's a sweet dear, but unused to our ways. Rustic, perhaps, we'll see."

The women had come to watch the size zero New York models strutting up and down the catwalk in their fancy hats and string beachwear. Mrs. Anderson said she'd have to dress Yazhi; buy her some appropriate outfits in keeping with New York fashions. What a strange name that was, Yazhi! A Navajo name, she didn't even like it.

"I'd want to call her Sasha, but that may anger Patrick. After all, he's strong-headed like his father. I'll have to brainwash the girl with some gentleness," she told her friends another time as they sipped tea.

Days later, Patrick arrived in the city with the girl. Church bells fascinated the twenty-three year old Navajo. Yazhi, her name meaning, "the little one," loved the jingle of little bells. She grew up to the sounds of the mystic humpback Kokopelli playing his flute in her head. She stomped around in the Arizona desert near her *ungee's*, her grandmother's, adobe. She chased the storms and the clouds, and prayed to the rain and the earth for guidance. The wind against her face energized her; and as she followed the rays of the sun through the seamless sand, the Kokopelli flute and the jingling of little bells brought a smile on her face. Yazhi, the little one, had not been inside any church until her wedding day. The height of the church dome amazed her, as did New York's broad streets and high rises through which the wind whistled.

Young Patrick, a roving artist from New York, had appeared outside her adobe one morning five years ago. He was searching for a sign, some meaning to his nomadic life when he came upon Yazhi, and there he paused. He watched her for a few minutes as she stroked the feathers of a wounded sparrow. Then he positioned himself to paint her portrait.

The notes of a mystic Kokopelli playing his flute drifted into her imagination and she smiled at Patrick. Then giving him a shy look, she ran inside. She let him paint her only after he asked her *ungee's* permission. Yazhi, then eighteen, had never lived anywhere else but that desert, and had not slept, not even on cold nights, without the stars gazing down on her youthful body.

Patrick returned every morning and painted her until the sun went down. She cried when the portrait was finished and Patrick said, "I must leave tomorrow."

She asked shyly, "Will you come back soon?" gesturing with her hands and speaking the little English she had learned at school and from the travelers who had come that way before him.

He nodded.

Her *ungee*, who had watched her face every day for two months while Patrick painted her, mumbled, "Good he's going away. Let your tears flow, my child. He's not coming back."

Yazhi pouted, and climbed the dunes, where she sat alone until sunset.

Day after day, she walked the sand with her eyes on the horizon. Then one morning, months later, he returned and asked her, "Come away with me. I've missed you so."

He had painted nothing in the time he was gone, and now all he intended to do was capture her on his canvas. So she left with him, and this time her tears flowed for the old *ungee* she had left behind.

They traveled by foot, in crowded buses, and on dusty roads. He made a little money by selling that first portrait to a man somewhere in Colorado. They passed through cities with big cars and large malls and crowds on the streets, and everything frightened her, so she clung to Patrick. He laughed at her innocence and held her close. They slept in cheap motels and she managed the confines of four walls only because Patrick was with her.

He captured her simplicity in the next portrait he painted. Later, he brushed her in many different poses, and sold his eighteenth painting of her in a seductive pose to a rich man in San Francisco, who wanted it for his mistress's apartment. The rich man said he owned an art gallery in New York and would like to exhibit Patrick, the artist, there. That's when Patrick told him he was from New York.

Patrick decided to abandon his wanderlust and take Yazhi to the city in which he grew up. He said nothing to her that night. He watched her eyes as she lay in bed singing a simple melody.

Next day, he threw away the patchwork skirt he had painted her in so many times. He told her they were going to New York to meet his mother.

She said, "I'm so happy because your mother will love me, just like my *ungee*."

Finally, she threw away her worn-out mukluks and wore the jeans and sneakers he had brought her weeks ago. She insisted on wearing her colorful beads, as always.

In New York, there were constraints. Mrs. Lily Anderson took Yazhi to many fashionable boutiques and got rid of her travel "rags" as she called them. She shopped at Cartier's for her accessories, and matched her dresses with colorful sandals with high heels. Yazhi had a hard time walking in them and felt frustrated. Yazhi hid the beaded jacket her ungee had made for her under her bed, because she was afraid Mrs. Anderson would not like it.

Somehow, Yazhi enjoyed the attention given her. Her face blossomed and her simplicity and elegance drew attention at cocktail parties and art shows. Mrs. Lily Anderson and her son and the new daughter-in-law, after the affluent church wedding, made their appearance on society pages. She was his muse. The demand for his paintings increased with time.

They argued as she became more of a city girl. She took longer to bathe and to dress. She needed more. Nothing serious, but a war of words all the same because she had less time for him. She cried when she felt cornered in their two-bedroom apartment or his studio in Manhattan. The stars and the sun never reached her window.

Patrick earned fame. The critics reviewed his talent and her portraits. He, who had grown up in New York, adapted to his Versace suits and Saks Fifth Avenue ties without much trouble. His schedule got crowded, meeting people, giving publicity statements, and attending luncheons. He said he loved her, but it didn't help.

She was lonely and felt dried up. She seemed not to hear the flute as often. She talked about the deserts of Arizona with a yearning in her voice. A discussion, which later became "words with raised voices," ranged from what he liked, and what she disliked.

On his choice of wing-tipped dress shoes, "You look like a clown," she said.

Her favorite rice, "Horrible chow," he'd say. They did not talk to each other for hours and then they made up.

They left the city and stretched on the beach on weekends. She rubbed his back with oils and tanning lotions, which made him happy. In the beginning of their courtship and later, after they were married, she did it with love. Months later, it upset her because he demanded.

She said to him, "The city has changed you. Your mother can never love me like my ungee." Then she rubbed him hard, scratched him too, with a bit of vengeance bursting from her fingertips. One day, she accused him of not caring enough for her, but along with it, she expressed her suspicion, "Is there someone else?" Her straight mind became a tangled web.

"Patrick is a different person here," she told Mrs. Lily Anderson, who said, "What nonsense, Patrick has always put himself ahead of everybody else. Especially you. He has to. You'll never understand city life."

She wished to lay her face in her ungee's lap and cry. She missed her *ungee's* rough, calloused hands. Her mind heard the twittering of little birds in the desert. She decided the mystic

Kokopelli and his flute, the humpback who brought her luck, had deserted her.

She hated it when he spent his afternoons sleeping and not painting. She posed for him when he asked her to, but her smile wilted on her face and eventually from the painting. They met the rich man at his studio a couple of years later and he asked, looking at the paintings, why the smile on Yazhi's face had aged. Patrick didn't know it had. He said he hadn't noticed.

More than a year later, they went for a walk in Central Park. They sat on the grass and Yazhi dug up varieties of stones from the gritty soil. She split her manicured nail; the polish chipped off, but she couldn't stop the digging. For the first time in many months, she felt connected to the earth's softness. She moved her fingers through the beds in which the stones lay. Slowly, she cleaned each little stone, as if polishing it, and she showed him their shapes and different colors. She placed them on the ground and heaped them like little bells. The bells of her soul were ringing happiness at that moment. She thought she had exchanged her adobe and her *ungee* for something so different that this fairyland offered. She looked around in a daze. All that glamour had come her way because she loved Patrick. It happened because he'd plucked her soul and placed it on his canvas. Suddenly, she realized she had lost it. She gave Patrick a sad look.

Next day, they were walking through another crowded art gallery. She saw a couple of her portraits there. A few people recognized her and stared from her to the portraits. While Patrick talked to somebody important, she stood in the corner of the room, observing the New Yorkers. A young man in his early twenties came up to her, and asked if she was Patrick's mistress.

"Wife," she said coyly, "for many years."

"Oh," said the boy-like man. "Now I understand."

She asked. "What's it you understand?"

"Never mind. Come and pose for me. Nude. I'll explain then. I can do better than him. I'm from the desert too. Arizona. I carry the blessings of the humpback Kokopelli with me. His flute keeps me alive. You and I belong together."

"You don't even know me," she said, as she backed away from him to where Patrick stood. She was aware the boy was watching her. She tried to take Patrick's arm, but he ignored it, perhaps because he was in a serious conversation, negotiating a big contract of his most sensuous painting of her, the one that had inspired the young man to make his offer. She had seen Patrick watching her minutes before. He must have noticed the boy. She wondered if it was anger in his eyes when he brushed her hand away. She became certain Patrick thought the man was her secret lover. She smiled at Patrick and left the room. She kept looking at him from the doorway. Patrick must want the wind and the rain to blow her away to where she came from.

She thought of how happy Mrs. Lily Anderson would be when he would tell her how much money was being negotiated. Her wanderer son would make a mark someday. The lights in the large room dipped transiently as closing time approached. There were too many interruptions in an art gallery for serious business.

Yazhi noticed Patrick look at her with a strange eye. She thought the painting looked dull in the dim light. Her smile was not as stunning, her posture not quite right. Her muse had left the painting, as she left the room. She knew he would convince himself that the light was wrong; that the gallery had not placed the painting in the best location. He'd want to speak to the organizers. The crowds thinned out. She saw Patrick looking for someone; probably the boy she had been talking to, but he was nowhere to be seen. Ten minutes later, she felt alone and decided to go out the front door. In the gardens with the sculptures and the fountains, she lay stretched out on the grass, scratching the earth with her fingers.

She smiled as Patrick approached. He was visibly upset. She showed him a stone she carried in her hand.

"I've been looking for you," he said. "Why did you run away?"

"I've missed the sounds of the Kokopelli flute," she said. "I was trying to hear it out here."

He sat down beside her. He stared at the stone she carried in the palm of her hand. She had scratched bells on it with her fingernails...church bells. She'd tried to make a humped Kokopelli too, but the stone was too small to contain everything; it carried only the symbol of the flute. She gave him the stone.

Yazhi said, as Patrick tried to take her hand," I'm going back to listen to the jingle of bells and the Kokopelli playing his flute. I want to feel the wind in my face and the earth on my fingertips."

Patrick asked her, "What will I do?"

"I don't know," she said. "I must go back to the place where my *ungee* is now buried."

"Will the boy come to see you?" he asked.

"I don't know," she said.

Years later, Patrick died a wilted old man, with diamond rings on all his fingers...an inheritance from Mrs. Lily Anderson. They said he had waited every day to hear the jingle of little bells and the sound of the Kokopelli flute ringing in the wind.

Mountain Guerillas in the Philippines, 16th Dec. 1941
9 days after Pearl Harbor

My mother labored for long hours in our small cottage
up in the mountains when I was born.
Father carried me everywhere, hugged me close.

A Japanese soldier knocked at our front door,
his gun pointed at me. Said to my father,
"You a guerilla hiding up here? I kill you?"

Father, putting his left arm up in surrender,
he was holding me with the right, said in a soft voice,
"I, a family man, sir, I do no harm."
Then he looked at me.

The soldier stared at me, then at him,
His deep-set eyes steady, the gun still pointed at us.
He searched him up and down, and poked the muzzle
into his chest.

Then his eyes wandered to the baby.
A stillness followed.
Father prayed with his eyes closed.

Minutes passed
Before he heard gunshots next door.

Sukhatme-Sheth 188

My Mother's Journal, 1947-2002

My Indian birth name is Meghana Multani, but for ease of the spoken language in Cleveland, Ohio, where I live, my friends call me Megan. I'm a freelance journalist by choice, a civil engineer by education, and the mother of two girls, both adopted from India.

This is my mother, Uma's story starting from the year, 1947.

Uma, a Hindu, and her best friend, Salma, a Muslim, were separated that year at age ten, when India achieved independence from the British, and was partitioned into the two countries of India and the newly formed Pakistan.

Unexpectedly in 2002, more than fifty years later, a newspaper assignment took me to Karachi, Pakistan. I promised my mother, who lived with us in those days, that I'd visit her friend, Salma, if I had the time.

I arrived at my hotel in Karachi and looked up Salma's step-daughter's telephone number in the directory that very hour. The daughter answered my call. She knew exactly who I was. The reserve in her voice bothered me. We exchanged pleasantries, but she would not invite me over, even when I said I'd like to meet her family. Then I asked if I could speak to her mother, and a silence followed. In my zealous happiness, without waiting for her answer, I invited the daughter to visit me at the hotel, but she said, "I don't get out much, and I'm not allowed out alone." An awkward long pause followed by, "My Ammijan talked of going to America to see your mother, even when she was very frail. We knew it was just talk; my *abba* would never have allowed it." She choked up in tears. Before the call ended, she said softly, "She is with Allah now. I wish you had visited us six months earlier. We'll stay in touch, God willing, *Inshallah*."

I tried calling her one more time, but she was not available, so her maidservant, who answered the phone, told me. Nor did she return my call. I didn't know what to make of this, but I felt that after her initially welcoming me, the reality was she may not have liked me because I was a Hindu, and an American. So I drove around Karachi in a taxi. I took photos of women in burkhas in the shopping areas of Elphinston Street and Victoria Road, and then the residential areas on Tariq Road. I didn't know the exact house. Some visual images to show my mother, I thought. Later that week, I returned to Cleveland without meeting Salma's daughter, but with news for my mother that Salma was no longer alive.

Several weeks later, a large packet from Karachi arrived for me in the mail. A cover letter from Salma's daughter said that her Ammijan had wanted my mother to have her letters back. She wrote that there were many more, but these were the letters her Ammijan had put aside. She had been told to burn the rest. A last sentence said her Ammijan did not want her father to read any of the letters after her death.

My mother took one look at the stack of paper and handed me the box right away. I noticed tears in her eyes, when no words came out. The next morning she brought me her journals, the wads of paper she would not share with us for all these years.

"All yours," she said. "Fancy up your own stories from what you find here."

Mother does not talk much these days. She seems quiet and to herself. I often find her writing at the kitchen table, scribbling in her journal and perhaps, penning her letters. It keeps her busy, although she has not mailed out a letter for months. She says she has nobody to send them to, since Salma stopped writing.

I did tell her details about my trip to Karachi, but she has lapses in her memory since Papa died, and may not remember that I said Salma is no more.

Over many weekends, I have sorted the letters and excerpts from my mother's journals. They weave me through my mummy's and Papa's life; through the story of my aunt, Durga, and into my uncle Dilip's capture in the India-Pakistan War of 1972. They reintroduce me to my feisty mother when she was sixteen, to a phase in her life she has talked little about to us. Her letters to Salma were her outlet.

Now, I have stories to tell the world.

154, N Block,
Conway Place
New Delhi
3rd March. 1953

Dear Salma,

When we were little, you asked your ammijan if I could sleep over. Your ammijan said no. She said my grandmother would be upset if I spend the night in a Muslim household. They separated us even then, but we knew our parents loved us and they let us be friends. I still remember how things changed when we were ten years old. Those horrible riots, war and killings during the Partition in 1947 changed our lives; those events will never be forgotten.

Salma, are you happy in Pakistan? Do you have kind friends? Have you started wearing the burkha? I miss you a lot. Love from Uma.

Memories of the Riots from 1947
-excerpt from Uma's Journal

This warm Saturday morning in April 1947, the sound of shattering glass and breaking window pane made me sit up in bed. The rhythmic clanging of metal against metal gritted in my head. I shuddered with fright and although I did not know it at the time, my world started to change as I buried my head between my knees and pressed my hands over my ears. I looked up to see checkered shadows from the cement lattice-work of our covered, second floor verandah on the walls, as they flit before my eyes. My favorite rag doll Lulu still sat slumped over at the foot end of my bed. The noises subsided and started off again as I looked around, perplexed and confused. It seemed later than my usual hour of waking up.

I ran across the cement courtyard with no particular thought in mind. My grandmother, Motiba, and Mummy were in the kitchen. I crouched up close to my mother who sat on a very low wooden platform by a knee-high coal stove, stirring a mixture of water, tea leaves, and milk to which she had added sugar and spicy tea *masala*. I hated the strong aroma of cardamom and cloves from the *masala* every morning, but I savored the sweet tea when Mummy offered it to me on Sundays, our day for a special treat. It tasted sweeter than the warm glass of milk I was usually told to gulp down. My eight-year-old brother, Dilip, clung to Mummy too, for just minutes ago, he, too, had woken up with a sudden fright.

Mummy was getting breakfast ready on a second coal lit stove, while she waited for the tea to boil. Motiba and she were making a stack of delicately spiced flat bread...*theplas*, which the family ate either with pickles or dipped in warm, sweet tea. With great deftness, Mummy rolled balls of wheat flour dough, spiced with salt, turmeric, chili powder and cumin into small, plate-sized, circular discs. Motiba roasted these flat pancakes on a hot iron griddle without edges, the *tava*, turning each one over, adding oil and making them crisp. The kitchen air was smoky from fumes of burning oil and made my eyes water.

Dilip spoke up before Mummy could say anything, "Uma, Uma, a war has started! Papa said so!" Dilip used a high-pitched voice of tension. "People are running in the streets with guns and sticks and the police are out there. Come now! Let's go peek from the verandah."

My eyes widened. My two long braids were partly undone from my tossing at night, and loose strands of dark brown hair hung down my forehead. I was still wearing a much-washed, flowery frock I slept in at night. Dilip, always with neat hair, a contrast to mine, and bright, shining eyes, grabbed my hand and we ran back over the cement courtyard, and crossed our living room to the covered verandah, which was also our dining room. We dragged high backed chairs away from the dining table, climbed on them, and peered out of the cement lattice-work that formed our windows to the street down below. Minutes later, Durga, my thirteen-year-old sister joined us, for the noises heard outside were frightening.

Durga, I thought, acted like an old lady. She wanted to know everything about looking pretty. "What perfumed powder can I use on my face," she asked Mummy from time to time.

Mummy looked to Motiba for answers, knowing full well that Durga's skin would not lighten so easily.

Motiba, as usual, had plenty of advice for Durga. She told her to do religious fasts on certain days, like the first day of the new moon, and to take solemn vows to forego some of her favorite sugary and fried foods. She made herbal poultices which Durga applied to her face for long hours. I, too, tried the poultices and then put various fragrant talc powders on my face whenever Durga did. She said it added a smooth, healthier glow to my already radiant complexion. We both liked the feathery powder puff, and I sometimes overdid the powder because I liked the feel of it. At the end of our session, Motiba said Durga's rough textured skin had not changed.

Papa worked long hours at his clinic and often times, came home after Dilip and I were in bed. Sometimes he helped Durga with her homework and he played "Snakes and Ladders" with Dilip and me on Sundays. We asked him many questions about his patients and what happened when war raged in far off places.

Dilip wanted answers to questions about World War II. He glanced at the newspaper headlines over Papa's shoulder, read out the few words he could, and listened to the radio with Papa. "Why did Hitler kill people from other countries?" was a question that bothered him. It fell on Papa to explain the reasons in simple words.

In our second-floor flat in Conway Place, we played cricket with a soft tennis ball. It left dirty markings on the whitewashed wall of the courtyard. Our flat was spacious, one amongst several similar ones in the model city of New Delhi, built by the British. The buildings were constructed in a circular fashion around a large, central area of green. The wide boulevards were lined with large acacia trees. Shops occupied the ground level frontage with large signs displayed over the front. Conway Place housed many affluent offices as well as private flats for middle class families such as ours. The likeness and symmetry of Conway Place strongly contrasted Old Delhi, a city of several hundreds of years, where I knew that the downstairs tailor, Miaji, and his son, Faizal, lived.

We had gone to the circus with Papa in Old Delhi. Salma with her sister, Naaz, went with us, as had one of Dilip's friends. Seated in a *tonga*, we passed haphazard, narrow streets which had never seen any sunlight and were overcrowded by hawkers, bicyclists, and pedestrians. Narrow windows with small balconies and crooked floors projected into the streets. Washed clothes that had been hung out to dry made the balconies and the streets even more claustrophobic. Paint peeled off the long ago painted walls, exposing gray cement. Rain stains marked the exterior walls and smudged the faded graffiti already there. Smells of garlic, fried onions, and sautéed lamb filled the air. Salma whispered to me that she had eaten the street vendor's ice cream at that corner last month and it was excellent. Papa hated us eating street food and would be angry if we asked. It would make Dilip cry if he said no.

I whispered back in Salma's ear, "Mummy has prepared a special party for us after the circus, with balloons and everything, so we have to eat at home."

Salma did not mind. She told the plan to Naaz.

This morning, the wide street facing our flat was chaotic. Through the octagonal openings in the verandah, we saw people rush around; bodies lay in the street, some curled over in pools of blood. Large knife gashes across faces and arms made for an ugly sight. Sounds of anguish interspersed with shouting filled the air. Five or six men raised their wooden *lathis* on a man with a red fez cap, the kind Muslims wore. The man's cap fell as he was beaten and got trampled on without even being noticed. Police in khaki uniforms and big turbans shouted "*Ghar jao, ghar jao*," telling the crowd to disperse and go home. Bullets zoomed through the air and left behind a smell of burnt flesh.

"Look, look!" I screamed. "Those men are robbing the music shop and throwing phonograph records out. Look, Dilip, they are turning the cart, and throwing vegetables on the street. See those oranges rolling away. Ugh, they're being squashed!"

"Is he a Muslim?" Dilip asked, pointing to a man with a beard and a cap. Then he continued, "Two men are ripping the roll down shutters from the shop window. Why, Papa? What's happening? Will they come into our house?" Dilip looked poignantly at him and then looked the other way. He did not want his papa to see him about to cry.

Papa stood behind us in silence. After a while, he said, "The Hindus and Muslims are fighting like they've never before, but we saw it coming." He paused. "It's all because of what the British are doing to us. Too much division, too quickly." He shook his head. "All this is going to get much worse before things settle down," he said quietly. Papa was always a man of few words, and carried authority in our household.

Four men on the street below wailed and chanted as they walked along, "Hey Ram, hey Ram," the Lord's name, every few seconds, as they carried a body completely bundled in a white bloodstained sheet. I tugged at Papa's shirt.

"Look," I whispered, pointing my finger at the covered body so Papa would look in that direction, "That man is dead." I added that sentence with a sense of superior knowledge and nodded to Dilip as I said it. I'd never seen a dead person before. Our whole family had gathered on the verandah, including Motiba. She told us to go inside; the body was being taken to a crematorium and this was not a sight for young children. We ignored her, and everyone talked and each one pointed to something different from the safe perch inside our home.

There were many unsettling questions in my mind. This was not just another day; something momentous was happening around us.

"Papa, I can't tell who's a Hindu and who is a Muslim except from what they wear. I do know my friends Salma and Naaz are Muslims, as is the tailor Miaji from downstairs, because they pray to Allah and do namaz five times a day." I tugged on Papa's arm.

Dilip whispered, "Remember, Uma, when Motiba shouted at Mummy when she let that bearded man who came to repair the taps, into the kitchen? She said, 'Don't let that *mussalman* step into my kitchen ever again.'"

I nodded. I did remember Motiba's loud voice.

Mummy stood behind Durga and put one hand around Dilip's waist to make sure he didn't fall off the chair as he watched the outside world. Papa said little to appease us. Over loudspeakers we heard a curfew being announced.

"All these people should be indoors," Papa told the family. "The Muslims are in real danger around here." We lapsed into silence thinking of what was yet to come.

Dilip said to me in a hushed tone, "No school today, no homework!"

The citizens of New Delhi witnessed many such episodes of fighting and looting in the streets in the next couple of months. People rumored to have left for Pakistan were unaccounted for, and said to be victims of large massacres at border cities in both India and Pakistan, because anti-Muslim and anti-Hindu sentiments were high. Hearsay or truth, nobody really knew how many thousands became refugees.

August 15, 1947 was the big day to come when two-hundred-year-old British rule over India ended, and India was to be divided into two nations based on religious affiliations. Commonly referred to as, "The Partition," people were in a frenzy, forced to leave their own homes and move to other cities. Friends and neighbors fought each other because some were Muslim and some were Hindus and Sikhs.

Dilip and I sat quietly at the dinner table the evening of 14th August, and listened. Papa said, "At last we have freedom. Now we can be a progressive nation in our own right."

"Papa, did the British really treat us so badly? Were we their slaves?" I asked.

"No, my child," Papa said. "Not slaves, but they treated us as their inferiors. Every country is entitled to be free, so their own people can rule. Every individual has a right to be free.

Pandit Jawaharlal Nehru will be a good first Indian prime minister and Mahatma Gandhi will advise him well.

"We have lost many lives because of our Gandhian nonviolent principles before the British finally decided it was time to let us be a free nation. Mohammed Ali Jinnah will be Pakistan's first president."

"Papa, I don't like Pakistan," Dilip quipped out of nowhere.

"You don't have to live there," Papa retorted and laughed his loud, raspy laugh. "Why worry? Just be happy we are getting our independence from the British."

Motiba said, "Riots are bound to break out because there is such a big rift between the two religious factions. Think of what will happen to the Muslims who decide to stay behind in India because this has been their home for generations. Can you blame them?"

"Many Muslims will choose to stay; many are being uprooted overnight. They are entering Pakistan as homeless refugees. What about their plight?" Mummy said. "Remember, the new post-partition India will also give refuge to millions of Hindus and Sikhs from cities in Pakistan like Lahore, Karachi, and Rawalpindi," she added. "Big problems to come."

Dilip asked, "Papa, if Muslims leave, does that mean Faizal from downstairs will go away? What about Uma's friends? Salma and Naaz?"

"We don't know what Miaji and Faizal will do," Papa said. "I presume it will be safer for them to be in Pakistan, but they may choose to stay on like so many others have decided to do." Papa let out a long sigh.

The year 1947 stood out as strange to me and affected me for the rest of my life. My birthday was in August and I remembered the events that occurred around then. An air of celebration pervaded in our city, New Delhi, the nation's capital. It was the day before 15th August, 1947. The streets were crowded and noisy. Loud music played at street corners. Tricolored Indian national flags were hoisted on public buildings. Colorful fireworks shot up into the air from time to time, leaving behind trails of smoke.

At dinner that evening, Papa said to me, "Do you think we should go to the Red Fort to see Pandit Nehru raise the flag?"

"Yes," I said.

"We must go. We'll take the children with us," Mummy said.

Papa said it would be too crowded and Mummy should stay home with Motiba. That way, our servant could go to the festivities if he wanted to, and Motiba would not be left alone at home. Mummy said Durga should go with her father to help him, because Dilip and I were still little.

"Please, please, Papa, we'll be good," we said simultaneously.

Dilip, with his well-combed hair and starched short pants, held Papa's right hand. His excitement could not be contained and he couldn't stand still. I was all smiles in my new yellow cotton dress, which Mummy allowed me to wear, and held Durga's hand tight because I was afraid to be left behind.

Pandit Jawaharlal Nehru, India's first prime minister, gave his ceremonial speech from the Red Fort that warm, sunny day of August 15th, 1947. Dilip and Papa led the way. A sea of people extended across the green maidan in front of the Red Fort. Colorful crowds in good humor laughed and joked and rushed forward even when there was no place to go. Young adults perched on tree branches and looked triumphant over others who stood at ground level. Loudspeakers for miles across echoed speeches, and cheers rose as the saffron, white, and green striped flag was raised. Dilip sat perched up on our papa's shoulder from where he got a good view and was protected from getting trampled. A wave of noisy people swayed back and forth in the hot sun, savoring each moment of their newfound freedom. Durga and I stood on a large boulder and took in everything.

Our faces flushed from heat and excitement as we saw the distant figure of Pandit Nehru at the lectern, and Lord Mountbatten, the Governor of India, towering next to him. What we heard distinctly over the broadcasting system was Nehru's clear voice in eloquent English, "Long years ago we made a tryst with destiny, and now the time comes when we will redeem our pledge...Are we brave enough and wise enough to grasp this opportunity and accept the challenge of the future...it is the future that beckons to us now..." etc. etc. One long speech heard in total silence by a crowd of fifty thousand or more on the Red Fort grounds, and all over India through loudly played radio sets.

Dilip and I, in our childhood wisdom, did not recognize that we had witnessed history in the making. I realized, too, much later that those chants and words for independence had stirred something deep inside of me: a personal goal of being free is what I wanted to strive for, no matter what the obstacles.

One afternoon, a few days after the August celebrations of Independence, there was a persistent, hollow knock at the front door. Riots and curfews were still going on. Who could have come up from the streets in the midst of such silence? The thought of police coming to grab my papa alarmed me, for I had seen men in handcuffs. I was frightened for my papa because my friend Salma's father was in hiding.

Our servant, at a nod from Papa, went across the courtyard to open the door. There stood small built Miaji, the Muslim tailor who had made his shop under our stairs. He wore his small, round, wire-rimmed glasses. Dilip admired Miaji's little goatee and black cap. He always wore a white starched jhaba, or long shirt, over his white pajamas, but this day his white clothes were soiled with blood. I knew him only as Miaji, and his then ten-year-old son, a miniature replica of his father without the beard, as Faizal. Miaji, with a pale, mask-like face, clutched his sewing machine in his arms. Faizal stood beside him, and Miaji rested his injured elbow on Faizal's right shoulder. I saw a woman, presumably his wife, standing a few feet behind him, wearing a black *burkha*, a long black gown that covered her from the hair on her head to her toes, except part of her face. The woman's frightened, dark eyes glimmered from the depths of a deathly white face. A black silky veil covered her nose and mouth.

I had seen women with *burkhas* on the streets. A picture of subservience, of captivity, a body smothered in a shroud. At ten years of age, that is how that woman in a *burkha* looked so sad to me. I knew my friend, Salma, would have to wear one when she was a little older. I savored the word independence that seemed to crop up everywhere, and it gave me a sense of pride. The fighting between neighbors and separation of friends hurt, but I did not want to be helpless like this nameless woman in the *burkha* who stood at our front door behind Miaji.

Our servant looked at Papa again, not quite sure what to do. Papa stepped forward and pushed him to one side. He grabbed Miaji by the hand and quickly pulled him into the house. His wife in the black veil and young Faizal followed in behind Miaji, and Papa closed the door. He took the heavy Singer machine from Miaji's arms and put it on the floor. He sat him down on a low wooden chair with plush cushions in the living room.

Mummy told the servant to get a bucketful of warm water while she fetched some towels. Papa told Dilip and me to leave the room and we felt dismissed, but we stood aghast in the doorway and watched. Papa ripped open the torn pajamas around Miaji's leg. Blood stained the white cloth and made spreading finger-like marks on it. The servant brought his doctor's bag.

Papa washed the wounds on Miaji's leg and examined the gash. He straightened and bent the leg a couple of times to make sure nothing was broken. An ointment and bandages seemed adequate.

"Get some warm tea right away," Motiba said. Miaji drank the tea with a deep, sucking action, noisily smacking his tongue between his lips. The three of them looked a little more comfortable as time went by.

Miaji's sobs were loud. "My shop was broken into. They pushed a crowbar through the metal bars in the door. All my customers' clothes are destroyed. They've vandalized all my things, Sahib." Miaji paused and took a deep breath.

"I have nothing left. My child has nothing!" he said, looking at Faizal. He pulled him closer and stared at his son's torn sleeve. He tried to overlap the torn edges with his fingers.

Papa said nothing right away but his face was sad. Slowly, he spoke up in a low tone, "It's not safe for you around here. Your shop was looted, but you are lucky. None of you were killed. Go back to your home and think about somewhere else to relocate."

"Our home in Old Delhi is burnt down, Sahib," Miaji cried. "I'm ruined. I came to ask if you will keep my Singer machine safe for me."

Papa assured him that he would take care of the sewing machine, but he did not know how else to help the tailor's family. It was too dangerous for them to stay in New Delhi. Papa's face was one of stern determination, and it silenced us. There was an uncomfortable pause as they all waited for Papa to make some kind of decision. Dilip and Durga and I looked at our father. He was the head of the household with all the answers.

Papa said, "There is danger beyond these four walls. Let me think." He walked out into the court yard and paced up and down and Mummy followed. We heard their hushed voices. A few minutes later, Papa sat down next to Miaji. I didn't know what all this meant, except that Faizal and his family were in grave danger.

"You will stay in our home till it's safe for you to leave. The riots and looting may go on for a while. When things settle down in a few more days, we'll buy you train tickets to an Indian town near the Pakistan border. After that, you may have to walk across the border, if no buses are running. Perhaps you will be lucky to find some truck driver to give you a ride. We'll take you to the train station and then you'll be safe on the train."

Mummy added her own support, once she knew what her husband had decided to do. "I'll give you some clothes and pots and pans to take with you; also, you'll need some money. So don't worry now, we'll help as best we can."

Papa looked around at all of us. His eyes stern, his face grim, he said with authority, "Be assured, Miaji, that nobody, absolutely nobody in my family will say anything to outsiders about your staying with us."

Whenever Papa expressed an opinion, we all accepted it, mostly because we dared not protest. Sometimes Dilip and I defied our father's decisions and could get away with some of our wishes, but Mummy and Durga always listened to him. Papa spent some time every morning performing various religious rituals, as did his father before him. It was a traditional Hindu household. Papa was a tall, dark, somewhat big-boned man with large eyes and sparse hair. He wore a little mustache, under which he curled his upper lip from time to time. With a penetrating gaze that addressed nobody in particular, I heard him say, "We don't know how long these riots in the city will last!"

Papa knew the consequences of giving shelter to a Muslim family, but his mind was made up.

"What if Miaji and his family stay in our house for a long time?" I asked Dilip. "You'll have to sleep in Motiba's room." Then I had another thought. "What if somebody tells the police?" For now, small as we were, I knew what we all had to do to protect Miaji and his family, and I felt important to be part of this conspiracy.

"Miaji and his family will use the servant's room," Mummy said as she continued with the arrangements. "Let's get some snacks for them." She went toward the kitchen and Motiba followed her.

Dilip and I had a good time playing cricket with Faizal, although our play was restricted to the small, cement courtyard in our flat. Dilip told me he had heard Papa and Mummy make plans for Miaji's escape but he didn't quite understand.

I worried about Salma and her family too. Mummy would not let me go to Salma's house, and we had stopped going to the park since the riots started.

New Delhi, 15th. March.1956

Dear Salma,

This time I write to you with a completely new reason. Shock! With urgency I tell you that I, too, will have changed overnight because a good man (according to my family) has been interested in marrying me since last year. He came to visit us and looked me up and down.

I dreamed I'd be a teacher someday. Now it won't happen, and I'm so angry with everyone. You are still my blood sister, no matter what the rest of them say.

Just hear this, Salma. I'm seventeen and engaged to be married to Parth. I can't stand it. He has big ears. You would be unhappy too, if you were in my place, so don't even try to say it's okay. It's not. Papa is even more determined than Mummy. Motiba wants to get rid of me, and Mummy won't say a word and speak up for me. She acts like she's happy. When will I go to college and when will I ever get a chance to become independent; to have a career? I have no one to talk to, but you.

On the other hand, let me give you more news. My sister, Durga, is content because she will be married soon, three days before me. That is Papa's plan. That's all she wants to do. Be a happy housewife and have twenty children, I bet. Tell me what to do.

Your most unhappy friend,
Uma

About the weddings to come, 1956
excerpt from Uma's Journal

I heard my papa's pretentious laugh, the made-up sound he seemed to produce on those infrequent occasions when we had company of any importance. His voice resonated above me as I darted up the dark, concrete stairs leading up to our flat on the second floor. From the faint streak of light at the top of the steps, I knew that our front door was open. I heard my parents saying good-bye to several people. I gathered my frilly dress in one hand and held my books in the other, my tall legs carrying me up with momentum. Turning the corner on the middle landing, I collided into a neat-looking, young man of slight build, wearing a white dress shirt. A bit pompous, I decided in a fleeting moment. With such big ears too! I lowered my eyes to the books I'd just dropped.

The man descended the stairs ahead of the others. Instinctively I knew! These people had come to judge Durga. To evaluate Durga's face, her walk, her talents. It had to be one of those bride-viewing sessions, where the visitors, between smiles, grilled Durga before they would decide if she was a suitable bride for their son.

I stooped to pick up the books that lay at my feet.

"Sorry," I said as I looked straight on, standing still, colour rising in my high cheekbones. The man was quicker than I. He turned the books around, and with an amused look on his face, he read their titles out loud. Then he handed me the books without a word. He also stared at me a second or two longer than I deemed necessary, and I, as always, conscious of my looks, wondered what he thought of me. I was amused by his big ears, but his muscular hands holding my books aroused my interest.

"Thank you," I said in a soft voice. Then I began to walk up the steps, with what I hoped was poise. An older couple descended the stairs at a slower pace and another younger man, perhaps sixteen, my age, walked two steps behind them.

My papa, an imposing man with fierce eyes, looked at me angrily as I reached the landing. "Haven't I told you not to run up the stairs," he shouted. I walked past him without looking his way or saying anything. Once inside, I threw my books and pencil case on the study table next to the door, slouched into a low armchair, my legs stretched, and my midi dress trailing the floor around me. Our living room looked crowded with additional chairs brought in from the dining area.

"What an awkward young man this time. What's his name?" I asked of nobody in particular. My mother and my frail Motiba with a strong voice, paid no attention to my theatrical posturing. They continued their own conversation. Durga, standing at the door, heard me.

"Uma, his name is Parth Shah. He works with his father in a textile business they own. He's twenty-eight years old. They were uprooted from Pakistan just after the Partition in 1947."

I looked at my sister.

"Like Salma and her family moved to Pakistan, these people came here."

I wanted to hear more details from my sister. She gave me a broad smile and said no more. "You like him, don't you?" I asked.

Durga was dressed in a bright, blue sari with little silver stars embroidered on it. She nodded, and then picked up the half-filled glasses of water from the coffee table and placed them in a tray. I faced Durga and clasped her hands.

"What if he wants to marry you, Durga?"

"Then I'll marry him," Durga said, a little shy but without hesitation. She freed herself from my grasp and gave me a big grin. Even the pockmarks on Durga's face didn't look so bad at that moment.

I was about to tell my sister that this latest suitor of hers had big ears, but on second thought, fearing I would hurt Durga's feelings, I kept my opinion to myself. Dilip, who was not in the room, would enjoy the story the most. I'd tell him and then the two of us would have fun laughing at Durga's suitor.

There had been many of these bride-viewing sessions over the past couple of years. Papa and Mummy never talked about it to me, for after all, I was just sixteen, but Durga's face and moods conveyed the circumstances. She had just turned twenty and completed her three-year home-science college degree. She had a pleasant smile and thick, well shaped eyebrows. But the skin on Durga's cheeks, scarred from a severe case of small pox in childhood, gave her dark complexion a rough, textured look. Some of the marks on her forehead were hidden behind her bangs. She wore her straight, well-oiled, long hair in a single braid. Out of habit, she played with the end of her braid, continuously splitting hair ends with her fingers.

When Durga was in a good mood, she hummed lively tunes from popular film songs. We sisters bantered back and forth and laughed. At other times, Durga copied my mother, busy trying to please Motiba and Papa. I never heard Mummy voice an opinion, even when it came to choosing her own saris.

"I like your papa's choice," she'd say to us, when we rolled our eyes and said Papa could have chosen a nicer color. In keeping with tradition, Mummy never called her husband by

name. She always referred to him as "Dilip's papa," no matter
who she spoke to.

After dinner that evening, with just the two of us in the
room, I asked Durga, "Why will you agree to marry any person
Mummy and Papa choose for you?" I, although younger, felt I
had to speak for my sister. I was ready to rebel on Durga's
behalf. This matter of marriage was far too serious for her to be
so accepting.

"Uma, I want to have my own home. I want to please the
man I marry," Durga said thoughtfully, still playing with her
hair.

I was furious. "What about you? Don't you want him,
the person you marry, I mean, to please you? You think Papa
will worry whether he is good looking or not? No chance! Papa
doesn't know a thing about it."

"I trust Mummy and Papa's judgment. Mummy says they
will choose the best husband they can for me."

I had magazine cutouts of young, handsome actors we
saw dancing and singing in Hindi movies, and wistfully
imagined that one day soon, some such handsome prince would
whisk my sister away. I was so annoyed by her passive attitude.

"I hope it's somebody handsome, really handsome, not
like the man with the big ears from this morning," I said. When
Durga showed no reaction, I threw down the pillow I held
between my hands and walked away in disgust.

The next evening, I sat on Motiba's charpoy feeling sorry
for myself. Motiba, my biggest ally against my parents in day to
day matters, for I was always trying to defy them, had just said
to me, "Your obstinacy and independence are going to make it
difficult for us to find a good match for you, Uma. You must
study hard and be serious about your education."

I pondered over Motiba's words.

"I'm the tailless lizard of the family," I said and laughed, but Motiba didn't get it. I was the only one in the house who had nightmares about the deformed lizard that dwelled in captivity on the high ceiling of our bathroom.

I had noticed the lizard when I closed the bathroom door. Several weeks ago, I had seen its severed tail flop around in a puddle of water on the cement bath floor. Mummy told me the tail must have been trapped in the hinged door, and that the lizard would grow another one.

"Look what Uma's scared of," Dilip laughed and ran behind me pretending he held the tail in his hand.

I told Motiba then, as I had repeatedly before, "I'm different from my sister. I want to finish college. I'll become a doctor, or a teacher, or a writer, you'll see." As usual, I watched for Motiba's reaction, but there never was any. Motiba ignored my protests, as if to say, "We'll just have to wait and see how things turn out."

Charles Dickens' long-winded novels or Emily Dickinson's romantic poems interested me. I read old romantic classics like *Pride and Prejudice* late into the night, and wondered about the lives of the eighteenth century women in old England in that story. The degree of dependence upon the men in their lives made me feel caged in. They seemed to have no opinions of their own. Durga should have been born two or three hundred years ago, I thought; or were we in India, still stuck in the same old-fashioned thinking? Whether we molded ourselves on British influences, or traditional Indian heritage, I didn't know if the outcome for a woman was any different. I woke up with haunting thoughts that when I turned twenty, my parents would make wedding plans for me, as they did for Durga.

At school, I complained to my friend during lunch.

"Durga's on parade like a prized cow. This bride-viewing business has been going on for so many months. She'll be led to the first bidder who asks for her. I feel so sorry for her."

It was a cultural norm. My friend changed the subject and reminded me about the movie they planned to see. It was the latest movie with Devanand, the hero of Hindi films. We had talked about seeing this movie for months. We needed to arrange a meeting time and place.

I walked home preoccupied with thoughts of college for next year. I washed up, changed out of my school dress, and sat down at the dining table in the enclosed verandah. The back of the chair leaned against the common wall we shared with the flat on the other side of our apartment. At first, a low murmur and sounds of conversation came through the thick wall and then abruptly changed to loud words and screams of heated dialogue between a man and a woman.

"They're arguing again," Motiba said as she walked in slowly from the kitchen, holding a big glass of warm, sugary milk for me. All of us at the table, Durga and Dilip too, pretended the noises on the other side were normal happenings and no more comments were made. We crunched on our biscuits and gulped down our milk.

I said to Durga, "She's getting you ready for marriage, Durga. She's telling us how much more freedom we have." Durga shrugged her shoulders in indifference and walked away. A glint in Motiba's eyes made me search her face again. I sensed Motiba was troubled, perhaps wrapped up with matters I knew nothing about. At times, our house help and Motiba got into wordy arguments. She always complained about his hastiness and how in his rushing around, he'd broken another teacup, or sometimes it was a saucer. I kept the thought to myself until I finished my snack.

"What happened today when we were at school?" I asked, picking up my last biscuit.

"I worry about you, Uma," Motiba said. "You are a girl of modern times."

"Well, so? What's wrong, Motiba? You're worrying about my future again, aren't you? How many times have I told you not to?"

"You becoming a teacher or a doctor is your childish fancy. There may be other plans in store for you." Then she gave me one of those long looks with no more words. Sounds from the other side of the wall had also subsided.

"Tell me now!" I shouted. "What exactly do you mean? What happened? Did that *sadhu* from your home town come again?"

There was an old man from Motiba's far away village, supposedly a wise man, who claimed to be an astrologer and, therefore, a fortune teller. He came to visit her about twice a year when we were at school. He stirred up all sorts of strange worries about what the future held for us children. Dilip was convinced this man was a fraud with a sweet tooth. He came because he liked the special sweet, *mithai*, that Mummy prepared not only for him to eat when he came to visit, but also packaged for him to take home.

"Your mother just walked in. She'll tell you when the time is right," Motiba said.

Motiba remained silent and was, I could see, very troubled. Mummy thumped her big purse down in the front room and walked into the dining room, her face flushed from the heat of the afternoon sun. She asked if we had a good day, but she seemed not to hear our answers. Dilip must have anticipated that some important talk was about to start and he left the table with his glass of milk in hand, hoping to go unnoticed.

Mummy sat down next to me. She looked exhausted, sighing and wiping wetness from the tip of her nose. Once she'd settled back with a glass of cold water, she turned to me.

"We have a reply from the Shah family today. Parth's uncle came over with a message."

I waited for the next sentence. Perhaps it was good news for Durga; news different from the usual, or was it the same reply this time too, as so many times before, "Circumstances are not quite right for our two families." The fact that Mummy wanted to say anything of importance regarding Durga puzzled me. I worried about my sister. If only there was a better way to make her skin look pretty, I thought. In my eyes, Durga was such a good-hearted person; she would never harm even a fly. Nobody seemed to understand my sister.

"Uma, don't be too hasty in what you say," Mummy said as she looked at me with stern eyes. "Just listen."

She paused.

"Parth and his parents have sent a message that Parth would like to meet you again. Uma, Parth wants to marry you."

"Never," I exploded before she could say more. "What! That man with the big ears."

Mummy ignored me.

She said, "I knew a major development was about to take place when his uncle stopped by the house in the morning. He sat comfortably on the sofa, his head high as if wanting to make a statement of dire importance. He waited for a while, surveying the room."

She had offered him a glass of water. "Dilip's papa will be out in a minute. Will you have some tea with us?"

The senior men in these old fashioned households conveyed important messages to other senior men in the house, always a man-to-man talk when it came to important events. Messages, negotiations, money arrangements, marriage deals, all the subjects that only men made decisions on.

"His uncle said he was in a hurry, but perhaps, half a cup of tea would be refreshing. He said he had an important message for our family."

Papa had walked into the living room just before he was to leave for the clinic. He looked formidable with his well-groomed, small moustache, and crisp khaki shirt and trousers. Motiba, a small figure in a soft, white cotton sari with a plain green border, followed him in. Papa greeted the uncle with a *namaste*, done by folding two hands together, and then they shook hands with each other. He waited to hear what the visitor had to say.

"Stars are not suitably matched for Parth and Durga," the uncle announced.

Mummy said she kept her gaze lowered. She didn't want my papa or the uncle to see her disappointment. The uncle remained seated, as if in no hurry to move. Usually, a negative message was given very briefly and the person disappeared. She wondered what remained to be said.

He spoke up with authority, "Parth would very much like you to consider another matter. He wants your approval for his marriage to your younger daughter, Uma. Our family wants to visit you again and see Uma, and then fix the details, if it is a workable solution to both parties."

Mummy and Papa's eyes met briefly. "Uma's not even seventeen yet," my mother managed to utter.

There was total silence for the next few moments.

"We'll have to think about this proposal for a while," Papa said, and then let out a noncommittal sound, an artificial laugh, as if that would ease his tension. "I'll let you know in two days time."

Mummy said that's where the conversation ended.

"Mummy, that's not possible." I burst out in loud sobs. "I'm much younger than him and I haven't even started college! What's wrong with this man! Why me? Doesn't he know I'm only seventeen?"

I wanted to scream and kick my feet; but with great effort, sensing Durga's eyes on me, I managed to stay quiet.

"Uma, say no more. We adults will talk it over and decide what's best for you." Papa spoke up in a voice of authority when the talk came up later that evening. He sat down on the bench by the shoe shelf. Without saying another word to anyone, he picked out his black leather shoes, put them on slowly using the shoehorn, tied his shoelaces into neat knots, and went out.

I ran out of the room in tears and did not come to the table for supper that evening.

The following week, I was told to wear a sari since Parth and his family were to come to our house for the official bride-viewing. This was something Durga had experienced over the past many months, and suddenly it was my turn. Motiba insisted that I wear a traditional sari. It would make our family appear orthodox. As if it were not already so, I thought to myself! Durga said I looked elegant in a sari, but I hated wearing it.

Motiba knew the customs of these old fashioned, traditional households. She had judged this Shah family as being orthodox from the time she met them. It was a very traditional move in which a family elder brought the message back to them. Motiba was confident about their interest in me and said she was sure a quick agreement would be reached. So she wanted me to look my best. I was to behave ladylike, be mild mannered, and then she said I'd look elegant wearing a sari.

I gritted my teeth till my jaws hurt. Everything around me was moving too fast. Even to be home for a kind of showing made me rebellious, but there was no more protesting I could do. Tempers were high. Nobody was interested in my opinion. Most of all, I feared Papa's loud voice and what he would say.

Motiba told Mummy she liked Parth because he seemed a mature, young man and she conveyed her opinion to her son also.

"Uma is young, impulsive, and immature," she told Papa the evening before the showing. "With Lord Ganesh's grace,

Parth has come along. He seems responsible. He's more than ten years older than she, and will be good to her. We must make the commitment if they show the slightest interest."

Motiba, with the servant's assistance, fried some savory snacks and enriched them with salty peanuts and cashews. Mummy made sweet, round, gram flour *laddoos*, a little different from the ones she made when we entertained the Shah family two weeks earlier for Durga's bride-viewing afternoon tea. Our household was busy on the morning of; that is, everyone except me. Motiba made *upama*, from semolina with sautéed onions and peas and ginger. Normally, Dilip and I relished all the leftovers after such occasions, because there was always plenty left over even after the guests had savored the spread. This day, I couldn't think of food.

Durga and Dilip had been told not to come to the front room, where the guests were entertained. So Durga sat in Motiba's room, pretending to read a magazine. I was almost in tears when Durga fixed my two braids into loops with ribbons at the ends and said I looked radiant. Dilip would get a spanking from Papa if he'd teased me. I heard the two sets of parents exchange greetings, the traditional *namaste* in the living room. They sat down and covered awkward silences with political jargon. Then Motiba joined them.

About fifteen minutes after their arrival, Motiba left the living room, saying she would fetch me. I entered holding a stainless steel tray carrying four small, porcelain cups of tea, delicately balanced in the same flowery patterned saucers. My magenta colored sari *palloo* draped my left shoulder, and its soft folds covered part of my left arm. I picked up each saucer with a cup full of tea with my right hand, and placed it on the table in front of each guest without directly looking at them. Then I sat down next to my father, my head slightly lowered.

Shortly thereafter, Mummy brought in a heavy tray full of crunchy, savory snacks. Along with it, she had prepared the same sweet *barfi*, which Parth's father enjoyed on their previous meeting, and the sweet *laddoos* she had spent time preparing. Papa encouraged his guests to have more tea and talked loud, putting on his boisterous laughter.

Parth did not say a word to me, but his glance wandered around the room. He laughed at Papa's jokes and ate from the spread before him, merely picking at the food. I sensed his eyes on me several times in that hour. This was an arranged marriage; this is what girls had to expect.

"Did you make the *laddoos*?" Parth's mother asked of me in a slightly probing voice.

"No," I answered, and said no more. I wanted to be rude, without letting my parents notice. Parth's mother did not pursue the conversation, but picked up one more *laddoo* and bit into it. After an hour or so, they left.

Two days later, Parth's younger brother stopped by. He told Papa he had come to invite them to their home, so they could fix an engagement date and discuss some details. The seventeen-year-old added, with a certain amount of assertiveness, that his family understood that as required by tradition, the elder sister should be married first; and it was agreeable to the family to wait till a suitable match was found for Durga.

"Of course," Parth's brother added in a sure tone, "we can only wait for up to one more year." We, as in royalty, ha. The younger brother was enjoying his important role in this, I could see.

I was a pawn in all these dealings. I hated it, but how could I escape this snare? I just couldn't fathom my way out of all these quick changes that were happening around me. I was a trapped, tailless lizard.

New Delhi
10th Sept. 1957

Dear Salma,
 I emptied out the silver trinkets and rings that cluttered the top drawer of my dresser today. I found a little bracelet in the back corner. Its shiny beads and bright blue and yellow color made me think of the yellow frocks you and I wore when we wanted to dress alike.
 I remember you gave me this bracelet for my eighth birthday. It was before the 'Partition.' The Partition made you move away but some strange bondage keeps us together. I laugh when I think it may be because the two of us exchanged little bracelets and tied friendship threads around each other's ankles then. We'll keep our friendship strong. Keep writing. Tell me everything. You sound like you are happily married? You are content, aren't you? I guessed it. I'll be married next year, I suppose. Your letters give me delight for your sake. I'm different. Write to me about the time you left so suddenly. I'll never know what happened to Miaji, the tailor and his family...remember, the one who lived under our stairs. They may have been amongst the hundreds of thousands killed during those times. What horrifying statistics!

Always your friend,
Love, Uma

p.s. Please don't show this letter to anyone in your family. Trust me; your husband doesn't like me, because I'm a Hindu.

My Sister Durga, 1956-1958
excerpt from Uma's Journal

The morning after my engagement was formalized, Papa wrote to his relatives across the country that there was a certain amount of urgency to rush Durga's marriage. He also gave news of my engagement and explained the circumstances in a few sentences; the least amount of words he could get away with.

My father's cousin, Gita, a well-endowed woman with six children, and one never to be seen without her large, diamond earrings, responded to his letter within a few days. She lived in a town in Gujarat, much smaller than Bombay, but they owned a spacious apartment in one of the suburbs of Bombay. No matter the occasion – weddings, baby naming ceremonies, baby showers, wedding showers, or memorial services – Gita would use these as excuses to shop for saris, and oftentimes, to pursue her passion for custom-designed, handmade jewelry, which she ordered from places of good repute. She had three daughters on which to lavish such luxury. On one such recent excursion, she heard through a friend in the jewelry shop that an acquaintance of theirs who knew of a young man ready to take a bride.

"His parents live in Paatadi," she wrote back to Papa immediately. "Their only son, Kishore, although not educated beyond high school matriculation, has a small business with a good income and is smart looking. The family doesn't want a daughter-in-law who would go to her parent's home on the slightest excuse, and are therefore, looking for somebody from another city. Your Durga may just be the right girl, who knows!"

A few weeks later, Kishore Vakheria, with his well-oiled, black hair and bright, red bush shirt, stepped into our living room with a superior air about him. His parents, two people seemingly without voices, sat indifferently and said nothing. It happened to be a Tuesday when Mummy had wanted me to help her in the house because important guests were coming. I had purposefully defied her and gone to enjoy the weekly fair.

Kishore came alone the second time on a Sunday. Because there had been many such bride-viewing sessions before, Dilip and I took this as just one of many. We were not enthused about this man in the gaudy shirt. In fact, we took an instant dislike to him when we saw him through the crack in the door. We went on to other things and thought nothing more of it. Mummy had given me explicit instructions that I was not to come out in to the living room this time. A second visit meant there was a possibility that he might have liked Durga.

"It's just a matter of formalities! The quicker he goes home, the better for Didi," I told Dilip.

Were we wrong! Kishore, the man with the smirk on his face, and his mousy parents sent word the next day that they wanted Durga as a bride for him.

I knew all along that my sister would agree to marry the first man who showed an interest in her. After more than two years of being on show, Durga had developed a defeatist attitude that nobody would want her. When Kishore expressed an interest, Papa and Mummy just couldn't believe that the right person had shown up for their Durga after all. They sent a message to Kishore's parents giving their blessings for their son's marriage to their daughter. I wondered if Durga harbored a grudge against Parth. If she secretly did, she never showed it. Kishore and Durga were married within three months of seeing each other for the first time, and Parth and I were married three days after them.

Their one-week honeymoon was at a place Kishore chose. Durga told me she enjoyed the hill station, Simla, north of Delhi, where Kishore had booked them in an expensive hotel. Later, she wondered why Kishore never asked about her choice of places for their honeymoon. She glossed over it quickly by saying he may have wanted to surprise her. He decided where they would go, what she should eat, and what he wanted her to wear. Very conscious of her dark skin, Durga always liked to wear lighter colors in shades of pale yellow and blue. Whenever the saris had large colorful *palloos*, she chose to wear them Gujarati style, so the color and designs were beautifully displayed, but Kishore said to her in a stern voice, "This is too old fashioned."

"I'd like to wear *salwar-khamiz* sometimes," Durga had the courage to say. "Mummy didn't want me to wear them outside the house."

"Yes, you must," Kishore told her, and she was pleased he was being so agreeable. Then he went on to say, "Looks like I'm going to have to give you a real overhaul. Your parents are so not up-to-date. They've made an old-maid out of you." Kishore laughed when he said this, and Durga said she felt an abysmal hurt deep inside. My sister had tears in her eyes when she confided in me and I disliked Kishore even more.

Kishore liked to show off when he wore a new shirt, and he liked to brag about his various club memberships. They had met a young couple in the early days of their marriage and admiringly, Durga had wondered how Kishore could make easy conversation with people he didn't know.

Durga did not like the hot sun because it tanned her face. She was very aware of her dark complexion, more so because Kishore was crass about it, and then she cried. At other times, Kishore talked and joked and loved to eat out in restaurants, and they seemed to enjoy their evenings out.

I was a quiet spectator looking in on Kishore's and Durga's life and wondering about my own future, for I, too, was married at the same time as my sister. I wondered if Parth's patience with me would run out, or if he had even noticed my indifference in our marriage. I was an obedient housewife, doing all my duties as expected of me, but I was aloof in my heart and didn't care if Parth had noticed or not.

Without saying it out loud, because it would hurt Durga's feelings, Dilip told me that people around considered Kishore a pompous fool who talked only of himself. I told him I already knew that. I hated the way he treated my sister. Somehow, Kishore never seemed to realize this, nor did he ever feature Durga in any of his conversation. It angered me that my sister was such a doormat; but then, thinking about my own marriage, I was not any different. Parth owns me, I began to think. Parth owns me. I'm a slave to him, not my own person anymore. That's what he envisions a wife to be. I am imprisoned.

A hideous crowing sound, along with the twittering of hundreds of other birds, woke Durga up every morning. When she looked out of the bedroom window of her fourth floor flat, she saw a large, black crow sitting on the ledge below her window and making a horrendous noise. This morning in September, her eyes drifted across to the opposite side of the narrow street and into the kitchen of the apartment across from theirs. She ran to the bathroom, feeling nauseous. The sight of the servant there, squatting by a hot *kadhai*, made her want to puke. The doctor had said another two or three weeks and she'd be fine when the second trimester starts.

He stirred the contents of a pan in continuous, slow, circular motion. Whatever he was mixing, the mistress of the house went back and forth between the kitchen and the dining room, serving her husband, who sat in his sleeveless, white undershirt at the dining table, reading the morning newspaper. The scene was a reminder to Durga to get a start on her own day, although she wanted to lie down for a few more minutes.

Kishore did not stir, even with sunlight pouring in and the crows raising a racket by the window. He did not have to go to the office at a regular hour, as one would for a regular paid job, and Durga looked forward to those few hours in the morning with him on days when he was not rushed. Most days, Kishore even had time to do a nominal *puja*, and say prayers after his morning bath. Durga always got the *puja* necessities ready for him in a little antique silver tray, which was our Motiba's when she was younger, and which she had gifted to Durga when she got married.

Durga cooked the morning *nashta*. Every evening, she told her servant what she wanted to make for Kishore's breakfast the next morning. It was to be *masala puris* this morning, and she had told him to keep the dough ready. Eventually, when Kishore seated himself at the dining table, she rolled the dough into small, round circles and fried them in hot oil. These *puris* puffed up with hot air trapped inside of them and then floated up to the surface. Kishore loved his hot breakfast *puris*, eaten with various sweet and sour pickles.

Kishore spent long hours at work or at the club, and Durga was alone most of the day, waiting for the baby to come in a few more months.

"Durga, you must go to the club with Kishore sometimes. You'll get to see what goes on there," I said to her.

Naive and soft-spoken Durga answered, "Kishore never asks me. Mostly he goes straight from work. He's always very busy." She would add the last sentence defensively and all I could do was smile, trying to enter Durga's world of make-believe.

12th Oct., 1960

Dear Salma,

Even after we have been writing so many things, finally I understand why you never wrote to me, to this day, about your move to Pakistan. The details you mention are sad beyond words and it is a lesson in history that will be told and retold for years. Thousands of Hindus and Sikhs were hurt too, Salma, and killed, when trainloads of corpses, instead of live, breathing people, arrived from Pakistan at train stations in Delhi and Amritsar in India.

Now I know your personal family story and it is sad, but great to hear that all is well. So much time has gone by, now I must be ready to live the rest of my life, as you must. I'm so glad we're friends. I can't say the same about being married to Parth, he has no romantic bone in him.

How nice to hear that Naaz is happily married. My little boy, Sunil, is a joy, but I'm restless and discontented. I want more than feeding and clothing him and holding him in my arms. Gosh, I'm being needy. Parth and I never go to the movies, do you? Life is dull for me. I try to find good books, so I won't be bored or depressed, but I am.

Naaz and you must have changed a lot. We're all caught up in an adult world, trying to make sense of what life has to offer. I want to cheer you up but I grumbled instead, sorry. It hurts me when you write that you're old at twenty because you have no children. Your mother-in-law has no right to say unkind words to you. Please Salma, learn to smile. I'll try also.

Your friend forever, Uma

What Salma said in her letters about their escape to Pakistan, 1947

excerpt from Uma's Journal written in 1960

We had seen pictures of refugee camps in India and how people who fled from Pakistan had to find new homes in the big cities in India. When I was a child, I wondered if there were lizards in the refugee camp, and if the other children were afraid of lizards like I was. Dilip and Durga always made fun of my fears, especially the tailless lizard. Now much older, I tried not to talk about it, but it was still a haunting memory. Salma had written long details of how they arrived in Pakistan years ago.

When her family left New Delhi, I immediately imagined Salma in a house similar to the one they had lived in. Her mother's raspy voice was still strong in my memory. I liked the sweet Urdu words with which Salma's mother offered us a snack after we ran around in her back yard playing hide and seek. Sometimes the snack was a mouth-watering, doughnut-like sweet, the *gulab-jamboo*; at other times she offered us spicy meat *samosas*. As years went by and I grew taller, I reflected on how tall Salma and Naaz might now be, what Salma looked like, whom of the two was prettier?

Salma wrote that she couldn't bear to verbalize any of the details sooner.

Sitting in their house in New Delhi in 1947, Salma's father, Mr. Syed Ali, was angry about the decisions the politicians had made for the people of India. Syed Ali was born and brought up in Delhi, as was his father before him. They prayed five times a day to Allah, as was required by the Quoran. The family worked hard and lived cohesively with their Hindu neighbors and friends, each respecting their own religions and one anothers. He felt Mr. Nehru and Mr. Jinnah, Prime Ministers of the two new countries of India and Pakistan, had not given enough thought to the day-to-day situations that would arise with partition. Syed Ali made no plans to move to Pakistan, for Delhi was his home. With all the political action around them, arguments always got heated and militant opinions arose during their office morning chai time. Mr. Ali said that the British were leaving behind a very inept India, not yet ready to take on the responsibility of an independent nation.

What once was peaceful co-exsistence led to a wave of dissension that rose through the different strata of people. Hindu-Muslim antagonism simply became worse. Hindu employees in his office objected to Mr. Ali's statements and Salma wrote word must have spread; for one day out of nowhere, angry Hindu militants threw stones at the Ali house. Then the militants went round to the back of the house to the servant's quarters and bound and gagged a Hindu servant who had been with the Ali household for many years. They dragged the servant to the front yard, beat him up, tied him to a tree, and left him there. These were Hindus punishing a Hindu for working under a Muslim master.

Syed Ali and his family were badly shaken up by many other threats that followed and ultimately, with advice from Hindu and Sikh and Muslim friends, they decided to move to Pakistan. That was a common happening amongst the Muslims who had been settled in India for four and five generations and were suddenly being attacked. Their Hindu friends were upset and suggested they go to Pakistan, but that plans to move should be kept a secret.

Mr. Ali got a large sum of money out of the Bank with the help of the bank manager who was a friend, so the paper transactions were kept private, without any of the bank employees finding out. Every night, after the servants were in their own quarters at the rear of the house, the family put all their precious belongings into small bundles that could be hand carried without the need for a porter or coolie being hired. For all appearances, the door-to-door vegetable vendor who stopped by the house in the mornings, and the woman who came to wash pots and pans later in the day, saw it as a normal working household. There were potatoes and onions in the pantry and a big pan of cooked lentils, and *daal*, on the kitchen stove. Washed *kurtas* and pants were hung out on the clothesline to dry in the backyard.

One night just two days later, Syed Ali shaved off his little goatee, the usual practice of Muslims, so he would not be easily recognizable as a Muslim. His wife had shed her long, black *burkha*, and instead of walking two steps behind him as she normally did, she walked beside her husband for the first time in all the years that they had been married. She wore a printed sari in bright colors, put a *kumkum* on her forehead, like a Hindu, and carried some bundles of clothing, as did her husband; a kind of appearance that would make people on the street think that a Hindu family was going to their village for a brief visit. Their loyal Hindu servant accompanied them with Salma and Naaz in tow. Salma had been told to answer to the name of Samira, a Hindu name, and Naaz was called Neena. Mr. Ali and the servant both carried rolled mattresses on their shoulders, each one tied neatly with thick rope. A *tonga*, a horse-driven carriage, had been ordered to take them to the local bus stop, and the bus would take them to the train station.

Friends had assured the Alis that they would go back to the house later that night and pack up their suitcases and bring their luggage to the train station. Syed Ali and his family were to wait inside the train for the luggage to be delivered to them.

I was in tears as I continued reading Salma's letter.

Syed Ali and his wife got on the train with Salma and Naaz. The servant standing on the platform handed the mattress to Mr. Ali, who stood in the door of the train, when a needy traveler grabbed it as it was about to change hands. Mattress in hand, the man ran to a compartment some distance away from the Alis and disappeared into the crowded train. There was utter confusion on the people-packed platform. They stumbled over one another, everyone shouting and talking at the same time. The suitcases from the Ali home had not arrived and Salma's father looked around frantically for the friends who were to come with the luggage. Minutes before the train was to leave, a long time neighbor and friend, holding two big suitcases, pushed through the crowd toward the exact train compartment and propelled the luggage through the train window into her mother's lap.

The passenger who had grabbed the mattress threw it in the corner of his train seat and was about to unroll it, when his wife needed to poke her head out of the window and spit out the bilious contents of her upset stomach. Then she rested her head against the rolled mattress and fell asleep. More people rushed into the compartment and there was no place to move or unroll the mattress and lie down. People wanted to get away from the smell and started to move in the opposite direction. After awhile, everyone settled down and dozed off. In the middle of the night, Naaz stood up to look, and in a split second, wandered off to the next compartment and then the next. She saw a little place by the woman who had puked, sat there and fell asleep in an awkward, twisted position, pressed against the weight of the woman's body that rested on the mattress. Salma thought Naaz might have recognized her mattress and snuggled behind it.

At first, when Salma's father woke up, he thought Naaz might have been in the bathroom, and waited. Then he walked through the train calling her name, but must have walked through the other side.

The crowded train was bound for Lahore. At night, famished and exhausted, Naaz wet her pants. Heat added to her mental confusion. She started whimpering and having nightmares. She screamed when what she thought was a cockroach entered her dark space and started to crawl up her leg. That when the passengers noticed her. They were all stunned to see this five-year-old in their midst, separated from her family, and not able to say how she got there. She would not even tell them her name. After sitting in the corner of the compartment for a long time, refusing even water, all Naaz managed to say in a weak voice was, "Ammijaan, Ammijaan," calling for her mother.

The train was well into Pakistan by now, and so the travelers believed they were safe. At Lahore station, crowds of refugees from the train emerged in a state of exhaustion, dirt, and hunger. Refugee camps had been set up some twenty miles away and people were sent there by the truckloads. The man and his sick wife had a distant cousin whose house they were to go to. They could not leave Naaz at the railway station. They looked around to see if anybody would claim her. They waited awhile, but not long enough and quickly walked away, not being able to recollect the face of the man he had stolen the mattress from. Naaz searched through the crowd with anxious eyes, but with the rush and pushing and shoving, all she could see were feet and legs and bundles of luggage that came right at her face. Salma's mother and father were completely bewildered as they searched and waited. Salma said she wanted to run up and down the station but her father wouldn't let her. Crowds for the next train filled the platform.

Naaz cried for days. Then gradually, she started to eat, but she stopped speaking. The family was kind to her, told her it was a mistake, and soon she would be with her own family, but the child just did not smile and would not utter a word. She kept opening the front door and stared out at the street in front of their house. Salma said that as an adult, Naaz still had deformed nails from picking at them. It was the result of her continuous anxiety during those initial months of being lost.

The man and his wife had no children and became very fond of Naaz, but the man had guilt written all over him, thinking he had not tried hard enough to find her parents. He did not know why in a moment of greed he had held the child's hand and walked away. He had wanted to make his wife happy. He suspected that she was sick because she was expecting their first child. Their fifteen-year marriage was at last to bear fruit, and he was desperate and anxious because the timing was so stressful and wrong for such a momentous occasion to come into their lives. The man soon found out that they were not to have a child of their own. He wondered if bringing Naaz to them was Allah's way of bringing a child into their home, and he graciously thanked Allah for letting that happen. Yet, he felt he hadn't done enough.

Salma wrote it was so fortuitous that Naaz finally came back to them. There were many horror stories of children being lost, kidnapped and sold, even killed. Many were estranged from their families at the time of Partition and had never been found. She said many people had died of cholera and other high fevers. She knew that thousands of Hindus had also left their homes in the big cities in Pakistan. Those who stayed behind were asked to convert to Islam. Salma said they knew of a Hindu who pretended to be a Muslim, so he could do business like before. Several thousands had been killed on both sides in the name of freedom and independence. "At what cost, Uma?" my Muslim friend wrote me.

From the overcrowded refugee camps where all efforts were being made to provide the basic needs to each family, Syed Ali was finally sent to a small town where many, small, temporary houses of mud and corrugated steel had been set up. A few provisions were given and these then were their living quarters for the next few months, until Syed Ali finally moved them to better lodgings.

Syed Ali found work as an apprentice to a cloth merchant. In Delhi, he owned a cloth factory and had employed thirty people under him. This working under somebody was hard for him, but as Salma said, he was grateful for a new start. Between husband and wife, they had managed to carry out most of her gold jewelry and a large sum of money. They had been lucky not to be robbed of their valued belongings, but they had lost their most precious, little daughter in this journey, and it weighed heavily on their minds. Day and night, Naaz was in their prayers and somehow they kept hoping for her return. Once there was a steady income, Mr. Ali began to look at other opportunities. He could afford to make a small down payment, borrow money from a pawn-shop and start up a small business on his own.

An acquaintance told them to advertise in the local Urdu paper that their daughter, Naaz, was missing. Many such columns filled up the daily papers of missing brothers and sisters, fathers and sons, mothers, daughters, grandparents; there was no end. Syed Ali gave the exact date of their journey and a description of the little girl who answered to the name Naaz. Naaz with her big, brown eyes wearing a blue dress at the time she went missing. They waited many months.

A few weeks before the advertisement was in the paper, a traveling *fakir*, a holy man, dressed in white clothes and with a long beard and gray hair stopped by Syed Ali's house. Mrs. Ali provided the man with food, and as they got talking, Syed Ali told the *fakir* the story of their missing daughter.

"My *bacchi*, she's only five years old, my Naaz! Will I ever see her again!" Mrs. Ali moaned and tears welled up in her eyes daily as she thought of Naaz.

"Fear not," the *fakir* had said when he heard the whole story. "Naaz will come back to you."

The *fakir* had raised his hands to bless her as she fell to his feet.

Nine months went by and the *fakir* happened to be traveling in the next village when he stood at the door-step of a man and his wife. The wife had her hands loaded with washed clothes that were to be hung on the line, when she saw the holy man at the door. She dropped the clothes into a nearby tub, wiped her hands on the sides of her *kurta*, and went into the kitchen to get food. As she crossed the courtyard and headed back towards the *fakir* with food in her hands, she beckoned to Naaz, who was sitting in the corner, playing with her plastic dolls. The woman called out to the girl by her pet name, Guddie, to come with her and give the *fakir* food. The girl ran up to the *fakir* and helped the woman put roti pieces in the alms bowl. Then she stood in front of him with her eyes lowered and her head bowed to accept his blessings.

"What is your name, child?" asked the *fakir*.

The child stood still and looked up at the *fakir* with her big, brown eyes.

"She does not speak," said the woman. "We do not know her real name. We call her Guddie. She came with us accidentally on the train more than a year ago. It's like Allah meant us to have her for our own."

"Go play, child," the *fakir* said to Naaz. He continued speaking, still looking in the direction of the child. "Bless you, woman. The child will be happy again. You have done a great thing looking after her as you would your own. Send your husband to the mosque this evening to see me."

It was a difficult transition for Naaz to get reacquainted with her own family. There were hidden feelings of anger and abandonment, and for many weeks, the *fakir* was the only person Naaz listened to without a temper tantrum. Gradually, she played with her sister with a little bit of shyness in her step. She stared at her mother with great intensity, and Salma said in her letter they wondered if she was remembering something. Their house was different and it took her quite a few weeks to figure out that she was back with her family. The *fakir* took her back to see the man and his wife often and she was happy when they hugged her. The man asked for forgiveness from Syed Ali, who saw that his daughter was well fed, wore clean clothes, and had been taught to pray to Allah regularly. All Mr. Ali said, with extreme gratefulness was, "Only Allah forgives. We have to accept what comes our way. Let us be friends." Saying so, he took the man's hands in his.

11th Dec. 1972

Dear Salma,

The India-Pakistan war has affected our world again. What a pity that countries fight each other in the name of religion, and destroy so much of our country's youth. My brother, Dilip, is a medical officer at the front. He would have been happier continuing his practice in Delhi and being with his wife, but he had no choice. Nobody has a choice in wartimes. I worry for him.

My daughter, Megan, is ten years old. Sunil doesn't enjoy school as much as Megan does. She writes well, whereas he's good at fixing things. Both children adore their father. Parth is tired when he comes home from the shop, but always finds the energy to play with them.

Having had a woman prime minister in power has done good to the morale of women in India. I'm wishfully thinking that even Parth will see that and let me help him. So far, I have not succeeded, and I remain a mouse in the house. Keep writing. Love, Uma

My brother Dilip's capture, 1971-1973
excerpt from Uma's Journal

I was at my parents' house that fateful day when we got bad news about my brother, Dr. Dilip Multani, the Army physician. Sunil and I had just returned from an English matinee movie, while Megan stayed home with her grandmother learning to embroider roses on her little handkerchiefs. I treated Sunil to two scoops of ice cream and he seemed content, more so because he was the only one to get the treat.

Papa walked into the flat, his steps weary after a long and tiring day at the clinic. Ten minutes later, he rested his bare feet on the coffee table, newspaper in hand; keen to find out what the latest event in the war across the border was. Anti-Pakistan sentiments were high in all Hindu households. Many of our friends also had enlisted relatives. Papa drank his chai at a leisurely pace. The empty teacup sat beside him on the table. He glanced up from behind his newspaper as he sensed the servant come into the living room and stand by the door. Papa suspected he had come to collect the empty tea cup and saucer.

He said apologetically to Papa, "A *bada* sahib, an important big sahib is at the door and wants to see you urgently."

Papa stood up right away, concerned that he had not heard the knock. I saw him walk to the front door. He shook hands with the sahib and invited him in. Papa then called out to me, "Get some tea, Uma. We have a visitor." Papa spoke English whenever an important visitor came to the house. It was his habit from his younger days under the British Raj. Somehow, all official and important exchanges occurred in English.

The man in a khaki army uniform was very matter-of-fact and cold, and after a few pleasantries, spoke up in a thick Punjabi accent, "Daactor-sahib, I have news for you, sir, and it's not good news." Then he waited for Papa to say something, as if giving Papa time to assimilate all that he had to say after this.

"Your son, Dr. Dilip Multani, had been specially called to give medical help to a commander-in-chief, who had a heart attack at the front three days ago. On their way there, it was already becoming dark, ji, when guerrillas attacked the jeep; and from what information we have received, Daactor Dilip was taken hostage across the border to Pakistan. It was a setup, Daactorji Sahib. They killed the two sergeants in the jeep there and then. They captured the driver and the daactor. Our sources tell us that daactorji is not too badly injured, ji, but we can't be sure, ji. We are currently not able to locate these two missing people."

Papa listened, stone still and expressionless. He cupped his hands over his eyes and put his head down. A hasty exclamation escaped him, "Hai Ram! Oh my God! Shanti, O Shanti! Come quick!" Mummy entered with two cups of tea. She set the tray down, her ears set on the conversation already in progress. As she sat on the chair next to me, the army man went on to say that they were trying to locate Dilip. Mummy's eyes rolled up and circled the room and her neck became limp. Papa looked at her just in time to hold her up and then gently laid her head down on my lap. We heard Mummy's loud sobs, in the middle of a dense silence.

Papa looked up after a few minutes. His face was drawn; the veins on both his temples pulsed high and fast.

"Why Dilip! Why my son! What can we think from all this? Dilip is a doctor, not a fighter. Will he be released when the war is over?" Papa asked of the army commander.

Motiba stood by the door and heard the news. They knew that when an army man came to the house, there was news of great importance. It could be good news, but most often it was bad tidings that the army sahibs came to deliver personally. The family had seen it happen in the neighborhood.

The officer nodded indifferently, and it wasn't quite clear what he meant. His face was expressionless.

"God willing, he'll be released soon," the man in the khaki uniform said. "Let him be released quickly. Our army knows his value as a good medical doctor. If given a chance, the Pakistanis will realize that too."

There was nothing more to be said. The clock clicked away loudly on the mantelpiece. A few minutes later, the bada sahib took his leave, "Do let me know if there is anything else I can do, daactorji. We'll give you information on his whereabouts as soon as we hear anything. It might take a long time, we just don't know. We'll try our best, ji. Just so you know."

The Army sahib left. The Multani family sat in silence for a long time. Nothing was the same again. I was pleased when Parth suggested to my parents that I could stay with them in time of such pain. We changed schools for Sunil and Megan, and all three of us stayed on in Delhi. Parth came to visit every three or four weeks, and talked with Papa and Mummy, but it could only be words. However, I was grateful, for what else could any one do? My own life became of little consequence. I was pleased Parth was being so considerate.

A growing part of me appreciated Parth, normally a man of few words. At home, I had seen him interacting with the merchants who stopped by the house. He asked about their children. Parth said to my parents that everything was all right at work and at home, and sometimes I felt he was being a hypocrite. I tried not to show it, but I still carried a grudge against him.

Mummy wrote to Durga in Bombay about what had happened to Dilip. Kishore allowed Durga to go to Delhi for a week. She came with her daughter, Rina.

Staying at my parents' with the children was a good way for me to show my concern for the family, and an excuse for me to be away from Parth. Yet, something within me had changed. It might have been Dilip's capture that made me anxious, so I had no time to focus on my own problems. A few times I even convinced myself there were no problems. Sunil and Megan brought some sense of an everyday routine into our days. Their playing and laughter helped. But, more importantly, I wanted to do something to help Dilip's cause.

Mummy tossed her head and dug her hair deep into her pillow, every time she turned on her charpoy next to Papa's. Their bedroom window frame rattled gently from the cool night wind. She would sleep lightly and wake up startled. She could hear a door opening and closing from a flat next door, and the sound of toilets flushing from the flat upstairs. The nights seemed long, and all noises bothered Mummy; sounds she was unaware of in all the years they had lived there, so she said when we sat down for tea in the morning. The shock of not knowing where her son was! She said constant thoughts of what could have happened to Dilip tormented her. She covered herself with the thin, white, cotton sheet and kept tugging it loose and covering her ears with it in the hope that all bad thoughts would distance themselves. Papa snored a soft, rhythmic beat on the charpoy next to hers, his bulky body nicely blanketed beneath his cotton sheet and his warm, cotton-filled *rajai*. Nights in Delhi were cold in December, but somehow in her restlessness, even the weight of a single cotton sheet felt heavy on her body.

We got details of the capture a month later. The same *badasahib* returned with news of Dilip's life in the army and the circumstances of his capture. We sat around him and listened to the official version.

"War is so unkind to all," Dr. Dilip muttered, as he entered the tent. He sat tense at the edge of his cane chair and planted his heavy, leather army boots firmly in the dust floor. His back was unsupported and he ached all over from the long hours he had spent in performing surgery last night. The patient chart that lay open in front of him was not complete. He could not even begin to decipher the multitude of thoughts that paraded through his brain. The blood encrusted, crushed face of the young soldier he had just attended to stirred up different experiences. The young man had groaned in agony as Dr. Dilip set his broken leg and steadied it in plaster.

Dr. Dilip had to probe his crushed right cheek bone to assess the depth of the wound. The youth gave him a wistful look, and screamed in pain, as he fainted. Dilip called for the nurse, and ordered intravenous morphine for the boy. Dilip kept looking at the boy. There was not too much more he could do for the distorted, burnt face, other than run saline over it and dab it clean as gently as he could.

What had shocked Dilip the most was that the twenty-year-old's home town address was Conway Place, New Delhi, the same area where Dilip grew up. Dilip had noticed in the chart that this young man also had the last name, Sood, a name he was familiar with. Dilip had been an army doctor at the military base camp for the last ten months and had treated thousands of casualties. War experience had calloused his feelings. To find somebody from his hometown upset the delicate framework he had built around him. He felt disturbed when he thought of how different this young man's life would have been if India and Pakistan were not at war.

Then, Dilip remembered the building at the corner of M block, where Theme House, the music store, was located and where he and his college friends stopped almost every evening on their way home. The shop was a favorite haunt for all the university students because the Punjabi owner, Mr. Sood, took care to bring in the latest English music from abroad. Elvis and the Beatles were the big names that kept coming to his mind. He had bought all his Elvis records from there.

He did not remember seeing this boy in the store, but he surmised he was one of the family. He didn't really know if he was from the same family, but Dilip felt a certain kinship just from knowing that he grew up in the same area as himself. Here they were at the India-Pakistan border in the northern most part of the country, about two thousand miles away from where they lived. What a pity that the youth was not able to talk to him.

Sadly, Dilip looked into the boy's future; this young man was ten or twelve years younger than he. The young man would stay disfigured for life. Dilip knew he would be blind in the right eye, where the fractured eye socket pressed into the cheek and displaced the eye, so its blood supply was shorn off. With luck, the other eye would have partial vision. It haunted Dilip's imagination to think that this young man would stay crippled after the war, and hate Dilip for saving his life.

"Perhaps I'll see him again in peace times," Dilip told the orderly at hand. He went on to say that he was a man from his own hometown. Not just that, there were many soldiers from Delhi. Dilip made a mental note to write to his papa and Mummy about this incident. They would remember the Sood family.

Dilip glanced at the pile of papers beside him. His desk was stacked with files of unfinished charts. He picked up his pen and wrote several post-operative notes and summaries. From out of his tent window into the hazy dusk, as the evening sun sent its last glow, he saw tents and heard a continuous buzz of helicopters landing and taking off. Revved up trucks moved in and out, bringing injured victims from the front. It was not hard for Dilip to be part of the war, even though he was away from the front. He was stationed in a safe zone at the base where he, as a medical doctor, had to stay and take care of the ugly aftermath from the border area.

"Dr. Multani, Dr. Multani!" a sergeant came running up and thrust some papers in his hands.

Dilip glanced at the papers with a certain degree of urgency, and even before he had finished reading the last sentence, said, "*Jaldi karo*. Hurry, quick! Get the jeep ready. I'll get my surgical bag."

The order was for him to be taken to the front where a commander-in-chief had suddenly taken ill with severe chest pains and needed medical attention.

"Yes, sir," saluted the soldier in a disciplined, no-nonsense voice, and ran out of the tent.

Within minutes, Dilip handed over his patient's charts to the Medical Officer in the next tent, with special instructions regarding the two soldiers who were seriously ill, and a third one who needed surgical amputation of his right leg right away. Then

Dilip and the two soldiers, all three dressed in camouflage fatigues, left in the jeep.

As the sun set and darkness spread across the skies, the jeep bumped along unpaved roads, leaving a trail of dust in its wake. The winding road took them through hilly country and disappeared through areas of tall bush and dense trees.

Further down, the road flattened and became narrow for about a mile, and was bumpy and uphill again. They crossed a dry riverbed and entered what seemed to be dense forest. The jeep slowed down. Dilip sat subdued, wondering what the condition of the commander would be and if he could really do much for him out there. He might need to be transferred to the base unit, but the ride back was not easy.

Dilip gazed into the forest darkness, watching the fleeting shapes of trees. The jeep moved along in a slow but jolty rhythm, and his body moved back and forth in harmony with the sound of the tires. An hour or two later, despite repeated jolts, Dilip dozed off. All of a sudden, the jeep jerked to a halt. He sat up with a start, as did the two sergeants sitting next to him. Peering into the darkness, he saw the outline of four men blocking the narrow road. Their guns were pointed at the jeep, while a fifth man emerged from behind the trees and walked over to the driver, his gun poised to the driver's head. Two of the shadows moved and became vicious men who walked to the back of the jeep and shouted for the doctor to get out. The sergeant in the jeep fired a shot at the guerrillas as they approached. There was instant havoc. Dilip stood by the jeep when a sharp pain in his leg made him cringe. He reeled over in pain as he realized he had been shot. He attempted to press his hand against the gush of blood from his leg when everything around him blacked out.

He did not know how long he had been unconscious. When he woke up, the jeep still jolted back and forth but he could see nothing. He lifted his fingers to his face and was aware of a sweaty cloth tied over his eyes. He called out the driver's name, but instead heard voices that were different, and then he recognized the Peshwari-Urdu slang of Pakistan.

"Don't move," one voice said, "If you value your life, don't move."

Dilip's head felt heavy, as did his left leg. He seemed to have been there, a prisoner, for a long time. He had no idea if it was still the same night.

1975

Dear Salma,

My children are growing up. Parth keeps himself busy, earning money to feed all my fancy. He's doing well, and my disgruntled self is a little more content. Still, even if he does everything for me, he's not the light-hearted romantic type, and I feel lonely. If only we could talk and open our minds to each other; if he would let me help him a little in his business, I'd be happy. So days go by, I see movies with Durga once in awhile; we're both being good, the way our parents like us to be.

Dilip's release from the Pakistan hospital took two years, but we're so grateful he came home. His left leg prosthesis is fitting much better, and like I told you before, he and his wife are settling well. No sign of their becoming parents yet, a big disappointment for my mother. You must keep busy with a teenage step-daughter and a step-son to take on. You are a truly kind person, Salma, and I love you dearly.

.   Sorry, I left the letter half written...

I always thought Durga was such a contented person and could take whatever came her way. Her husband Kishore was her 'God.' So much has happened since, hence my delay in writing to you. I'm greatly saddened as life shapes up so differently for each one of us, but I've found a new strength. Is it only because we are women that we endure? I am born with a new courage, almost overnight. I'll fight with all I've got. I'm not making sense, but I'll write you everything soon.

Love, Uma

Life's ups and Downs; My dear sister Durga, 1975

excerpt from Uma's Journal

It was a warm, sunny afternoon when the boy rung the bell twice in succession and waited for the door to open. Hearing no one, he started pounding on the door with his fists. He banged incessantly and with increasing intensity. At just this time, the servant, Bhimji, had lain down to rest for ten or fifteen minutes.

"What's the big rush, I'm coming, *bhai*," said Bhimji, as he limped toward the door on his arthritic knees.

Bhimji, their servant from when Kishore was a little boy, finally reached the front door and saw a very flustered errand boy from his sahib's office. The boy breathed heavy and appeared to have run most of the way.

"Call *sahib jaldi*, quickly, I've an urgent note for him," the boy said to Bhimji.

Bhimji crossed his arms on his chest and shook his head, "My sahib is at the office. He works very hard. He's never home this early in the afternoon. What do you take him for?"

"But I'm from the office, *budhoo-mia*, you fool. Otherwise why would I have come here? Where did he go? Ask *Bibiji* (the lady of the house)!" the boy demanded.

The boy clutched a folded piece of paper in his thin hand. His dirty, unkempt fingernails were a poor sight. Durga heard the commotion and came to the front door, still holding the magazine she was glancing at as she and I conversed. I was visiting her that afternoon and followed behind her to the door, just from curiosity.

Durga told the boy that Bhimji was telling the truth and sahib was not home. The boy said the office manager said to hurry with the message and not stop on the way for chai.

"This is so urgent, *bibiji*, you read the *chitthi*," he pleaded. "If you don't tell me what is to be done about this message, *Bibiji*, I will get a thrashing from the manager sahib in the office."

Durga was alarmed as she unraveled the crumpled note and read it. She handed it to me. In hushed tones, we discussed what answer to give the boy right away.

The errand boy had heard parts of the phone conversation between the manager and some other contact at the other end saying, "*Lorry ulat gai*, lorry is overturned." He started to tell Bhimji about it, while Durga and I read the contents again. The boy said the manager was going to wait in the office till he brought back the reply.

The note said one of their company trucks had been in an accident and this would lead to big delays in the delivery of the goods. He didn't think the driver would survive. One of their other truck drivers coming from the opposite direction had just walked into their office and informed him of these details.

The manager wanted Kishore's permission to change the priority for delivery of the goods. He was told the overturned truck's driver had his head cut open and was taken to the hospital for stitches. Kishore would have to make some decisions and act quickly. The manager wanted to send out another truck, which would mean the need to pacify another customer who would not get his goods on time. The *dukkan sahibs*, the shopkeepers to whom the goods had to be delivered, did not particularly care for the cause of the delays. Kishore would personally have to intervene and keep the contracts going.

"Sahib must be busy with some other clients," Durga said, after some thought. "Perhaps he forgot to tell you in the office."

I heard this. I could not look at Durga. I had seen Kishore with an attractive woman in the pale yellow Lucknow *salwar-khamiz* years ago, and not told my sister. A thought flashed before me. Was she the only one or were there others like her?

Durga turned to me, "Is Kishore really getting so forgetful? Why did he not tell the office where he was?" Then she went on to tell me how the other day when he was late, she had asked if he was so busy at work and he had snapped at her, "Since when have you started to question me?" Durga said this in a light-hearted way, not too concerned about the incident.

I told Durga in a very assertive tone to make a decision as best she knew how, and tell it to the boy. After a few more seconds she went to the door and said, "Tell the manager sahib to send out the extra truck and make the necessary changes. I'll tell sahib when I see him. He will be home later in the evening."

Durga and I went back to the living room once the crisis was averted. She asked Bhimji to make some chai for us. She put on a tape of Indian film songs and listened for a while. We each had some thinking to do. Then it was time for me to go home.

That evening, Durga hemmed her daughter Rina's dress, intermittently looking at the clock, and then again listening to the radio that blared popular Hindi songs. The tic-tic clock noise was a constant drone in her ears, yet time was still. She waited for Kishore's return. She had told the boy that the manager should go ahead and take action. "Before that," she had said to the boy, "Check in sahib's club in case he is there for a meeting." She was sick with worry, in case Kishore had been in an accident.

Next day, she, and later Rina, told me how events unfolded that evening. Kishore came home very late. Durga had waited up for him, as she always did. His eyes were bloodshot. He was belligerent and yelled at her. He was angry because Durga had sent the boy to the club and interrupted 'his meeting.' He said he did not think it a matter of such great significance as the manager and Durga had deemed it to be.

The next morning, Rina noticed her mother had a black eye and she asked out of genuine concern if it hurt. She suspected the worst.

All Durga said was, "I ran into the wall on my way to the bathroom last night. How stupid of me!"

Rina, a young teen, had seen how her mother waited on her father and tried so hard to please him. She saw, too, that he rebuffed her mother's attention. Sometimes Rina could smell his strong breath and had noticed his vague expression. She had told me she felt uncomfortable when her father looked at her with hunger, as if she were one transparent being, and he watched her insides with a sense of possession. It made her want to leave the room, insecure and uneasy. Often, she would ask her mother if she could visit with her friends, where she would sit and talk even if the hour was late. Rina hoped her father would be asleep by the time she came home. At times Kishore shouted at her for being out so late, but mostly he took it out on his wife, and Rina was unable to defend her actions except to start crying. Kishore hated a scene, so he backed off when Rina cried. Rina did not know what went on behind closed doors.

Two nights later, Durga rubbed her hands and paced up and down. The bruise on her forehead seemed to be getting bigger. She was afraid Bhimji may come out of his room when he heard footsteps, thinking she needed something. She went to the bathroom and opened the cold water tap. Placing a wet hand towel on her forehead and then patting her cheeks eased the sharp pain. She knew the bruising would become black and blue in the next few days, and this time she could not make the same excuse to Rina or me that she had walked into a door. I would ask questions, she knew that. Sometimes I wondered if she would tell me the truth, but I knew it hurt her too much. She knew I was even more disillusioned with my own marriage, a fact to which I had not quite reconciled, and perhaps never would.

Even when they had company, Durga tolerated his crass remarks.

"You're a fool, you don't stand a chance. You don't deserve this luxury I keep you in," and on and on. Durga never answered back. It seemed she flinched under the stone hand that seemed to just fall on her.

Two weeks later, I noticed Durga was in a bad mood. She became very silent after some outburst on inconsequential matters. She had, very discreetly, wiped the tears that welled in her eyes. Of late, I knew that Rina seemed more perceptive and very aware of what went on in the house, more so than Durga had ever realized. Rina was becoming a little more sensitive in her own daily interactions with her friends, so her own moods were never predictable and she seemed to take it out on her mother at various times.

Durga was a very patient person, calm, low-keyed, and never assertive. Motiba had always said women have plenty of listening to do in life and she seemed to follow that. Say less, react less, let the man do the talking in public. Rina had seen her mother deal with household crises, just as the one with the truck accident. Every crisis passes eventually, Durga said, and she listened to Rina's teenage lament with patience.

Rina noticed that her mother was quieter than usual for the next few days.

"Na, no, just thinking," Durga said, when Rina asked if she was upset at her.

Quietly, Rina resented her father even more.

I, too, had noticed the change in Durga; her quiet demeanor and something in her eyes bothered me. I wondered whether this would be a good time to tell Durga that I had seen Kishore with another woman. I worried about her constantly and waited for the right moment when I could tell her.

A few weeks later, for Kishore's birthday, Durga decided to make a special evening dinner for the three of them. At first she thought she would send her young servant to the other side of town to the big vegetable market, but then the servant would be out all day, and nothing else in the house would get done. If she went, she would also visit the Mahalaxmi temple there on this occasion.

I happened to be busy that day with an activity in Megan's school and could not go with her. Things might have turned out different if I had been with her, but I will never know. Durga told me she'd also get a fresh coconut, which would add good flavor to the curried vegetable dish, *undhio*, she was planning to make. After her shopping, she would be home in time to cook the special meal. Kishore and Rina both liked the coconut dessert she made. They'd also have cake that she planned to get from a bakery near their home. To share in the celebrations for later that evening, she had invited my family. Rina would be happy too, with Sunil and Megan visiting.

Not an unusual occurrence, but when Durga's young servant did not show up for work that day, and Bhimji was too old to go anywhere by bus, Durga had no choice but to take the bus and go herself. She called me again once her plans were made and asked if I wanted to join her. I told her Megan would be very disappointed if I did not go to her school, but we would certainly stop by for cake after dinner.

I did not like to go to Durga's house in the evenings, and neither did Parth, each for reasons of our own. I wondered if Parth would be conveniently late coming home from the shop, so

I would go alone with the children. Parth had made these types of excuses before when it came to going over to Durga and Kishore's flat.

I could not believe the note Durga left me. The note was on the dresser by her bed. I grabbed it before Kishore got there. What a drastic step my sister had taken! My head hurt, my heart was numb, even my arms throbbed, and I kept thinking, I could have done something. I should have realized what a sensitive human being my sister was and that she would not be able to take Kishore's infidelity. Kishore was her unconditional world. I understood the depth of what Durga had to say because of what I had seen several years ago, and it came back to haunt me. Papa, far away in Delhi would be affected. Little Rina! Left without a mother, and with a father who didn't care. Between what Bhimji said and what Durga wrote in her letter, the facts unfolded like this.

Durga had got down from the bus at the other end of town and went back and forth trying to locate the spice store from where she wanted to buy some fresh *masala*. By chance, she spotted Kishore's car parked on the street. Pleased that he was somewhere nearby, she thought he must have come there for business. She looked up and down, in case she saw him coming; she would ask him to go to the temple with her. It was his birthday and a visit together to the temple would make it a perfect day. Perhaps he could give her a ride back if he had time.

She finished her shopping, keeping an eye on the car. Finally, she saw Kishore come out of an alley with a lady friend, holding hands and laughing. Durga stood frozen. Kishore walked right past the store doorway where she stood, without looking her way. They got into his car and drove away.

Durga was faint from the shock of seeing Kishore. She went home in a daze, not fully aware of how long she was on the bus or what she had gone to buy. She did not make it to the temple. She just got home and handed her shopping to Bhimji.

Bhimji said she didn't want to talk and did not answer his questions, something that had never happened in all the years he had worked at their house. Bhimji thought she was probably very tired from the hot sun, and needed to rest.

She wrote in her note that Kishore had told her in the morning that he would be working late that evening and she had reminded him that for his birthday, they were having a special celebration. He had nodded to her happily, and as always, she believed him and chose to forget what had happened the previous night. Never in her life did she question his feelings for her.

Her note said, "What I saw before my very own eyes simply leeched the blood out of me. I am a shattered woman, Uma, and don't want to live this way. You must look after my Rina for me. You can give her a happy home."

Durga must have walked into her bedroom and closed the door. Half an hour later, when she did not come out of the bedroom, Bhimji knocked and told her he had left a glass of cold *lassi* on the table for her, and that he was going down to the market to buy some onions, which they would need for their evening meal. "Be sure to latch the door when you get up," Bhimji muttered as he left.

Durga answered from behind the closed door that he should take the money from the side table, where they always left some change in a platter for the servants to take on their many errands. After Bhimji left, Durga must have gotten up and gone into the kitchen. She emptied a gallon can of kerosene on her nylon sari, spilling it on the kitchen floor. Quickly, she lit a match and must have let it fall on her lap. The flames flared high on all sides of her. She sat there, perhaps praying and screaming till she was unconscious against the kitchen cabinet in the midst of more flames. The neighbors in the flat opposite heard the screams and walked in, just as Bhimji returned and saw the fire spread. He screamed for water. The neighbor woman pulled a bedspread off the bed and threw it on Durga. A maid-servant and the mistress from the flat next door both pushed Durga to the floor and rolled her over. The maid ran to the bathroom and brought a bucket of stored water and threw it over Durga. Another neighbor called for a doctor. Someone phoned Kishore to come home right away, but he was not in the office. A neighbor phoned me to come very quickly in a taxi.

By the time the doctor arrived, it was too late. He said they would have to get an ambulance and take her to the hospital to get a death certificate.

I sobbed in a corner, angry and defeated. I was shocked into grief...grief over my sister's death and guilty about the secret I carried. Months ago, I had seen Kishore with another woman and I had not had the courage to tell my sister. I gave Durga pep talks and observed her and offered her advice about how she should open her eyes to what Kishore was like. But I did not tell her. At that moment, I did not know what caused Durga to take her life. All was lost now. Minutes later, I found the note in the bedroom and read it.

Parth came quickly after he was informed. I showed Parth my sister's note and I told him everything I knew. Parth held me close. Rina, who was at a friend's house, came just then, and stood at the door in disbelief. In tears, she flung herself on her mother's body. After a while, I led her away and we both cried.

Parth and I waited a long time before Kishore was finally contacted by the police. Later, they talked at length to him when he finally seemed to be in control. He told the police it was a tragic accident and he looked remorseful. After the police left, he pleaded with Parth and I not to tell his family or my family, for the stigma of suicide was severe. I had read the note to him. In many ways he told us he would mend his ways and be a good father to Rina. That night, Rina wanted to come home with us. The next day, Parth went to Rina's school to talk to the head mistress and told her Rina would be absent for a few days.

After many discussions and arguments with Kishore, Parth and I as one voice, maintained that Rina was to stay with us. Parth watched my strength in dealing with my sister's affairs. My being so self-reliant, and confident in what I said to Kishore, must have made him see me in a different light; I sensed that. I felt stronger too, seeing Parth's loving eyes on me. They might have always been there, only I had never made the effort to believe it. His letting me talk and argue with Kishore, guiding Rina with my newfound strength, healed my own hurt.

1986

Dear Salma,

Parth and I are a team at last, as family goes, but at what price? It happened ever since Sunil left home, because Parth and he had an argument. Sunil's wife is a Muslim, I've mentioned that before in my letters. Rina tells me she is a very nice person. If only Parth would accept that marriage, I'd be happy, but knowing how his family suffered in the Partition long ago, he'll never forget it. I think I told you in my previous letter that we did not go for the wedding.

After Durga's death, a lot has happened in our lives. I guess we were meant to be together. Parth knew it from the first day he set eyes on me. I took much longer to understand him. People start with love and drift apart. We merged with the years, but enough of me.

I can't believe what you are telling me. Did you not have the courage to tell me before? You say it is the custom of your times. Muslim religion allows four wives, but I can't imagine that

happening in your family. So, your status as the first wife stands, and the three younger ones respect you. How strange that his youngest wife is about the age of your first step-daughter? You say it is okay because you couldn't bear him children. Why is it your fault? I just cannot comprehend your placid attitude. How old is the second son from your husband and his third wife? You enjoy playing with him, and his sisters. Are you really like an older sister to all those co-wives, or are you just convincing me? I've to admit I was very upset when I first got your letter. After a week of thinking it through, I have the courage to reply. If you are happy, Salma, that is all that matters. Parth and I celebrated another wedding anniversary last week, with some happy news from Megan and her husband. They seem happy in America.
Love, Uma

My Children, Sunil and Megan, and Rina 1986.
Our driver Sen Singh

excerpt from Uma's Journal

I stood by the open window of my dining room and, as was my habit, gently massaged my right hand over my left arm. I liked the look of my long painted nails. Megan's letter lay unopened on the table. Parth had his own idiosyncrasies and one of them was that he liked to open his letters with meticulous precision, with the silver, sword-shaped letter opener the children had given him for his birthday. I had learnt to wait. His car appeared in the distant space beyond the confines of my colorful garden. In April, the heat was already oppressive and it would only get worse until the rain started in the late summer months. The air was humid and settled heavily around me, as the car drew near.

My starched, off-white cotton sari with its broad, crisp, purple and green striped border felt damp. My mother said green was the color of new growth. Odd sayings, different thoughts, forgotten images surfaced every day. I felt hot and flushed as I dabbed at beads of moisture at the tip of my nose and around my upper lip.

Playing with my wedding necklace, the *mangalsutra*, I remembered it as my wedding bond from exactly thirty years ago. Was it just maturity and understanding, or was it simple resignation that had carried us through the years? I smiled as I thought now of how Parth and I had learned to lean on each other and, in our own determined way, had come to love and respect one another. Unlike Salma, I had my space and my independence. Salma was happy in her home, I was happy in mine.

I believed Megan's letter to contain greetings for our thirtieth anniversary. I thought of the joy on Parth's face, for without doubt, he would not have remembered our special day, at least not by lunchtime. Few Indian husbands ever did, not with such ease, so I remembered my friends saying.

Parth's car pulled up into the driveway. Our driver, Sen Singh, in a khaki safari suit and a large colorful turban, quickly got out and held the door open for his sahib. Sen Singh always hid his emotionless, straight face behind his big mustache and beard; looking at him, I always felt a pang of sympathy for him and for his wife, Surinder Kaur.

A long time ago when Sen Singh was first employed by us to become our driver, I had asked about his family and he had told us he had a wife in the village and their two boys were with her. He had not talked about his little girl then. With time, Surinder Kaur joined her husband. I got to know them both well, and it was on one such summer afternoon when the lunches were done and Sen Singh was driving Parth back to the store, that Surinder talked to me with great frankness.

"We're from the Punjab area, *bibiji*," she said. "He (she never called Sen Singh by name, but neither did I call Parth by his name) came by train to Delhi first and in the night time, he learnt to drive from a friend who was a taxi driver from their village. In the daytime, he walked all over town looking for a job. After many days of walking and searching, he found a job in the cement factory. Then he sent a money order every month to his father in the village where we lived."

Another time, there was great sadness on Surinder's face as she talked about her daughter, Sujata. For a brief moment, I imagined Sujata's fate was like my sister Durga's. People in villages married their daughters off very quickly with whatever money they could afford. This way there was one less mouth to feed.

It had all started fifteen years ago, she said. Sen Singh was a young man and they lived in their village that was eight miles away from the Dhartipur Bird Sanctuary. Sen Singh drove a bicycle rickshaw owned by a big sahib and took tourists around the bird sanctuary in his rickshaw. The sahib paid him a fixed salary. All the money earned, including the tips he got when he drove tourists around, were given to the manager, who sat at the rickshaw stand at the entrance to the park and kept tabs on the fares each driver got. Sen Singh, with time, learnt enough English, so he could name the birds, talk about their habitats and guide the tourists to the right spots.

"One day, a not so young, rather big built *phirangi* couple of pale skin sat in his small rickshaw, and he showed them the crane birds and miniature owls hidden in remote areas of the sanctuary. They seemed very pleased with his knowledge. They talked and asked him if he could show them his house. They wanted to meet his family, they said. With great hospitality, he brought them to their one room hut in the village.

The foreigners sat in the courtyard on the charpoy for a while and talked to their three children, the older two boys of seven and nine, and their youngest, little three-year-old daughter, Sujata. She sat on Mrs. Cooper's lap and showed her a rag doll she cherished. I made hot chai with plenty of milk and sugar, and I fried cut up potatoes and onions dipped in thick, savory gram flour batter, the *pakodas* for our guests. I served these *'pakodas'* and then took the tea out to them. The foreigners enjoyed the afternoon. He took them back in his rickshaw to where their taxi was waiting for them outside the bird sanctuary."

She said two days later, the same couple returned and asked for Sen Singh's rickshaw. They wanted to drive through the area again, because they said they had read about the *'neelguy,'* a large mammal rarely found in other parts of the world. Her husband told them that it was a cross between a deer and a cow and it might be possible to see one if they toured the sanctuary early in the morning and took a longer time. They said that is what they wanted to do.

"During the conversation, Mr. Cooper said to Sen Singh, 'I have an important question to ask of you. We want to adopt your little girl and take her back to our country. Do you want to give her to us? We'll pay you ten thousand rupees.'

"My husband kind of understood that this was serious but did not understand the word 'adopt.' He thought they wanted him to go on a tour with them to some of the other places. When they got back, Sen Singh asked a *babu* at a bus stop if he spoke English. When the *babu* said he did, Sen Singh asked him to explain what the sahib was saying.

"At first Sen Singh was very angry and waved his shoe at them. Absolutely "No Sir," he said, and started to walk away, but stopped because he realized he had been so rude. He felt bad about getting so angry.

"They went on talking to him as the *babu* kept explaining. This was not something they could force him to do,

Mrs. Cooper said. He should think about it, and he should explain it to his wife. 'Also, think about the future of your little girl,' Mr. Cooper said. 'We will provide her a good home, her own room, pretty clothes, plenty of milk, and food and toys and a good school. She will be happy with us and we will bring her to India to visit you often.'

"*Bibiji*, when he told me all this, I could not sleep at night thinking what we should do," Surinder said. "He and I and our parents and the entire village had an opinion about what we should do. Everybody, poor people that we are, felt their Sujata had brought good luck to the family she was born into, to be asked to live in a foreign country with plenty of money. A daughter is considered a 'Laxmi' Goddess of Wealth, and their fellow villagers felt she was bringing them that. Only her mother's heart in here," she said, pointing to herself, "felt the anguish of separation. I suffered silently for many months and many years, and he did too, but we never bring it up and we never take Sujata's name now.

"True to their word, the Coopers came back in six months with some important papers for him to sign. I put my thumb imprint also. Sujata went with them happily in the taxi thinking that she was going for a ride. Her brothers also got into the taxi with them. So they all went for a long ride very happily, had ice cream, and then the Coopers very quickly told the boys to get off and that they would give Sujata an extra ride. The boys were content with the ice cream and the candy and the car ride and kept talking to their father and me about their adventure. My sari palloo covered my head and I pulled it even lower to shade my tearful eyes.

"Three years later, the Coopers came back with Sujata. They called her Susie now. She wore pretty dresses, *Bibiji*, she spoke another language and she looked happy and healthy. She came to me shyly with what I thought was recognition. I understood nothing of what she said to me. In a little while, still happy, she went back to her foreign mother and hugged her.

"Even my husband's English, she did not understand, nor could he understand what she said."

Sen Singh told Surinder their daughter spoke like a *phirangi*, a foreigner now; she was no longer their daughter. There were too many people around who had come to see her Sujata, and they were happy, so she could not even cry in front of them after she had left.

"Sujata came back to visit one more time when she was ten years old. I rejoiced to see Sujata happy. My heart bled but I was brave and I did not let her foreign mother see my torment. My husband told me Sujata had asked who we were. Outside in their dusty courtyard, her foreign father had sat on their charpoy with Sujata in his lap and talked to her for a long time, but we understood nothing. I busied myself making the chai.

"Come to think about it, *Bibiji*, by ten years of age, we would probably have found a good match for her, paid a small dowry and got her married, but we are poor people and our dowry would have been small, so who knows if she would have found happiness. Her life is so different now; we could never have given her that. So we take solace and imagine that she is at her mother-in-law's house and is treated well.

"After we moved to Delhi, we asked a *babuji* to write a letter to the foreigners who have our Sujata, so she will know we are here, in case she comes back again sometime to see us. She'll be a big girl now."

Surinder told me that Sen Singh bought his own bicycle rickshaw with the money he received from the *phirangis*, so after that he did not have to give all his hard-earned earnings to the master. Gradually, he put some aside in a post office account. As the boys grew bigger, they spent a lot of time playing *gili-danda* in the streets and went to school when they wanted to. Sen Singh and Surinder had heard life was better in the big cities. A neighbor who had moved to a big city had come back to the village one time to see his old mother and told them, "You can earn more money in a big city. There are more jobs. Come, I'll find you a room to sleep in. You can look around and find somewhere to work."

This very Sen Singh stood so stately beside their Fiat, and opened the door to let my husband out. I wandered how much he missed his little girl and I wondered what she looked like, what she did and if she remembered her brothers. I thought all this and more because we missed our Megan. It could be no comparison to the ache Sen Singh and Surinder must have felt.

Parth glanced at the dining table as he entered. All letters were usually placed at the entrance in a glass platter with a silver rim, and the silver letter opener with an intricately carved handle was placed beside it. I wanted to tear open the envelope, especially when it was a personal letter, and read it quickly, more so when it was Megan's. The excitement of holding my daughter's handwriting in my own two hands and reading the contents! There is a bond there, a connection, an impulsive hold and release, but I waited, for over the years I had learnt to be patient. It was our tradition that Parth opened all the letters as master of the house, neatly, with the letter opener that Megan gave him one year for a birthday present.

My thoughts went back to the days when Megan had told us in a letter several years ago that she had met a fellow civil engineer, Arun, and, "Mom, I'm very serious about him." In a letter six months later, she told us she and Arun wanted to get married.

We held the wedding reception in Delhi since Arun's parents also lived in India. It was a big, colorful wedding as all Indian weddings tended to be. On the large open lawn of a five star hotel, more than five hundred guests mingled and talked and exchanged pleasantries. Amidst colorful, blinking lights sparkling in the bushes, they gave their blessings to Arun and Megan, as did most of the older guests, for it was mainly Parth's and my friends.

Arun had come to India after seven years and had invited only two of his friends who were also visiting India. Megan had more of her classmates in India; several came with their husbands and children. Noise, perfume, glittering gold and glamorous brocade and silk saris pervaded the scene. Bearers in white uniform and maroon turbans carried wholesome trays of savory appetizers back and forth. Happiness abounded within me as I stood beside Parth, welcoming the guests. There were many bits and pieces of advice I had learned from my grandmother. My Motiba had been so right to say that what you make of your life is through your own efforts and God's grace. She had died five years ago and had ot been alive to see my happiness right now. I felt her presence.

Parth and I were together, and we were happy with our daughter and new son-in-law. The shadow in my life was Sunil, who did not come to his sister's wedding, because Parth did not want him invited. I felt that we overdid the celebrations at Megan's wedding to make up for Sunil's marriage. When would Parth and Sunil make-up, if ever they did? I washed back to the present as I heard Parth enter.

I tried not to show my impatience as Parth took off his coat and washed his hands. He then came and sat at the dining table. I served him the green chutney and the finely chopped tomato and onion salad as we waited for warm food to be brought in. Parth opened the letters in his usual methodical style, and glanced at Megan's letter. Suddenly, he stopped and gave me a broad smile. Reading the letter, he said, "You're going to be a grandmother soon, Uma. The title of Nani suits you. Look, read what she has to say."

We looked at each other. Parth never showered me with compliments, but in his own awkward style, he had told me that he always thought I looked even prettier when there was a glow of happiness on my face. He liked my straight black hair, now speckled with gray and tied back into a low knot at the nape of my neck. I always wore the gold bangles his family had given me on our wedding day. Some days I wore a special diamond stud in my nose, as I did today.

"Happy Anniversary, too," he remembered suddenly, "the diamond nose stud suits you." He held out both his hands while still seated. With hesitation, I placed my hands on his, afraid the servants would see us thus. He held them even tighter and pulled me towards him. As usual, he said little but I was content.

"Thirty," I said. "I knew you'd forget."

Then I heard a servant approach and looked to Parth. He quickly released my hands. I read the letter silently again and then said, "Megan wants us to go to America when the baby is born. Shall we?"

"Yes, yes, of course, we'll go. I'll have to come back but we'll get a four month visa and you can stay and help her."

2980, Maitland Drive
Cleveland, OHIO
29th July 1997

Dear Salma,

Parth and I have decided to live in America near our grandchildren for a few more years. We are both slowing down, Parth more so than I. Rina runs our business in Bombay with great aptitude. She's good at it. She and I took charge of the shop and have made it into a prosperous boutique, when finally Parth let us. It took a long time for him to trust our 'woman's' judgment, but when he did, it was a joy for all of us.

Mummy passed away a few months ago. A car accident. She died on the spot. Papa was devastated, but is better now.

Sunil's twins are doing well in Mumbai. Did I ever tell you that he married a Muslim girl? Navida is the sweetest thing on earth, and although Parth and Sunil were estranged for many years, we are now one family.

Salma, thank God, be it Ganesh or Allah, for our friendship and love for one another. Parth is almost bald, and stoops a little. We laugh when I tell him about how I thought he had big ears. I'm quite grey too, and maybe a little forgetful. Parth helps me get by. Send me your photo sometime, with your large family. No *burkhas*, I hope! Those days are past.

Love, Uma

My husband Parth, 1997
excerpt from Uma's Journal

I watched the hands of the kitchen clock move forward. It said eight thirty and the sun was already up in the sky. Sunshine crept into the dining room, onto the family portrait we had taken five years ago, soon after Parth and I had moved to the United States. I liked the way I looked then. I had insisted on wearing my sari and adorning my forehead with a big red *kumkum*; the way I always did in India. When I wore my Indian attire, I liked to wear my diamond earrings. Rightfully, Dilip's wife, Hansa, should have inherited her mother-in-law's jewelry, but Dilip was adamant about wanting me to get the earrings. He said we had to be progressive and change cultural taboos, and do what we, as a family, feel is emotionally right. Dilip and I had talked how I had been deprived of my ambitions when I was coerced into marrying Parth. He is pleased that life had turned out well for me. If only it had for our Durga, he said mournfully to me when the two of us reminisced about old times. Dilip worked hard at his medical clinic in spite of having lost a limb in the war. I admired his persistence.

A few months after Mummy's demise, Papa had said, "*Beti*, take your mother's diamonds and wear them with joy."

I had protested, but Papa explained to me that he and Dilip had already talked and again, decisions had been made for me. Wearing the earrings for the photo, in a sense, made me feel my mother's blessings were with our family. Blessings from parents who wished us well were all that remained of Papa and Mummy.

The photo had been taken too soon after Parth and I had arrived in America. I was not used to the Western attire then. No matter what, I thought to myself, I'm so glad I wore my sari in that photo. That's the way I wanted my grandchildren to remember me. I'll always be an Indian at heart.

I studied Parth's face in the portrait. He was thinner then and although he was just minimally taller than I, he always stood very upright. I scrutinized his face, stopping at what I once had thought were his big ears. A little smile escaped me. For the last several years, I had not noticed those big ears. They were just a part of Parth. Maybe it was just me, thinking they were big, I said to myself and chuckled.

Rina's letter was on the fireplace. She said the boutique was running well. That the Board of Gujarat Handicrafts had honored me for my work in initiating the sales of handicrafts made by people with physical challenges. Kutchy hand-stitched embroidery and mirror work, carefully done by these people from Kutch in Gujarat were a rage in Bombay. Rina had hired two young helpers. Navida looked good and the twins were growing well.

"I need your blessings, *masi* and *masa*, my Parsi man and I are engaged. We can talk about a wedding date when I call you next month."

Little Tara, our second granddaughter, was always the one who noticed her grandfather's new shirt or a different tie, and would lovingly cuddle up to him and say, "Nana, your tie is so soft." Tara even liked to comb her grandfather's hair, or what was left of it.

"Let's play beauty," she would say, and he would happily agree and let her mess up his head.

Lately, Parth had been content to just sit in one of his favorite chairs for hours. He said he felt tired. We went to the clinic for dialysis three times a week. I drove him there on days when the pickup van was not available, and while he was on the dialysis machine, I played with the children on dialysis in the adjacent unit.

We had done this for more than a year now. The doctors had started talking to us about a kidney transplant, but Parth had refused to let any of the family members think about it.

Parth had looked puffy last night when he went to bed. It was getting late for his clinic appointment and I needed to get him out of bed and give him his breakfast. I walked into our bedroom as quietly as I could and sat beside him. Slowly, I put my hand on his shoulder and shook him gently. Parth was wide awake with a smile on his face. There were birds outside our window.

"It's great you have time for me these days," he said.

"We have to get dressed and leave soon," I said. "Your clinic appointment is for ten o'clock."

"Yes, yes," said Parth. "I'm up now." But he did not move.

I paused for a while and then talked to him about what Tara said that morning before leaving for school. Parth smiled thinking of how he and Tara played their little card game of Bluff and how good she had become at it.

Parth sat up slowly and looked for his walking stick at the head of his bed. He shuffled around in his slippers and managed to get to the bathroom. I went into the kitchen and made him his tea and a slice of dry toast. That's all he had for breakfast every morning. I made myself a cup of tea, and at a slow pace, each in our own thoughts, we ate our breakfast. Parth, as always, buried his face in the morning paper for a few minutes. He looked at the headlines and then saved the rest of the newspaper for after breakfast. It's almost like he waited to hear what I had to say about the children. Like he wanted to say a lot more himself, but refrained from it.

I said, "Tara wore her new dress to school today. She wanted you to put her barrette in her hair but I held her back because you were fast asleep."

Parth had a very contented look on his face.

"Next time she wants me to put a barrette in her hair, wake me up. Just send her in and show me what to do. It's time for me to get up anyway."

We talked at leisure for a few minutes. Then we got ready and I looked at the clock, and told him it was time for us to leave for his clinic appointment. I found our coats in the front closet. I picked Parth's shoes from the shelf and brought them up to him. He sat down, exhausted, on the bench that Arun had specially placed near the shoe rack. Parth was breathless from all this activity; from having walked a few steps. He was having a hard time bending over and tying his shoe laces. I helped him tie them. Eventually, Parth stood up. I held out my left hand and he took it. Slowly we headed out of the front door. We did not speak. I placed my arm on his right shoulder and leaned into him, with the gesture that said, "I need you too." I handed him his walking stick, supported him at the elbow, and we walked out to the transport van that had come to take us to the hospital. Parth leaned onto my shoulder and looked at me for comfort. I smiled and walked half a step ahead of him. In his eyes, I saw our lifetime together.

4th May, 2000

Dear Salma,

My dear husband of 40 years passed away quietly in his sleep last month. I miss him terribly. I think of all the years I wasted before I finally realized that I'd grown to love him, like a fresh flower blooming in my garden, one I loved to look at but always took for granted that it would be there. Culture and traditions of those early times demanded male dominance. What is a man or a woman to do! All I know is that we had become good friends and spent many happy years together. When I helped our handcraft busines grow with Rina's help, I was fulfilled. Durga's sacrifice is what opened my eyes. I was too complacent before that, just wasting my life dwelling on things not available to me. I failed to see all that I did have. I wasted a few years of my life not living in the present. I miss him, my dear gentle Parth, with his big ears.

Love to you,
Uma.

Epilogue to my mother's story

Letters to Salma and excerpts from my mother, Uma's journal complete the picture of my parents' life together, as well as give us a depth of understanding about Uma's and Salma's friendship. Innocent friendship of decades, and being a Hindu or a Muslim didn't break that thread. They were merely ordinary people living in a world at war.

I admire my mother's courage after her sister died, and how my father stood by her. She was a victim of tradition of that time. They lived through many crises in their lives, overcame hard times, and as time, circumstance and traditions changed; she became an independent woman.

I never understood my parents' love for each other; no holding hands, no public kissing, no admiring looks. Yet day after day, she waited for him to come home and they would sit down and dine together.

Recently, my mother had told me how fondly my papa talked about my children, and for years, he carried that hurt look, almost anger, when my brother Sunil's name was mentioned. My mother would never have chosen the path she was led into...the path of an arranged marriage at seventeen. She hated her situation for years; years of youth wasted in being angry. Later, she found the strength to live the life given to her. My papa's simplicity, and I suspect, quiet admiration for my mother, made them inter-dependant.

My mother is grey, sits most of the time, and keeps her journal open. She stares at it, as if deciding what exactly to say. She doesn't seem to write much in it. The page is blank.

One of Salma's old letters to her lies open on the kitchen table, fluttering in the gentle breeze of the day, as if waiting for the time when it too will vanish.

Sukhatme-Sheth 266

272

273